LONESOME JUSTICE

JUSTICE SERIES - BOOK 3

DONALD L. ROBERTSON

COPYRIGHT

Lonesome Justice

Copyright © 2019 Donald L. Robertson
CM Publishing

Books@DonaldLRobertson.com

❀ Created with Vellum

ACKNOWLEDGMENTS

I cannot begin to put into words, even as a writer, how much I owe my sweet wife, Paula. If it wasn't for her, I'd still be trying to come up with a title for this book. But she thought of the perfect title, and this is not the first book she has titled. Paula is always my target audience. She reads chapters I have questions about, and she also is the first person to read the finished manuscript. She had strong negative feelings about the first ending of *Lonesome Justice.*

I reread the ending, with my reader hat on, and agreed with her. That produced a total rewrite of the last four chapters, making it, in my opinion, a much better book. Thank you, Honey. You put up with my moods, you come up with great titles, and you save my bacon. I love you tremendously.

When writing Westerns, I depend on either having been where I'm writing about or researching the area, looking at old maps, finding names of creeks, rivers, and major features. Sometimes it becomes difficult and time consuming to the point of delaying the book. When I see that happening, I pick up my phone and try to contact a person knowledgable about the area the book takes place in. This time I was extremely fortunate to have Brad Newton, Executive Director of the Presidio Municipal Development District, in Presidio, Texas, pick up the phone. Brad freely gave of his time and knowledge to me, someone he didn't know from Adam. He even took time to send me pictures of Presidio and tell me great stories about the country. Thanks, Brad. You were a great help.

If you'll bear with me one more moment, I want to thank another author. Steven Konkoly is a very successful author in a completely different genre—mystery, thriller, and suspense. I'm sure many of you know him and have read his books. He took the time to give me some suggestions on writing book blurbs and on covers, when I was first starting. In fact, he spent quite a bit of his valuable time and never failed to answer an email. Thanks, Steven, you helped a lot, and I'll not forget it.

1

Clay Barlow made his way along Congress, the bustling main street of Austin. He was dusty from the tip of his overrun boots to the crown of his worn, sweat-stained black hat. It had been a long ride into the city. Blue, the blue roan his pa had given him ten years ago, happily munched oats in Platt's stable.

It may have been a long ride back from his ranch, but it was also a happy one. The chance he and Adam Hewitt had taken on stocking the Hereford cattle was starting to pay off. They had made their first sale, the new breed proving much more profitable than the lean longhorns.

His eyes were drawn to a shapely blonde in a light blue dress that accentuated her slim waist, walking along the boardwalk ahead of him. Her arms, swinging at her sides, were covered with sleeves that ended midway down her forearms, with short white cuffs, exposing a portion of her golden, tanned skin. Something about her looked familiar. She wore no bonnet and her shoulder-length hair undulated with each step, shimmering in the afternoon sun. The young woman was striding past the swinging doors of the Iron Front Saloon when a large hand thrust out over the swinging doors, followed by the hand's owner, a drunken buffalo hunter.

He grabbed the young woman's upper arm. "Hold up there, blondie. Come on in and I'll buy you a dri—"

The man's words were cut short by the petite little fist that drove into his lips, smashing them against his teeth. He stood there in stunned silence, blood running down his chin.

"Get your hands off me, you lush!" the young woman snapped.

When he was too slow in removing his hand, the small fist flashed again, slamming against the big man's nose. Blood splattered over the front of the girl's lovely blue dress.

The buffalo hunter recovered and, drawing his right hand back in a fist, roared, "You ain't hittin' Ole Billie Byrd, you—"

Clay had started moving as soon as he saw the hand reach out over the saloon door. His right fist preceded his body's arrival, slamming the man under his left eye and splitting the flesh over his cheekbone.

During the altercation, the man had moved out of the saloon and onto the boardwalk. When Clay hit him, it broke his grip on the girl's arm and drove him against the door facing. The man stumbled out into the street, blood now coursing from his cheek, nose, and mouth. He shook his head like a bull, throwing blood on several bystanders who jumped back out of range.

Bent over, he looked up at Clay. "Mister, you may be big, but you ain't near as big as Ole Billie Byrd. Now, I'm gonna show you how smart it is for a cowboy to mess with me."

The man reached behind the holstered gun he wore on his right side to a scabbard, positioned immediately behind the holster, and pulled out a big Bowie knife.

"I'm gonna slice you up and serve you for dinner."

Clay was tired. The ride had been long, and the last thing he wanted to do was draw his Bowie knife and duel it out with the drunk. "Mister, you're drunk. Apologize to the lady and ride out of town, and I'll let you go."

"You'll let me go? Why, you young whippersnapper!" The big man charged Clay, the cutter, edge up, leading the way.

Moving so fast that few in the gathering crowd saw the action, Clay drew his Smith & Wesson from the right holster and stepped into the rushing man. He knocked the knife outside and away from his body with his left forearm and drove the barrel of the revolver into the side of Ole Billie's head, allowing the large, but now unconscious man to plow into the dusty street.

Clay slipped both revolvers back into their holsters. He had seen a deputy sheriff standing in the crowd. "Jim, can you throw this drunk into jail and let him sleep it off?"

"Sure thing, Clay. Glad to help." The deputy turned to a couple of men standing in the thinning crowd and recruited them to help him carry Byrd to jail. Clay turned back to the young woman who was still standing on the boardwalk. She was slightly flushed but showed no sign of nerves, only dissipating anger that was quickly hidden by a wide and beautiful smile.

"My hero, again."

Clay cocked his head slightly, looking at the girl. Then the clear and confident voice registered in his memory. "Dorenda Davis! Why, aren't you a pretty picture? What's it been four, five years?"

The smile disappeared from her pretty face. "You listen to me, Mr. Barlow. This is 1881, which makes it seven years since you rescued me and my mother from those bandits, and you know to call me Dee."

"Seven years," Clay said, shaking his head. "Who would've thought it?"

Then a grin creased his face. "You still planning on marrying me?"

The softly tanned face framed in golden hair turned a light

crimson, but she didn't lower her eyes. Those brilliant blue eyes stared directly into the ranger's. "I'm considering it."

Now it was Clay's turn to blush. "Well, yes—I mean no, I mean . . . how are you doing?"

Dee giggled at Clay's discombobulation. At that moment, just a few paces up the boardwalk, the door to The City Hotel opened. Niles and Nancy Davis stepped outside, saw the drunk being carried off, and spotted their daughter. They came running over.

"Dee," Niles said, "are you all right?"

She smiled at her parents. "Yes, Papa, I'm fine, thanks to this gentleman."

Nancy looked at the big man with the thick mustache for only a moment, then threw her arms around his neck and gave him a big kiss on the cheek. When she stepped back, she turned to her husband. "Honey, don't you remember Clay Barlow?"

Niles smiled at the man in front of him and thrust out his hand. "Looks like you're in a habit of saving my family, Clay. Thank you."

"My pleasure, Niles. Anybody else would have done the same thing. I was just in the right place."

Nancy, with one hand on her hip and the other hand's pointer finger extended toward Clay, said, "Clay Barlow, that is almost the same thing you said when you saved us from those bandits that attacked the stage. You listen to me, don't demean the courage you've shown, twice. You are a brave man. Take credit for it."

Clay looked at Niles. "Boy, these Davis women are tough."

Niles laughed and put an arm around each one of them. "You have no idea. They make me mighty proud."

"You should be," Clay said. "Let me tell you what your daughter did. That drunk reached over those swinging doors,"— Clay pointed at the Iron Front Saloon—"and grabbed Dee's arm. That was a big mistake. She hit him twice before he could turn her loose. Busted his lips and broke his nose. All that was left for me was to give him a little tap and he was done."

"Mother," Dee said, "that is not exactly how it happened."

"I'm sure," Nancy said. "Clay would you join us in The City Hotel? We were getting together for supper and we'd love to have you join us."

"Yes, ma'am. If it's all right with Niles and Dee."

"Of course it is," Nancy said. "Now, young lady, let's get that bloody dress off of you and soaking, or those stains will never come out."

She grasped her daughter's left hand and looked at it. "It looks like those skinned knuckles need a little doctoring, too."

Nancy tossed a glance toward her husband. "Would you grab us a table? We'll be down in a few minutes."

He nodded. The men followed the women toward the hotel.

Several of the hotel's clientele smiled and nodded to Clay as he walked into the lobby. There were a few who cast critical glances at the dusty cowboy, but most knew him either as Ranger Barlow or Mr. Barlow the attorney.

A waiter met them at the restaurant entrance. "Good afternoon, Clay. Looks like you just came in off the trail."

"Afternoon, Chester. Could you seat Mr. Davis while I go wash up? Mrs. Davis and her daughter will be joining us."

"Why, yes, sir. I'd be glad to."

The waiter motioned for Niles to follow him and Clay headed for the washroom. Passing the washroom door, he stepped out the back door into the alley. There, using his hat, he beat a substantial amount of dust from his clothing and looked around at the growing city of Austin. It amazed him how much the city had grown, even through the depression, and now it was almost booming.

Clay reentered the hotel and turned into the washroom where he washed his face, neck, and hair. The mirror reflected a young man of extraordinary build. Wide-set gray eyes stared back at him from a strong, sun-browned face and a dimpled chin, which he still had difficulty shaving. He combed his thick, black hair with his fingers, wiped the dust from his hat, and returned to the dining room.

"How's the ranching business?" Clay asked, pulling out a chair and sitting across from the older man.

Niles nodded. "Good. You may not know it, but you saved our ranch in '74 when you let us know about the coming depression." He looked around the restaurant. "In fact, it was right in here that it happened."

"Don't thank me. That was my grandpa's financial adviser from New York." Clay glanced over to the table where he had sat with his grandpa; Senator Barlow; Mr. O'Shea; and Mike those seven years ago. So much had happened over those years. It was later in that same week that he left with Mr. O'Shea and Mike for New York.

Clay pulled himself back to the conversation. "Mr. O'Shea had traveled to Texas to meet with several legislators, including my grandfather, and shared the news of the coming depression with us. He explained that the more people who knew about it, the better off the country would be. That's when I came over and shared it with you."

"Well, I'll tell you, if it hadn't been for that conversation, we would've lost the ranch. But thanks to you, we were able to sell off enough cattle to settle all of our debt. It wasn't easy, but we made it."

"I'm glad to hear it, Niles. A lot of ranchers and farmers lost everything."

Clay's head turned, along with all of the other restaurant patrons', as Nancy and Dee entered the restaurant. Nancy was still very attractive. Her blonde hair had more gray in it than seven years earlier, but she still turned heads. Her daughter, however, was a striking beauty.

Clay and Niles rose from their chairs as the two women approached. Dee, slightly behind Nancy, moved to her side as they entered the room. When she stepped out from behind her mother and Clay's eyes fell upon her, he was mesmerized.

She had grown into a tall young woman. She was almost five feet six inches tall, near as tall as a man. She had grown up on the ranch, working cattle alongside the ranch hands and her father, and her shoulders showed it. They were wide, tapering down to a narrow waist where her hips flared gently, swaying the yellow satin of her dress as she walked.

Dee had never been a town girl. Her face was not the milk white of the girls in town, but a soft golden tan from the kisses of the sun. Her long neck emphasized the gentle swelling at the bodice of her dress.

Clay was struck. The blonde hair falling about her shoulders framed a confident beauty. Her smiling lips exposed even, white teeth that completed the picture.

"I guess I don't have to ask if you like my dress?" Dee said, staring up into Clay's wide eyes. She laughed, placed one hand on his arm, and on her tiptoes, kissed him on the cheek.

"That's for my gallant rescuer."

Clay recovered and grinned down at her. Before he could say anything, Nancy spoke up.

Though she was smiling, she said, "Dee, that is quite enough! You know you're in a public place."

Niles shook his head. "Nothing my daughter does surprises me."

Dee winked at Clay and smiled at her father. "Oh, Papa,"

Clay looked at Niles. "She may not surprise you, but she sure surprised me."

Dee laughed again, then seated herself next to Clay. Nancy sat across from her.

It was hard for Clay to focus his attention on anyone except the blonde. A light fragrance of roses drifted in his direction. *She sure smells good,* Clay thought. *All my time in New York, I never met anyone like her.* He realized Nancy was talking.

"How's the rangering business, Clay?"

"Ma'am, it's too good. I find I have little time to help my grandpa at the *Barlow Law and Land* and keep an eye on my ranch north of Uvalde."

Niles leaned forward. "I understand you and Adam Hewitt are working together."

"That's right, although he's doing almost all of the work. I help out when I can."

"How are the shorthorns working out?"

Clay smiled as he thought of the success they were having with the Herefords. "Very well, Niles. The Texas winters don't seem to bother them, and they're taking the summers in stride. It's like they were made for this country, and they carry a lot more weight than the longhorn."

"Papa has some," Dee commented. "I like them. They're much easier to work than those wild old longhorns."

Her comment allowed Clay to give her his full attention without obviously staring. He wanted to reach out and touch her soft hair. He hadn't felt like this for a long time.

"You're right there," Clay said, gazing into those deep blue eyes. "Have you heard your papa and his cowhands talking about them?"

At this question, Nancy laughed. "Clay, if you could see her. She rides out with the men and works the cattle right alongside them. It's impossible to keep her inside."

"Really?" Clay said, his eyebrows lifting in interest.

"That's right," Niles said. "I guess I'd have to hogtie her to keep her home. She can ride and rope right along with the best."

A teasing grin creased Dee's face. "I can shoot, too."

"Yep," Niles said, "She's got most of the boys her age buffaloed. They all figure she's better than them."

"I am! They're just boys playing at being men." After this statement she gazed up at Clay. "Are you intimidated, Mr. Ranger?"

Clay threw back his head and laughed. He was joined by Nancy and Niles, although Nancy knew her daughter's plan, and was concerned for her.

"Yes, ma'am," Clay said. "You've had me intimidated for seven years, since that day on the stage."

Dee narrowed her eyes at Clay. "Clay Barlow, I was just a little girl then."

Clay grinned back at her. "I think you were probably more intimidating at twelve years old than the bandits who were trying to rob you."

She slapped him on his arm, letting her hand linger as her father said, "I'm hungry. Let's eat." He turned to Chester and waved.

Clay felt the warmth of Dee's hand on his arm and wanted to put his hand over hers, but controlled himself. She finally pulled her hand back, and Clay glanced at Nancy. It was obvious the interaction between the two of them did not go unnoticed.

Clay cleared his throat. "I'm with you, Niles."

The four ordered. One thing Clay liked about eating at the hotel was the large servings. Chester brought out the four platters, then returned with a big bowl of fresh, hot rolls, the steam still rising from the bread.

"Straight out of the oven," Chester said, placing the bowl on the table.

"Chester, you're a good man," Clay said.

The waiter grinned his thanks. "If you folks are in need of anything else, just let me know."

"Do you know everyone in Austin, Clay?" Dee asked.

"A few, but when I'm in town, I live in the City Hotel."

Nancy looked puzzled. "Not with your grandfather?"

"No, ma'am. He wants me to, but it gets a little crowded in his apartment. I help out in his law practice, but I'm a ranger. Often, I get called out in the middle of the night. Grandpa's a light sleeper, and, at his age, he needs his rest."

"How's he doing?" Dee asked.

Clay looked down at the beautiful face gazing up at him, reading genuine concern in her clear blue eyes.

What am I feeling? he asked himself. *Be honest. You've never felt this way about any woman in your life.*

Dee's soft lips parted and she said, "Clay?"

He could feel himself turning red. Under the sun-browned skin, it was only faintly noticeable. "Oh...uh, sorry." A wry, self-conscious grin broke across his strong face. "He's getting old. He's always been a strong, independent man, but I don't think he ever totally recovered from being shot. I'm sure glad Raymond has stuck with him all these years."

Nancy hadn't missed the look that had passed between Clay and Dee. She turned to her husband, a knowing smile gracing her face. Niles, his forehead wrinkled, looked at Dee, then Clay. He turned his head toward his wife as she gently laid her hand on his.

Clay, his composure recovered, cleared his throat. "Reckon we best eat before this good food gets cold." Niles and Clay picked up their knives, and before long their steaks had disappeared. Clay leaned back and grinned at Nancy. "It's been a long time since breakfast."

She smiled at Clay and patted Niles' arm. "I've lived with a big appetite for many years, and he's never let me down. It's always good to see a strong man appreciate his food."

Clay started to respond when the hotel door burst open. The telegrapher raced into the lobby and stopped. Looking around, he spotted Clay in the dining room and raced over, thrusting an envelope into the ranger's hand. "This just came in from Alpine."

Clay opened the envelope and pulled out the message. *Need help. In Presidio. Jake.*

Clay stood and handed the man four bits. "Thanks." He tossed a dollar on the table and waved to Chester. "Put this on my bill. I've got to run."

Chester, used to Clay leaving abruptly, said, "Stay safe."

The Davis family had also risen.

"Sorry," Clay said. He handed the message to Dee.

She quickly read the short message and looked up, searching his eyes. "You just got in. You're tired."

Clay smiled at her, then turned to Nancy and Niles. "I've got to leave. This message is from a ranger who's a good friend. He's in trouble. I've enjoyed seeing you again."

He glanced back down at Dee, then up to Niles. "Mr. Davis, I'd be obliged if I could call on your daughter when I get back."

Niles looked at Dee's pleading face, and then at Nancy who gave an almost imperceptible nod. "You have my permission, Clay, and good luck on your trip. If you don't mind my asking, where are you headed?"

"Presidio."

"Long ways. You take care of yourself."

"Yes," Nancy added. "We wouldn't want anything to happen to you."

"Thank you, both. Now, I've got to get going."

He looked down at Dee, seeing the worry laid across the face that just a few minutes earlier had been wreathed in happiness. Even with the frown, she was lovely.

"Don't you need to pack?" Dee asked.

"No, everything I need is still in my saddlebags and bedroll at the stable."

"Then let me walk you to the door."

Clay shot a questioning look at both Niles and Nancy, who nodded their consent. She took his arm. The tall girl and taller man strode toward the door. He opened it for her, and she glided through. Stepping onto the boardwalk the couple stopped. People passed, hurrying to their separate destinations, but neither of them noticed.

Dee looked up at Clay and placed her hands on his shoulders, pulling him down slightly so that she could place her soft lips on his cheek. Clay felt the touch of her lips course through him like warm sun on a winter day. With both of his big hands on her arms, he looked into her deep blue eyes that were close to tears.

"Do take care, Clay. I want you to come back to me. I'll be at the ranch."

"I've got a lot to say to you when I get back, but now I've a favor to ask."

"Anything."

"Would you stop by the Barlow Law and Land office and tell my grandpa I'm sorry I couldn't see him? Give him the telegram and he'll understand."

"I will."

"Thank you. Now, I've got to go." There was so much more that he wanted to say, but now wasn't the time or the place. One last look at the girl he had so immediately and thoroughly fallen in love with and he turned, hurrying through the rush of people, his mind on the long ride ahead.

2

The dry rawhide cut deep into Clay's wrists and ankles while the red ants gnawed incessantly on his body. Stripped down to his trousers, the July sun joined in to slowly roast his upper torso and feet.

The men responsible for his plight turned their horses and rode off down the dry riverbed. Clay's hat disappeared around the bend, now on the head of Apache half-breed Shifty Joe Beck, while his boots dangled over each side of Earl Griffin's saddle. Those boots were old but broken in and comfortable. He hated to see them go. It wasn't bad enough that Griffin had his boots, he also had his Bowie knife, Smith and Wesson Model 3 revolvers, and Roper Repeating Shotgun. He was alone in the northern Chihuahuan Desert, aside from the giant red ants.

The irony of it all was that Clay Barlow, Texas Ranger, had not even been after them. He had been on his way to meet his pard Jake Coleman, in Presidio.

Three weeks earlier, he had reconnected with the little girl, now woman, who said she was going to marry him. Dee wasn't so little anymore, and he felt like, at twelve, she had been prophetic. That's what had gotten him in trouble. He was thinking about those few, wonderful minutes he had spent with her, and with his attention dulled, the bandits picked the perfect time to jump him.

Clay tried to lift one shoulder to ease the pain along his spine. Shifty Joe had slid a small rock, about the size of a silver dollar, between his shoulder blades right on his spine.

He knew he was in trouble. Besides the constant biting of the ants, his white skin that seldom saw daylight was turning red from exposure to the blistering heat. He figured he had been staked to the rocky ground for at least two hours, and as bad as his back ached, his heart ached more. Earl Griffin was riding Blue. That horse had been with him since before his folks were killed.

A shadow drifted over his face. Squinting against the sun, he could make out four buzzards circling—lower and lower.

Great, he thought, as another red ant started chewing on his neck. *Not only am I covered in these blasted ants, but now those buzzards are coming in for dinner.*

Glare and heat from the sun suddenly disappeared. He strained, twisting his neck, trying to see over his right shoulder and behind him. A line of dark clouds appeared, moving rapidly into his line of vision. Just as his gray eyes caught the leading darkness, a shaft of lightning lit the summer sky, crashing into the rocky point a short distance to the west. He could feel the cooling, almost cold, air caressing his hot body—too cool. *Hail*, he thought. *I've got to get out of this riverbed, and fast. I won't die here. I told Dee I'd be back.* The first fat raindrops hit him in the face.

Clay Barlow had been a big boy who grew into a big man. In stocking feet, he reached well over six feet. Hard work had put muscle on those bones with much of it residing in his massive arms and shoulders. With the bandits gone, it was time for him to get out of this draw. He gradually started increasing the pressure on the stakes holding his arms to the ground. Shifty Joe had driven them deep, all the while grinning at him. "You a big man. I make sure you stay," he'd said.

Clay pulled with all the strength he could muster. Lightning crashed again, close. *If I don't get out of here quick,* he thought, *a flash flood could rip me out with all the debris it pushes in front.* He relaxed. There was no slack for him to play with. His arms were stretched tight. Now, it was pouring. Up the dry riverbed, there had to be huge amounts of water cascading into it. It wouldn't be dry for long.

The heavy rain sluiced the huge red ants from his body, the one with pincers embedded in his neck was the last to wash away. Clay's body screamed for him to rub the bites, but to no avail. His hands were still tied—but not quite as tight. The dry dirt was turning to mud. Rawhide was stretching, ever so slightly, in the rain. His body arched as he applied all of his strength, straining to have his hands meet directly above him. The rain was washing the blood from his wrists where the rawhide cut through the skin, but he didn't release the strain. Harder. I've got to pull harder.

With the strain, the veins across his forehead stood stark against his sunburned skin. Below the protection his hat normally provided, the skin was the color of well-tanned leather, down to his lower neck, and from there the red continued. He relaxed again. Had the left stake moved, just a little? He rested his body so he could regain his strength. Several deep breaths and for the third time, he mustered all of the strength available to him. This time, he pulled from deep inside himself. It was like he could hear his pa saying, "Picture what you want to happen, boy, and work for it, hard. You can do it."

So he did. Slowly at first, the right stake moved. Maybe it was because of the rain softening the ground, maybe he changed the angle just a little, but the small movement gave way to total release. It ripped from the earth, and Clay, his arm outstretched, saw the rawhide and the stake dangling from his wrist, directly above him.

He grabbed the stake in his hand, and rolled over as far to the right as his tied legs would allow. He started digging. As he jabbed the stake into the ground, he heard it—a roar above the rain. Flash flood! He didn't take his eyes from the stake he was digging around. Finally, he ripped it from the ground, immediately sitting and working on his tied feet, first his left and then his right.

The roar increased. He could picture it in his mind as the left stake released and he went to work on the right. The flood would be pushing every piece of debris that had accumulated in the dry riverbed. Logs, rocks, prickly pear, carcasses, all of it would be pushed ahead of the irresistible force of the water. Now the sound was deafening.

The last stake released, and he leaped to his sunburned feet. A quick glance told him all he needed to know. The roiling water, tossing logs and boulders up and then sucking them back down, pushing, almost like a thick soup, was nearly upon him. It was so close, there was no chance to dash for the bank. He would have to angle, hopefully gain a few feet on it.

He took off. The cut bank was steep through this portion of the no-longer-dry riverbed. He would have no chance to climb it before the water and debris would be on him. About fifty yards down the riverbed, just before it started to turn, he saw a sloping bank. It wasn't the best, but it was the best he could hope for. One thing he had always been able to do was run. As a young boy and early teen, he'd had a Tonkawa friend. They had spent a great deal of time together and had run throughout the hill country where his pa's ranch was. It had paid off before, and now it was paying off again.

He hit the sloping bank and, on all fours, scrambled to the top where it leveled. Once there, he looked back and into the now-racing river, as it tore around the bend. Clay's body hurt all over, but right now, the part crying the loudest was his feet. He scanned the rocky countryside. A short distance away, at the bottom of a prickly pear and ocotillo-covered ridge, was a small overhang. The rain was still pouring. Now that he was safe from the flood, his wet body started shaking. *I've got to get under some cover,* he thought, *before I freeze to death in the middle of a Texas summer.*

He started toward the overhang, gingerly placing his bleeding feet on the rocky ground. He had no sooner started than the first hailstone struck. It was big. When Clay made a huge fist, the hailstone was bigger. Another crashed nearby, then another and another. He hated to run on his damaged feet, but he had to get to cover. A hailstone hit him on the left shoulder and almost drove him to the ground, but he kept moving.

With a relieved sigh, he slid into the small space. From there, his body racked with chills, he sat and watched the monsoon move through. Another time, under different circumstances, he could enjoy the majesty of the sight. The lightning crashed over and over, thunder booming across the desert, declaring, "Here is water for you," to the plants and animals.

In the roar of rain, thunder, and river, only partially clothed and deeply chilled, sunburned and ant-bitten, Clay let his mind drift. What was happening to Jake? Why would he send such a cryptic message? Was he still alive? How could he, Clay Barlow, help his friend or anyone, now that he was darned near helpless himself? Here he was, no knife, no guns, his shotgun gone, along with Blue, the best horse a man could have.

Blue had been with him when his folks were heinously murdered. Clay had ridden him over a good part of Texas, and now he was carrying Earl Griffin. His horse had been stolen once before, and Clay had gotten him back. Hopefully, fortune would smile on them again.

The monsoon moved slowly, hanging around for several hours. A small stream had developed along a gouge in the overhang he was under, and cascaded over the edge. While it lasted, Clay leaned his head back, and, with the rain beating his face, he drank deeply. The rainwater was sweet and soothing to his parched throat. When he wasn't drinking, he had taken to holding his feet under the stream to wash out the dirt and debris that had collected in the cuts and gashes of his swollen soles. It felt good. He held them under the flow for so long they had turned white and wrinkly. *That's all right,* he thought, *the water seems to cool the sunburn.*

Finally, the rain stopped, and the sun came out. The clouds moved away, leaving only a few scattered around as a reminder of what had passed. He sat for a few minutes, taking in the country-side, rough country. Most people would call it barren, stark, unforgiving. It was that, but more. Much of the flats were still covered in tall grass, brown now, but still nutritious for cattle and grazing animals. The hillsides glistened, freshly cleansed. Prickly pear caught the sunlight, showing off their purple fruit and pale green leaves. He wished he had a knife. The fruit of the prickly pear was tasty. He'd eaten it many times, but without a knife . . .

Clay examined his feet. They were in bad condition. Besides the sunburn that covered most of his body, except his back and legs, his feet had numerous cuts from the run on the rocks, some deeper than others. He inspected each sole, then sat wondering what he could do to protect them. As he sat with one foot crossed to the other leg, he flipped the cuff of his canvas pants several times. Suddenly the idea hit him: use part of his pants to make foot coverings. The next question was, how could he cut them? He had no knife.

He had seen the Tonkawa shape antlers into dagger-type knives, using flint-like rocks to produce edges. When they started using the white man's steel knives, they maintained their tradition.

Clay eased out from under the protective overhang. Limping, he scoured the ground, looking for the correct type of rocks. He moved closer to the running river. Finally, he spotted a large rock, round on one side and tapered to a narrow width on the other.

He picked up a bigger rock and moved back to the shade of his overhang.

Once there, he began to rub one rock against the other. With an edge of the bigger rock, he started bringing it down on the smaller one. Finally, having found the correct angle, a chip flew off of the smaller rock. With his small success, he quickened his pace. Clay didn't notice the sun drifting lower until it was shining almost directly into his refuge. He stopped and looked around. It was getting late in the day. He examined his handiwork. It wasn't perfect, but it was time he tried to cut his trouser legs off using the shaped rock.

He removed his pants, stretched them out on a flat rock, and started cutting—or rubbing. His edge wasn't nearly as effective as he thought it would be. Gripping the rock on the rounded side, he scraped the blade across the tough canvas material. A couple of threads pulled, but that was it. More determined than ever, he started moving the edged rock across the pants quicker. This time, when he stopped and looked at it, he saw a slight cut. He thrust a thumb into the hole and pulled. The material ripped lengthwise, down the leg. He stopped. That wasn't what he wanted. It needed to cut around the leg portion, so he could slip the material over his foot like a glove.

Using his makeshift knife, he cut, hammered, and tore at the fabric, until he had separated the leg portion from below the knee. He chipped at his knife with the bigger rock until he had broken off some finer flakes. Running his thumb across the blade, he could tell the knife was sharper. Clay went to work on the other leg. This time it went quicker. He stood up and slipped the shortened britches back on. He grinned at the sight he made. It reminded him of the pencil drawings in the book *Robinson Crusoe*. Pleasant thoughts flooded his mind, of his ma in her rocking chair and him seated next to her near the roaring fireplace while she read. Then the sight of her, murdered, invaded his mind. The killers had paid for their evil acts, but it would never be enough.

He sat down and pulled one lower pants leg over his right foot. It covered the foot perfectly. He'd need to tie up the toe, and also tie something around his ankle to keep the new *moccasin* up. Clay removed the material from his foot and limped to the desert willow that was leaning over the river. He pulled several of the strands hanging from the tree and slowly made his way back to his spot. On the way, he picked up a stick and, using it as a club, broke off prickly pear pads. Gently, being sure he missed the thorns and the soft stickers that were waiting to imbed themselves into his flesh, he took them with him.

Using his sharpened rock knife, he managed to slice through the end of a pad. He scraped and sliced one side of the pad until he had removed all of the thorns and stickers. Then he worked the knife around the edge until he could leverage up the outer portion. Once he could grip it, he skinned the thorny side until he had it loose and threw it away. He worked on three more pads until he had accomplished the same thing. Once finished, he put two pads each into the leg openings, with the skinned side up. Then, slowly, so as to ensure the pads didn't move, he slid in a foot. Once in, he tied the end in front of his toes with a willow string, and then tied a string around the remaining leg opening above his ankle. When both were done, he stood.

The soft pulp of the prickly pear felt good on his feet. He tried a step. A little squishy, but much better than a sharp rock. He hoped it wouldn't tear apart too soon. It was late, and he was whipped, but he had to get away from here and find food and clothing soon. He didn't think the outlaws would be back—they probably figured he had been killed by the flash flood—but they could surprise him.

Stepping out, he headed southwest. If he was going to survive, he needed a place to rest and heal—plus weapons. He knew how to make a bow and arrows, or a spear, but required the right kind of wood. For that, he must head for a higher elevation. To the southwest the land rose considerably, but the air would cool as he climbed. Fire would become a necessity. It was hard to think about fire, with his body burning—he had smeared some of the prickly pear pulp over his burns and it had helped—but he knew the sunburn would only get worse if he couldn't find something to use for clothing.

He made a misstep and drove his right foot into a sharp rock. Fortunately, the rock did not penetrate the canvas and the prickly pear, but the pain was excruciating. He was a big man, and the weight that was placed on the lacerated soles of his feet was already painful. Now this. He stopped for a few moments. When the pain had subsided to a bearable level, he continued toward the mountains.

In the dim light remaining, he could see a tree line ahead. Slowly he closed on it. Ash, desert willow, and cottonwood trees lined the creek. This one was also running. He could see debris lining the lower edges of the creek. The brush was healthy and green, and there was more vegetation along the bank, indicating water was available in this creek for many months of the year. Determined, he moved through the gathering darkness beneath the trees, looking for particular items. He needed a fire. It was getting cooler. With little clothing, he would have an uncomfortable night without heat.

3

Clay found a short, hollow log that was starting to rot. He broke a straight limb, two feet long and about the thickness of his thumb, from an ash tree. Using the stick, he felt around inside the log, making sure no rattler or skunk had made it his home. Finding neither, he examined the log. If he had his boots, he would stomp the log to break it open, but his feet weren't stomping anything. His canvas pants-shoes had been much tougher than he had hoped they would be. The prickly pear pads had also helped in protecting his torn feet, but walking across the rough terrain had slashed the fabric in several places.

He looked for a large rock. In this country, it wasn't hard to find. Clay hobbled over to one that was about the right size, guessing it weighed about twenty pounds. Satisfied with his choice, he carried it back to the log and slammed it against the top side. With the third blow, the log started to split. He didn't want to smash or splinter it. He wanted access to the inside. He put the rock down and grasped the log with both hands, each hand placed on the end with his fingers inside, and pulled. Slowly the log cracked open, revealing its precious interior—soft, dry debris. Now he picked up the stick that he had broken from the ash and trimmed the bark down, almost forming a point.

He had found a perfect place in the trees for a camp. Two ash stood within six feet of each other, and the ground around was fairly clean. He finished cleaning a small area and laid the short, split log in the center. Through his many visits to the Tonkawa, he had learned how to use a fire plough. It had always been a competition between him and Running Wolf, and his friend had beaten him every time, but he had learned.

Clay knelt in front of the log, gripped the limb in his big hands, and started rapidly rubbing it in one of the natural cracks of the log. It happened quickly. After no more than two minutes, smoke started rising. The shavings rubbed off the log had gathered along the path of the stick and at the end of the crack. From the larger pile of shavings, smoke grew thicker. He kept rubbing. Finally, a glow, a small ember, and then a tiny tongue of flame lifted from the shavings. Clay gathered more of the dry kindling from inside the log, and carefully held it to the flame. It lit. Slowly he added more, until finally, he could start laying sticks inside the log and across the flame.

The warmth seeped into his chilled body. With his dwindling strength, he gathered more wood, and as the fire grew, was finally able to lay a few substantial logs across it, relaxing for a few moments. Leaning against one of the ash, he pulled a handful of young mesquite beans from his pocket, took a big bite, and started chewing. *Surprisingly good,* he thought. His stomach growled in anticipation.

The beans were sweet and hearty, but he needed meat. No gun, no knife, no bow or arrow. He was in a tough situation. He could make a bow, but he needed string. Making string from the leaves of a yucca plant was possible, but he needed to boil it first —no pot. Clay stretched his legs out in front of him. His face and upper body felt chilled, but the skin was hot to the touch. The sunburn on his chest, shoulders, and feet was developing into water blisters. His immediate concern was infection. In the fire-light, he examined his body. It was covered with welts. He was lucky the ants hadn't had time to make it to his face. The last thing he wanted was for them to bite his eyes or inside his nose.

He needed more prickly pear pads. Careful of his canvas shoes, he stood and moved to a large growth of prickly pear within the light of the fire. Looking around for a stick more substantial than the one he had used to start the fire, he spotted one in the shadows. Moving deeper into the trees, he looked the stick over. It was just what he was looking for. Close to six feet long, relatively straight, and not quite as thick as his big wrists. He leaned over and grabbed it, yanking it from the vines that entangled it. Immediately, the ominous buzz of a rattlesnake filled the night.

Clay froze. He carefully eyed the area the sound was coming from and could just make out the rattler. Coiled, its head was lifted almost a foot above the coil and pulled back, ready to strike. Clay grasped his new staff in both hands and waited. The rattler continued to vibrate its tail, the triangular head drawing farther back. And then it struck. Lightning quick, the thick cudgel struck the snake alongside its head, knocking it sideways and into the ground. Grasping the staff by one end, Clay drove the opposite end deep into the rattler's head, pinning it to the earth. The snake thrashed and writhed, twisting itself almost into a knot.

The staff remained, pinning the snake securely, until there was no further movement. The body had relaxed and now lay limp. Clay bent over, and, still holding the head down with the staff, he grasped the tail and pulled until the body separated from the head.

Continuing to hold the rattler by the tail, he lifted it from the dirt. *At least five feet,* he thought. *I wanted meat, and now I've got it.* He tossed the snake next to the fire and went back to the prickly pear, knocking off several pads. Using his staff, he flipped the pads near his seat by the fire. He picked up his newly found meal, located a flat rock, and laid the snake across it. With his makeshift knife, he worked at the reptile until he had two, two-foot-long sections. Then he grasped the skin, separating it from the flesh, and pulled, ripping it the length of the section. Using his fingers, he cleaned out the intestinal tract, laid the clean piece on the rock, and repeated his actions with the second piece. He had found another stick about three feet long. Impaling the pieces of rattlesnake on the two sticks, he leaned them across the fire, using the rocks to support the sticks, and had himself another mouthful of mesquite beans.

While he crunched on the snack, he cleaned the thorns and tiny pods of stickers from the prickly pear pads, taking a break occasionally to turn the meat. Finally, he had the prickly pear cleaned off, including the attached tuna, the red fruit on the end of each pad. By this time, the first piece of snake was ready to eat. He pulled it off the stick and took a bite. This was the first meat to hit his lips since yesterday—it was delicious. He'd never been a big fan of snake, but this tasted as good as a juicy steak. As soon as he finished the first piece, he pulled the second from the fire and started on it. After a few bites, he laid it down and picked up the remaining stick. He impaled one of the prickly pear pads and propped it over the flames.

After finishing off the last of the snake, he concentrated on the prickly pear, making sure every little pod of stickers and remaining thorns were burned off. He let it cool for a few moments, pulled the purple tuna from the pad, and carefully, using his teeth, ripped it open so that he could get to the inside. It was reddish-purple, tasting similar to a mildly sweet melon. He'd always liked them. As a boy, he would collect a sackful and bring them home. His ma would clean them and make a delicious jelly. Clay checked the pad to make sure it was clean before taking a bite. Tough and sour, it was a sharp contrast to the tuna, but still good.

Standing on his aching feet, he gathered more wood. The day

couldn't have started worse, but he was lucky to end it with a full belly. The monsoon had brought water to the desert, and for the next few days, all of the seeps and holes would be holding water, solving one of his problems. He'd never run out of mesquite beans and prickly pear, so he could survive. His big concern was his feet. They felt a little better, thanks to the medicinal aid from the prickly pear, but he hoped they wouldn't be worse in the morning.

Clay couldn't help but think of Dee, her wide smile, her golden hair, and deep blue eyes. He needed to help Jake quickly, so he could return to her. *Could this be serious?* he wondered. *It sure felt like it as far as he was concerned, but how could you fall in love with a girl that quick? Is it really possible?* Then, as he dropped into a deep sleep, his last thoughts were about Blue. *I hope they don't treat you bad, boy. You just hold it together. I'm coming.*

HE AWOKE TO DARKNESS. The fire was nearly out, and he was freezing. Even with clothes, it would be cold, and all he had was sliced-up britches. He moved to get up, and the pain from his feet made him drop back into a sitting position. He pulled one foot up and looked at it. He couldn't see much, because of the darkness, but it looked bloody and swollen. He slid the canvas shoe back on and stood, gritting his teeth. After standing still, the pain subsided until he took his first step. After a few cautious strides, his feet felt better. *I need fresh prickly pear,* he thought.

He picked up wood and gently placed it on the fire, careful not to scatter the coals. The last thing he wanted was a grass fire. Moving back to his spot he sat down and spit a prickly pear pad on each stick. Once the fire was burning again, he seared the thorns and stickers off, repeating his actions with three more pads. He had bent over to start his work on the makeshift knife when he heard a hoof turn stone and a dog bark.

"Hola, Señor."

Peering into the darkness toward the sounds, Clay could just make out an outline of a man, then he heard a bell and the "baaa" of sheep. Initially, his hand had automatically reached for his guns, but, of course, they weren't there. *In my condition,* he thought, *there isn't much I can do, no matter what.*

"Good morning, Señor," Clay said. "Come on in."

An older man walked into the camp leading a donkey, a large dog accompanying him. He dropped the lead to the ground and moved over to Clay. The man's eyes grew large as he came into the light. Clay, looking huge in the firelight, wearing only his cutoff pants, his body sunburned, swollen, and covered in ant bites, must have been a frightening sight. Then the man saw his feet.

"Señor, what has happened to you?"

Clay grinned up at the man. "You might say, yesterday was not a good day."

He couldn't be sure in the light of the fire, but the man's eyes almost seemed to twinkle.

"Señor, I would observe, if you would permit me my poor English, you are a master of the . . . how do you say, subestimación?"

This time, Clay laughed. "The understatement. Well, you may be right. I'd offer you something to eat, but all I've got is mesquite beans and prickly pear. I've already finished off the snake."

Sheep started drifting through the brush around the camp. "Sorry, Señor, my babies have few manners. Do you mind if I join you?" He turned back to the donkey, lifting a plugged gourd and a sack from its back. The donkey stood with its head down and eyes closed.

"Reckon it doesn't matter to me. I sure don't own this place."

"Señor, would you mind if I fixed us some breakfast? And I believe I have something for injuries that will help your feet."

"No, sir, I sure don't have any problem with you putting

together something to eat." At the thought of it, Clay's stomach growled loud enough to wake the donkey. He lifted his head and looked directly at Clay. Then, when there was obviously no threat, he lowered his head and went back to sleep.

"Por favor, Señor, call me Miguel."

"Thanks, Miguel. My name is Clay, Clay Barlow."

"Gracias, Señor Clay. Now, let me fix something before your stomach eats itself. While I am doing this, you can tell me how you ended up in this poor situation, a big man like you."

Miguel went to work, first digging into the fire, moving coals to one side. After stacking a sufficient number of coals, he picked up several rocks, measuring each in his hands for the correct size and shape. He surrounded the coals with the rocks, leaving a channel open to the fire. Then he moved quickly to the donkey and removed a pot and skillet. He poured something from the gourd into the pot, and from the bag he had first brought over, he removed several links of chorizo and six eggs. He broke the eggs into the skillet, ripped the chorizo links open, and crumbled the sausage into the skillet, all the while keeping an eye on the pot.

While he was working, Clay told him the story of what had happened.

"I left Fort Davis early yesterday morning, headed for Presidio."

"Ah, Clay, you are a little off the course."

Clay moved his feet and winced. The pain was increasing, especially the right one. Miguel looked up when a short exclamation escaped Clay's lips. Then he looked back at the pot and skillet, stirred the mixture, and put in several ingredients, setting both on the rocks surrounding the coals.

He stood and moved to Clay. "Let me look at those feet." He slipped the makeshift shoes from the big man's feet and, one at a time, lifted them up. As he touched the soles, Clay had to concentrate to keep from wincing.

"It is not good, Señor Clay. I must clean them before dressing them. I am afraid they have". . . . Miguel paused for a moment searching for the word.

"Infection?" Clay said.

"Si, Si, *infección*. I am sorry, my English is not good."

"Miguel, your English is excellent."

"Ah, gracias," Miguel said, as he gently lowered Clay's foot to the ground and moved back to the fire. From his bag, he removed two metal plates and cups. Of the eggs and chorizo, he scraped two-thirds into one plate and the remaining portion into his. Then he poured the hot liquid into two cups and removed two forks and spoons from the bag, placing a fork on each plate and a spoon in each cup.

Picking up one cup and plate, he took them to Clay. "Careful of the drink, it is *muy caliente*."

Clay looked at the steam rising from the cup. "I can sure see that."

Clay's stomach growled again while Miguel moved back to the fire to retrieve his cup and plate.

"Please, Señor, do not wait for me. I think your stomach is telling you it is time to eat."

Clay nodded as he shoveled eggs and chorizo into his mouth. It was delicious. It was better than the finest meal in the finest restaurant in New York City. He took another big bite. After swallowing, he picked up his cup and looked at it. He couldn't tell what it was until he held it up to his nose—chocolate. He shot Miguel a questioning look.

The little Mexican's face broke into a guilty grin. "Señor, at my age, I no longer have many vices, but chocolate is one of them. One of my devoted sons brings it to me when he visits me from Chihuahua. He is a very important man in the government. If you ever need help in Chihuahua, ask for him. His name is Rafael Lopez. Tell him I told you that he would help you."

Clay took a sip of the hot liquid. It warmed and caressed his taste buds, flowing down his throat and bringing warmth to his body. It had a bite to it. "Miguel, this is really good," Clay said, before taking another sip.

"Yes, a touch of the pepper gives it the extra warmth. It is good for a cool morning such as this."

The two men turned to their food. Silence enveloped the camp, broken only by the sheep that now surrounded them. Miguel's dog had disappeared into the darkness.

After they finished eating, Miguel brought the pot over, still steaming, and refilled Clay's cup, pouring what was left into his own.

"I believe you were speaking of your travel?" Miguel prompted.

"Yes," Clay said. "I was jumped by four men, not far out of Fort Davis. It was my fault. I'd been traveling hard from Austin. Basically hadn't stopped, except to grab some shuteye and to eat. So I was pretty whipped, and my horse, Blue, was plumb tuckered out." Clay stopped to take another sip of his hot chocolate. "A man could get used to this."

Miguel nodded. "As I said, it is my vice. When I leave mi casa, I make sure I have plenty of chocolate with me."

Clay continued. "I'm not making an excuse, being tired, I mean. I just let my guard down, and those outlaws chose the right moment to jump me. They had me covered before I could do anything. One of them was Earl Griffin and another was Shifty Joe Beck. I'm not familiar with the rest of them, but I won't forget their faces. They grabbed me and led me to a dry riverbed. I figured I was a dead man, and it wasn't going to be pleasant. Once we got there, they found a red ant bed and staked me down over it. I guess I was lucky. If Beck hadn't suggested they do that, they probably would've just shot me, but I'll tell you, those ants. . ."
Clay stopped for a moment and scratched several of the red welts.

"This medicine," Miguel said, "will also help with the sunburn and ant bites. Wait just a minute."

Miguel rose, took Clay's empty plate and cup, and dropped both sets into the skillet. He then picked up the pot and skillet and headed to the creek.

Daylight was slipping into the trees. The myriad of stars Clay had watched were now disappearing in the brighter light. He waited for a few minutes. Miguel, following an animal trail through the brush, came back up the cut bank with the clean utensils and the pot full of water. He knelt down by the fire and raked more coals into his makeshift stove. Then he placed the pot of water on the supporting rocks and found a large log. Demonstrating more strength than one would expect from a man his size, he dragged it near the fire and Clay, and sat.

"Now, tell me more."

Clay shifted his back against the big ash and shook his head. "I couldn't believe they didn't shoot me. Griffin wanted to, but the other men were against it. I think Beck just wanted to have some fun. He seemed way too excited about staking me out, which is what they did. Griffin stayed on his horse, grinning, holding his six-gun on me. Several times he invited me to make a run for it. I figured I'd be better off in the ant bed."

"Sí I have heard about this gang. They are worse than a pack of coyotes. They rob and kill the poor as well as the wealthy. This Earl Griffin is a bad hombre, but Shifty Joe Beck, he is the meanest. He likes to bring pain to a person. The other two are Emmett Knox and Flint Jericho. Knox, I think he is just a down-on-his-luck cowboy. Flint Jericho is from California. I've heard he has a big reputation as a gunfighter back there, but I know nothing else about him."

"That sounds like an awful lot. How'd you come to know so much, if you don't mind my asking?"

Miguel appraised the big man. "I make it my job to know

what goes on in my mountains. In this country, the ignorant man dies. I have lived for many years. It is my goal to die in my bed with my sweet wife by my side."

Clay nodded. "Makes sense. I'd say that's a worthy goal. Your wife is still alive?"

"Oh, yes. My fourth wife is Alicia. My first three, Isabela, Veronica, and Teresa, have all died." He took his sombrero off and held it to his chest. "May God bless their sweet souls."

Clay was taken aback. "You've outlived three wives? How old are you, Miguel?"

The older man smiled at Clay, sliding his big sombrero back on. "I have to admit, I do not remember. When I hit sixty, I stopped counting, and that was right after I wed my third wife. Maybe eighty, maybe ninety, but what is age? Only a number. I feel very good. My fourth wife has given me six children. We are all happy."

This time Clay shook his head in amazement. "How many kids do you have?"

A big smile lit up the man's face, exposing even, white teeth. "Señor Clay, a moment, I must count." He concentrated, ticking off each one on his fingers and mumbling names. "With Isabela, and she was so sweet, there were ten. She passed suddenly in childbirth. Then Veronica, ahh, my lovely Veronica, we had twelve before an evil rattler, on the path to the outhouse, took her from me. Teresa only had eight. After our last son, his birth was very hard for her, the *partera*, how do you say . . ."

Clay, like many men who had grown up in Texas, was fluent in Spanish, and said, "Midwife."

"Yes, midwife. The midwife said she must have no more children. She was brokenhearted and ashamed. I tried to tell her it was all right, but she just moped around the house, doting on that little boy. She was dead within six months. I truly believe she died from sadness."

His sad face lit up. "That brings us to Alicia. She is such a joy, such a beauty. She was twenty-two when we married, and she has been a wonderful wife. I fear, as sweet as she is, she is the one who will see me in the grave." He shrugged his shoulders and, with a casual air, said, "Although, that thought has been in my mind with each of my wives. Only God knows."

The water was churning in the pot. Miguel stepped over to the donkey, scratched behind the little animal's ears, and pulled a roll of clean, white muslin from the pack. He tore a long section off and moved back to the pot with it in his hand. Using the muslin to protect his hands from the heat, he carried the pot of boiling water over to Clay.

"I am sorry, Señor Clay. This will be quite painful. I must get all of the dirt from your cuts. I will work as rapidly as I can, but it is important I get them clean."

Clay nodded and leaned back against the tree. Miguel had seated himself on the log and now picked up Clay's right leg, laying it across his knee. Tearing another piece of the muslin, he made a pad of it and dipped it into the water, immediately pressing it against Clay's raw foot.

Clay's jaw clamped shut. His jaw muscles worked like straining ropes as he clenched and unclenched his teeth. The pain was greater than he could have imagined. He grabbed one of the sticks that he had broken the night before and clamped both hands around it.

Miguel worked quickly. In several of the cuts, he had to dredge the muslin through the open cuts to pull the debris from the flesh. He examined the right foot, nodded in satisfaction, and picked up the left.

"Are you ready, Señor?"

Clay gave a short nod of his head. Despite the cool morning, sweat ran down his forehead. He reached up and wiped the salty moisture from his eyes. "Do it."

Miguel again soaked part of the cloth and immediately went

to work on the left foot. This one was not as bad as the right. He was able to clean it quicker, with little required dredging. When he had finished with both feet, he said, "Now let them dry in the air for a few minutes. Then I will make them feel much better."

"I'm looking forward to that," Clay said, followed by a small, self-deprecating grin.

Miguel nodded. "Once I get this medicine on those feet, I'll wrap them, but you must stay off your feet until they heal."

At Clay's immediate objection, Miguel held up his hand. "Clay, I am old enough to be your great-grandfather. I have seen and doctored many wounds. Trust me when I tell you, yours are bad. You must stay off your feet."

The big man sighed. "Miguel, I have got to get to Presidio. A good friend is in trouble, and he asked for my help."

"I am sorry, Señor, but you cannot help him with no feet, or worse. You must rest. I will rig a travois for my donkey, and we will take you to our mountain home. There, you can heal, and then, when you are better, you can help your friend."

Clay said nothing, but his mind raced. *How can I help Jake? It's already been almost three weeks. What if he's already dead or injured? I can't believe I allowed those crooks to capture me. I have no guns, no clothes, no horse, and bad feet.*

He felt a cool hand on his shoulder and looked up.

"Señor Clay. Your friend is either all right or he isn't. You worrying about him or accusing yourself will do no good. Lift your spirits, my friend. You might even learn something."

"Thanks, Miguel." *He's right,* Clay thought. *Pa always said worrying does nothing except ruin your day.*

"Now, I am going to put this *crema* on your feet and then I will wrap them. After that, I'll rub some on your sunburn and ant bites."

Miguel went to work. Clay's feet felt better as soon as the cream was spread over them. Once they were wrapped, a thought hit his mind. *They feel so good, I bet I can walk on them.* He started to stand, and Miguel shoved him back.

"No, Señor! You cannot stand on your feet. Do not be a stubborn gringo. You must listen to me. Listen!"

Clay heard the authority in the man's voice. This man may be a shepherd now, but he hadn't always been. He nodded his head in surrender. "All right, Miguel. I'll listen. Reckon I won't like it, but I'll follow your direction."

A smile returned to the little man's face. "Good. Now, let me get this crema on your chest and shoulders. It will help the sunburn and the bites."

He made fast work of spreading the white salve over Clay's sunburn. Even the ant bites felt better. Clay had tried to ignore them, but the stinging would push its way into his mind no matter how hard he tried to forget they were there. After he was finished, Miguel was off to find some strong limbs to make a travois. He carried a wicked-looking machete. Clay had also noticed, when Miguel threw his serape back to cook breakfast, the butt of a Colt Army protruding from his waistband.

In a short time, Miguel was back. Quickly, he put together the travois, securing a blanket across the two poles that would support most of Clay's weight. The cross braces were positioned for minimum discomfort. Miguel loaded the cooking gear back on the donkey and led the animal close to Clay. He removed an extra serape and sombrero from the donkey, handing them to Clay.

"Thanks," he said. "And thank you for that delicious breakfast. Those eggs and chorizo were perfect. If you don't mind my asking, how do you happen to have eggs in this rough country?"

The old man grinned. "Hunger always makes food better. As to my eggs, my home it is not far from here, and we battle the varmints to ensure we have many chickens. I love my eggs too much to allow the skunk and coyote to have them. When I go to the mountains, I pack a big sack with straw, placing my eggs gently throughout the sack. I very seldom have a broken one. Of course, I have been going to the mountains for many years."

"I'm thankful for your skill, and your chorizo was probably the best I've eaten."

"My special recipe. Guests always brag on my chorizo, that and the chocolate."

"Yep, hot chocolate is hard to beat."

Clay started to stand to get onto the travois.

"No, Señor. As I said before, you must not stand on your feet. You must crawl like a baby to the travois."

Clay looked up in disbelief.

"I am very serious, Señor. You must stay off your feet. Forget your pride, and get on the travois. We must be off to the high country."

Swallow your pride, Clay thought, *and just do it.* He reached for his staff, rolled to his stomach, and brought his knees up under himself. Then, as Miguel said, he crawled to the travois and pulled himself up onto it.

"Good. It is a long walk. It will be slow with my sheep." Miguel let out a long whistle, and moments later his black-and-white dog came trotting up. Miguel led him up to Clay. "José, this is Clay."

The dog sniffed at the big man's feet, then moved up to his hand. Clay scratched him behind his ears. The dog sat next to him, his long tongue hanging out.

"José speaks Spanish and English, with some French. He is an international dog. José, sheep!" Miguel took the donkey's lead and started off toward the mountain.

The dog jumped away from Clay and raced toward the wooly beasts. The animals had already started following Miguel, the donkey, and Clay.

Clay looked around as the travois bounced over the rough ground. His feet were definitely feeling better, but he knew he should stay on the travois. He remembered the torture of running out of the wash yesterday.

THEY STOPPED ONCE for lunch made of corn tortillas, jerky, and a paste of something and peppers. Whatever the ingredients, it was good. Never having been in this part of Texas, Clay had just assumed that the mesquite, creosote, and prickly pear continued up and over the mountains. How wrong he was. As they climbed, the climate changed drastically. The sweltering heat gave way to a much cooler temperature. The serape Miguel had loaned him felt warm over his bare upper body, protecting him from the coolness. The trees had been the big surprise for him. He'd read about the aspen in the northwestern states and territories but had never guessed he would see them in Texas. But here they were. Stands of shimmering green leaves, flashing in the wind, scattered in patches among the tall ponderosa pines. The views, as they worked their way into the mountains, were impressive. He could see forever. Looking back over the country they had departed, he could see the heatwaves rising from the red-tan ground. Dust devils pranced across the desert like wild horses, going in one direction, then suddenly charging off in another. Stark country but encompassing a beauty all its own.

Looking down the slopes they had climbed, he could see the dry bunchgrass, changed to tall blue stem, the trees from mesquite to oak to pine. He was lost in the majesty of the country, admiring the wide openness and freedom.

"We are here," Miguel said.

Clay twisted around so he could see over his left shoulder, spotting a small, but well-built cabin with windows, a porch, and a chimney rising from the back.

"Looks mighty nice, Miguel. Did you build it?"

"Sí. Many years ago when my Veronica was still alive. She

used to love to come up here and enjoy the cool air and the violent storms."

"I guess you want me inside?"

"Yes, Clay. For now. There are two rockers in the house. We can move them to the porch later, but don't forget how you must travel."

Clay nodded, picked up his staff, and rolled off the side of the travois. Once on the ground, he crawled the twenty feet to the house.

"Watch for the splinters on the floor, Señor. The wood of the old house is very dry."

Clay nodded. He made it up on the porch, then rolled over and sat, his legs hanging off the edge. The view was breathtaking. It couldn't have been an accident. Miguel must have positioned the house to take advantage of the panorama.

"Mighty fine view, Miguel," Clay called as the man unloaded the little donkey and led him to the corral.

"Yes. I built it for Veronica. She loved sitting on the porch in the morning to watch the sunrise. I tell you, it is worth seeing." The old man turned to the east, enjoying the view for a moment, then went on to the corral and barn.

The grass around the cabin was almost as tall as a horse's belly. Bells tinkled, and sheep poked their way through the tall grass, much like worms snaking through newly plowed ground, visible, then disappearing, then visible again, causing the grass to wave at the blue sky.

Miguel was working in the barn, leaving Clay to sit on the porch in frustration, anxious to be working, helping. It was not in his nature to lounge around while others labored.

After a few minutes, the Mexican returned from the barn, humming to himself, carrying two bandoliers, one with ammunition for his 40-50 Sharps, the other filled with forty-four cartridges for his two Army Single Action revolvers. His revolvers were in his waistband, while he carried the Sharps in his right hand and a large canvas bag in his left.

"The grass is tall and good for the sheep's belly," Miguel said, walking up to the cabin. "It will make them fat.

"José will watch them now. Come inside and see your new home."

5

C lay started to stand, thought better of it, and switched to his hands and knees. Once inside, he looked around the one-room cabin. It was more spacious than he had thought, looking at it from the outside. At the back was a large stone fireplace with a horizontal rod extending across the full width, the ends buried in the rocks. Wide enough, the fireplace would hold at least three pots side by side. In front of the fireplace were two rockers.

To the left of the fireplace was an oak table and chairs for six. The table was worn smooth from use. Next to the opposite side wall was a large bed, big enough for more than one person. An unusual sight, in a cabin such as this, was the intricately carved bed frame and headboard. A person very seldom saw this kind of handiwork for a bed, much less the tall blonde headboard. At the foot of the large bed, against the back wall, was a bunk bed.

Miguel laid the rifle, bandoliers, and bag on the sturdy table to the left of the door. After dropping his gear, he unfastened and swung the heavy shutters open, flooding the cabin with light. A welcome mountain breeze quickly cooled the stuffy room. Clay moved to one of the rockers and pulled himself up. Once in the rocker, he examined the headboard more closely.

"That is mighty fine work, Miguel."

The shepherd smiled at the compliment. "Gracias, Señor Clay. It took me a whole season to make it. It was for my Veronica. She detested sleeping on the floor. The poor woman was deathly afraid of scorpions. After our first trip, she said she would not come up here with me again without a bed. So a man does what he must."

"The bunk beds?"

"I built those for my girls, for when they come up with me. The boys sleep on the floor inside, or if it is not too cold, on the porch."

Clay nodded at the hardware Miguel had placed on the table. "Looks like you're prepared for whatever might happen."

"Sí. I've found that being prepared increases a man's lifespan."

He pulled one of the Colts from his waistband, hefted it, then walked over to Clay and handed it to him. Clay took it, immediately opening the loading gate and checking the cylinder—five loads. He flipped the gate closed, aimed it at a small rock in the back of the fireplace, then placed it in his lap.

"Thanks."

"For protection. I will be gone for several days, demands of the sheep. Hopefully it will not be needed . . ." He shrugged and started taking supplies from the bag.

"You've got some nice weapons."

The old man smiled. "Yes. There was a time when I fought for a living. I learned that the wolf does not worry about the coyote, but the sheep does. I prefer to be the wolf." He picked up the Sharps. "Also, there are bear in these mountains. I must protect my sheep from them."

Clay, his hand roaming unconsciously over the Colt, said, "Do you lose many sheep up here?"

"No. José is an excellent sheep dog. I trained him from a pup.

His only fault is that he knows no fear. He will attack anything that tries to harm the sheep, including the bear."

Miguel picked up the other rocker and moved it to the front porch. Clay slipped out of the rocker he was in, and Miguel took it outside, Clay following. Once more seated in the rocker, he examined his surroundings. The sheep were busy eating, and several half-grown lambs disappeared into the tall grass.

Once Miguel sat, Clay asked, "How long have you been coming up here?"

Miguel rocked back, thought for a moment, then said, "Many years. Time has moved quickly, but the land never changes. Oh, a tree may fall, or perhaps a fire, but life soon returns to normal."

The men rocked silently. The sun dipped behind the peaks to the west. From the cabin's location, the eastern plains were covered by shadow, moving slowly, as if a giant blanket was being laid across the expanse. Finally, Miguel spoke again, softly, almost as if he were speaking to himself.

"I am a happy man. Life has been very good to me. I have fought in many wars, had many children, and loved four special women." A faint smile drifted across his face. "Maybe more than four, when I was much younger. As a young man, I yearned for battle. To fight was to live, but as I grew older, I realized that life came from my family. I have many wonderful children, maybe two or three that aren't so wonderful, but they will learn."

Quiet again cloaked them, broken only by the call of the quail, howl of the coyote, and the sheep bleating round the cabin.

Miguel again broke the silence. "Are you married, Señor Clay?"

The question jerked Clay from his reverie. Surprised at the question, he spoke sharply. "No."

Miguel nodded his head slowly, to the rhythm of the rocking chair. "Ahh. You have perhaps come close?"

Clay watched the shadows cover the desert floor, and a smile brightened his face. "There's a girl. Her pa owns a ranch near

Comfort. When I get back, maybe." His mind drifted. *Dee was completely different from the girl whom, at the time, he thought was his first love, Lynn Killganan. It was not just appearance, though Dee was a blonde and Lynn had black hair. Dee had beautiful blue eyes, and Lynn had dark violet eyes. The big difference was, Dee accepted him for who he was, and Lynn could never reconcile his having killed men, even though they forced his hand. He truly believed Dee loved him.*

"Señor?"

Miguel brought Clay out of his thoughts. "Sorry, I was just thinking."

The old man smiled. "Yes, they can do that to you."

The coyotes howled again, interrupting Miguel. He cocked his head and listened. When they were finished, he gazed into the darkness. "You have the look of a lawman."

"Ranger."

Now Miguel's head turned, and he examined Clay more closely. "Yes, I can see the look." His tone sharpened. "So you are a member of the *los diablos Tejanos*?"

"Reckon I've never considered myself a Texas devil. That seems a little strong."

"From many of my people's viewpoint, not strong enough." The sharpness left Miguel's words as he continued. "But the past is the past. Here, we are just two men in the desert, one with his life ahead of him, and the other . . . watching the sunset."

Clay could think of nothing to say, so he remained silent. The coyotes had stopped howling, and the quail were silent. The only sound in the twilight was the squeaking of the rockers.

Miguel rose. "I will return shortly."

Clay could hear rustling taking place in the cabin. Then the faint smell of oak burning was followed by flickering light reflected on the cedar columns supporting the porch roof.

Shortly, Miguel returned with cups of hot chocolate. In the

wavering light of the fireplace his smile was a caricature of infinite age. He took his seat and returned to rocking.

"Thanks," Clay said, taking his chocolate. He took a sip, burning his tongue, and waited for it to cool in the evening air.

After a few minutes of the men sipping their chocolate, Miguel spoke again. "Marriage to a good woman is a blessing, Clay." Miguel chuckled. "I should know, I have been married to four good ones who have brought great happiness to me, sometimes immense frustration, but mostly happiness. Do not let the years pass you by. When you reach my age, life will become primarily a memory. Don't let the bad overpower the good."

"Thanks, Miguel. I'll think on that."

The darkness attempted to steal the light from the sky, but even though there was no moon, the stars lit the heavens. *Jewels,* Clay thought. *Ma always called them jewels because there were so many different colors.* With no moon, he could clearly see the mass of stars in the Milky Way, the two groups running parallel and then joining. Millions of stars, each with its own brilliance.

A sound in the cabin caused his head to jerk to Miguel's rocker. He was gone. Clay turned his attention back to the stars, wondering how long it would be before he was on his feet again.

"Come in, Clay," Miguel called. "Time to eat."

Clay looked at the floor. He tossed the residue from his cup to the ground and with a sigh, eased down on the rough planks. *It won't be long,* he told himself as he crawled back inside.

TWO WEEKS HAD PASSED. Feet mostly healed, Clay was putting together a pack. Surprisingly, the time had passed quickly for him. Within only a few days, he was able to walk, carefully at first, but at least he could stand and walk. Miguel had some tanned elk hide, out of which Clay made himself three pair of moccasins and a shirt. His work was a little rough, but it fit. The shirt would provide protection from the sun. Thanks went again to Miguel as he gave Clay the extra sombrero and wool poncho.

As the morning sun rose over the western peaks, Miguel sat outside, rocking and singing. Clay had quickly gotten used to the old man's rituals. Every morning, after breakfast, he would go outside and sing to the sun as it rose. He told Clay that it was in gratitude for his wonderful life.

Clay had learned that the man's life had been anything but easy. The loss of his wives weighed heavily on his heart. Of his thirty-two children, ten had died or been killed, yet this man saw life as a blessing. Miguel had taught Clay more about life over the past two weeks, than he'd learned during the two years he spent at law school in New York. He caught himself humming along with Miguel as he packed. He stopped, grinned, and continued packing and humming.

The second week, he worked around the stable and corral, doing repairs that the old man could not quite handle. He had also mucked out the small stable, following Miguel's direction and piling all the straw and manure along the outside wall of the barn. Miguel said that Alicia loved to use it in her garden when she came up. She would be coming soon, so Clay cleaned out weeds and hoed the plot, getting it ready for her late planting when she arrived. Miguel had been thrilled at the work in the garden and around the property.

It was too bad Alicia couldn't come up with Miguel and stay longer. But the younger children would have to be left with her father and sisters. Though she wanted to be with Miguel, it would be too painful for her to be away from the younger niños for the complete season.

The rocker and singing stopped, and Miguel, slightly stooped, came back into the cabin. "Ah, Clay, I hate to see you go. You have brightened my life. Old like I am now, I get lonely quicker. It was good to have you here."

Clay scratched at one of his legs. Some of the ant bites still itched. "Miguel, you saved my life. I don't know what I would've done if you hadn't come by."

"You would have done what you must to survive. You are truly a survivor."

Clay laid the Colt revolver and the extra ammunition Miguel had loaned him on the table. The man had also given him a knife and scabbard, which now rested on his right hip, hung there from a piece of rope tied around his waist.

Miguel walked to the table and picked up the Colt. "What is this?"

"Amigo, I can't take your Colt. They are expensive, and you need all the firepower you can get, up here by yourself."

"First, I am not by myself. I have José. The second thing is that I want you to have it. If you ever happen by here or mi casa, you can return it to me. But for now, you must take it. No man should go into this country unarmed. Remember the wolf and the sheep, Señor." Miguel looked the big man over, noting the wide shoulders, big arms and narrow waist. "Although, I don't believe you have ever been a sheep."

Grateful, Clay picked up the Colt, sliding it behind his waistband. "Much obliged, Miguel. I don't know when it'll be, but I will get it to you."

"Here, take this," Miguel said, handing him a leather bandolier. "It will save you from having to carry the bullets in the box, which is already coming apart."

Clay took the bandolier and started filling it with cartridges from the box. It had forty-three loops for ammo on it, and he filled every one. Once filled, he slid the remaining seven cartridges, still in the box, across the table to Miguel.

"This should be more than enough." Dropping the loaded bandolier over his head onto his left shoulder, he slid the other end under his right arm. Out of habit, he left his right shoulder open for the butt of a rifle—which he didn't have.

"Take the trail through the mountains," Miguel explained. "It will guide you to Presidio. When you reach the end of the mountains, it will be about a day's journey. Turn west. Four to five days, on foot, should put you at Presidio."

Clay swung the pack to his back, moved it a couple of times to find the most comfortable position, and said, "Miguel, I can never repay you for what you've done. That salve of yours fixed up my feet, not to mention those ant bites and sunburn."

Miguel thrust out his hand. "I am glad I could be of help. Time passed quickly with you here. Now you go do your duty, and then get back to your señorita. I am sure she is anxious. As for me, in only a few days, my Alicia will be arriving with the children."

Clay took the man's hand in his. He felt an unusual attachment to this old Mexican sheepherder. This was almost like leaving family. "Take care of yourself." He turned and headed out the door.

"*Vaya con dios, mi amigo,*" Miguel called to him.

Just before stepping into a screen of aspen, Clay raised his hand in salute. The cool of the early-morning mountain air was invigorating. He felt like breaking into a run but thought better of it. Miguel had cautioned him about taking care of his feet. They were still healing and tender. The last thing he wanted to do was tear the new skin on the soles.

Distance fell behind him as he strode quickly down the trail. It felt good to be stretching his legs, feeling their strength pushing him forward, drawing him closer to Jake and Presidio with each step. With his thought of Jake, he hoped the ranger was all right. It had been over a month, almost five weeks, since he had received that cryptic note. Even maintaining his current long stride, another week would pass before he would arrive in Presidio.

The miles dropped away as he drew farther from Miguel's cabin, and Clay's mind stayed with the old man's kindness. He was deeply in debt to the man and would like to pay him back before leaving the country. Miguel had explained how to find his casa. It was located south of the southwest end of the Chisos Mountains. He hoped he would see Miguel again before heading back to Austin.

Time passed quickly. He slowed his pace slightly. It was time to watch for the turnoff to the west. If he kept going to the end of the mountains, Miguel had told him he would be looking at a precipitous drop with no trail to the bottom. Plus, he needed to be as quiet as possible. Miguel had explained that Apache raiders out of Mexico came through this area. He came to a clear spring and filled his goat skin. After carefully examining the surrounding area, he stretched out and drank his fill of the cold, sweet water. Once filled, he stood, pulled a piece of jerky from his bag, and visually checked the trail ahead.

Through the pine trees, he spotted a faint trail leading off to the west. This must be the one Miguel had meant. Starting on the path, it began to slope down almost immediately. Within a short time, he had dropped out of the big pines and aspen into scrub oak and juniper. Before long, those turned to mesquite and palo verde. He stopped and looked back up the mountain. The days there, in the cool air, had been pleasant. Now, as he traveled lower, the heat was returning. Clay continued out of the Chisos. On this side of the mountains, everything was turned on end. Jagged, vertical, volcanic, it thrust up at crazy angles, the earth and rocks, variants of red and orange, all shades from light to dark. It was majestic, threatening, and beautiful.

He must be careful crossing this land. Some of those rocks would slice through his moccasins like his Bowie knife through a tender steak. His hand reached to his right side to verify his knife was still there. Not his own Bowie knife, for it rode on Earl Griffin's saddle, but the knife given to him by Miguel. His mind drifting to the outlaws, a feeling of deep anger began to boil within. His hand drifted from Miguel's knife to the empty space under his left arm. He had gotten used to the weight of the shoulder holster containing his Smith and Wesson. Now it, as well as the two he normally carried on his hips, were gone.

He hadn't even been bothering them, just riding through. They saw easy prey and pounced. *We'll see who pounces when I find them,* Clay thought.

The sun was drifting low in the west, turning the reds, oranges, and yellows of the desert into a myriad of brilliant colors. Clay started looking for a place to camp. On the eastern side of a low ridge he was approaching, and well away from the trail, were some large boulders. He turned off the trail, picked a small limb from a creosote bush that still had its leaves, and lightly brushed out his tracks for twenty-five or thirty yards. Satisfied with his handiwork, he continued to the boulders.

Once among them, he could see that others had the same idea, for there was a pit dug, and dry logs and branches lay next to the pit. On the ridge side, where boulders backed against the slope, there was an indentation in the bank. It couldn't be called a cave for it wasn't that deep. But inside, it had been cleaned and obviously slept in. He looked around further. On the back of the wall were some drawings of antelope. Several men with bows and spears were attacking the animals.

He continued to look around and found small bones of other animals, remnants of meals. Having seen enough, he moved out from the boulders, continuing along the bottom of the ridge for at least half a mile. *I'll not be staying in such a popular spot,* he thought. *I'd rather not wake up with an Apache's knife in my ribs.*

6

Clay found a likely place among another jumble of smaller rocks. They were still big enough to hide him, but much farther from the trail. He shed his pack. There was no good reason to light a fire, and every reason not to, especially with such a popular campsite not too far away. He pulled some jerky from his pack, leaned against a sloping rock, and started eating. He watched the stars slip from their hiding places to become visible in the darkening sky. Just before rolling over and going to sleep, he slid the Colt from behind his waistband, keeping it in his right hand. The bandolier of ammunition lay on his right side, next to the goatskin. He thought about taking another drink of water, ruled against it since he had no idea how long it would be before he found another spring, and stretched out. His head on the pack, he was asleep before the first coyote howled.

He came awake to a moonlit sky and distant voices. Listening, he pinpointed the voices to his first camp selection. He quickly said a short thank you that he had decided not to stay there. With the bandolier, his knife, and his pack on, he eased to the nearest rock, covering him from the direction of the sounds. Opening the loading gate of the Colt, he dropped a cartridge into the remaining empty chamber, and closed the gate. He was ready.

Six shots and no rifle. The Colt was a fine handgun, but it had one big drawback. It took too long to load. First, a person had to open the loading gate, then select each chamber, press the ejector rod to kick out the empty cartridge, and drop a fresh round into the vacant chamber. That's why he loved his Smith and Wesson revolvers. They broke open by grasping the barrel, releasing the catch, and swinging the barrel down, which pitched the cylinder up. When it hit the stop, it tossed out all six of the empty cases. All you had to do then was drop the fresh rounds in and close it —ready for business. *Wish I had mine back,* Clay thought, and grinned, his straight, white teeth framed by the thick black mustache. Pa always said you could wish in one hand and stack cow manure in the other and see which one filled up the fastest. When Ma heard him, she would scold him for being crude. That was her French upbringing. Pa would just grin at her and kiss her on the cheek.

Clay listened closely. It sounded like they were speaking Apache. He had learned a few words, growing up in Texas. There were at least three of them, maybe more. He sat still behind the boulder and listened. He couldn't make out all the words, but he could tell they were arguing. At least one wanted to return to Mexico, but the others were for continuing deeper into Texas. It didn't make any difference to him what they did, as long as they loaded up and left, so he could get on with his travels while it was still cool. Then he heard the word for prisoner, quickly followed by a cry. The sound of a hand striking flesh followed by what sounded like a whimper drifted to him over the desert landscape.

He shook his head. They weren't arguing about going back to Mexico, they were arguing about killing the prisoner or taking him back with them. Clay immediately put his needs aside and started slipping toward the Apache camp. He brought all of the skills he had learned from Running Wolf and his father into play, slipping silently closer to the Apaches. He grew nearer and was able to understand them. They were drunk. *All the better,* he thought.

The quarter moon overhead cast few shadows but provided dim light for him to vaguely make out the ground. He stepped clear of a limb lying across his path.

Drawing near to the Apache camp, he caught glimpses of the men as they moved behind the boulders, waving arms and fists at each other. The trip across the moonlit ridge had taken more time than he would have liked. Daylight was sneaking in from the east, overpowering the weak light of the quarter moon. He reached out and touched the nearest boulder. Coming within feet of their camp, the only thing that separated him from the three men was the boulder he stood behind. He moved his gun to his left hand, carefully slipped his pack to the ground, and drew his knife with his right.

From Clay's position, he could clearly see one of the men throw up his arms in frustration and yank out his knife. It was now or never. Clay had done well on his stalk. Taking his time, being deliberate, feeling every step through his moccasins and his tender feet, he had cleared at least four hundred yards without detection.

The creosote bush is a most adaptable plant. Its sparse green leaves conserve the few raindrops that fall upon them through the years, surviving and slowly multiplying. This particular creosote was over one hundred years old. Unfortunately for it, in the fall of the previous year, a majestic mule deer buck, deep in the throes of the rutting season, had taken out its anger and passion on this small bush, ripping it apart with his antlers. What had once been a small but stately creosote was now a broken and battered little bush, with only one or two tiny limbs remaining.

Clay started around the boulder, and a thin limb from the almost invisible creosote bush brushed softly on his buckskin sleeve. At the sound, one of the horses snorted. Knowing the

Apaches had been alerted, he tossed caution to the wind and leaped around the boulder. Only two Apaches stood facing him, both with rifle muzzles coming level. He fired at one, striking the man in his chest. The recoil of the Colt kicked the barrel up, tilting the rear of the gun into the web of his hand between his thumb and forefinger. In one smooth motion, his thumb slipped over the hammer, and, as the muzzle came down on the second Apache, effortlessly brought the hammer to full cock. Once the muzzle leveled on the second man, he squeezed the trigger, driving a second slug into that surprised Apache's face, his rifle clattering to the rocks at his feet as he collapsed next to his dead companion.

As the second explosion of his Colt crashed in the surrounding rocks, Clay was driven to the ground from the weight of the third Indian. The knuckles of Clay's left hand hit the face of a broken rock, jarring the Colt from his grip. The Indian, riding his back, yanked Clay's head back with his right hand, and, using his left, brought the razor-sharp scalping knife in front of Clay to slice open his throat. No more than three seconds had passed since the first shot.

Clay's left hand, still tingling from the blow on the rock, shot up and wrapped around the Apache's wrist, pulling and twisting simultaneously. The knife was still in his right. He drove it up and behind him, feeling it grate across the man's skull. The Apache leaped from Clay's back, twisting his body in an attempt to break the big man's grip on his wrist, which succeeded, but left the Indian on his back. Clay was instantly on him, bringing his knife to the man's throat.

The instant the blade touched the Apache's throat, the smaller man went wild. He brought both feet up and kicked Clay in the groin. Exquisite, debilitating pain shot through the big man's body. Even with death so close, he could hardly keep from throwing up. In an instant, the Indian was on his feet, scooping up his knife and turning to attack.

Clay fought through the fog of pain. Fortunately, in spite of the pain, he had managed to hang on to his knife.

Seeing Clay distracted with pain, the Apache rushed forward, and, with his blade held high, thrust down, aiming for the junction between Clay's neck and shoulder.

The boxing moves that had been drilled into Clay during his time in New York came to his aid. He slipped slightly to his left, knocked the Indian's knife arm away, and drove the big Bowie deep into the man's chest. For a moment the two men stared at each other, then the light slowly departed from the Apache's eyes. Clay laid the man on the rocks and pulled the bloody knife from the inert body. He quickly looked around, seeing the captive for the first time. He moved to his Colt, picked it up with shaking hands, and reloaded. He was covered with blood, thankfully, none of it his.

Pain still coursed through his body. He looked around the campsite that had almost become his grave. Neat and peaceful last night, it was a battlefield this morning. Dawn was only now starting to brighten the day. It had only been minutes since he stepped around the boulder.

"Well, don't just stand there. Untie me!"

Clay had forgotten about the prisoner. Surprised by the sharpness of the female voice, he turned to see an older woman, probably in her late forties, maybe fifty. He moved quickly to untie her bindings.

"Am I glad you came along. I was done for, you understand? Done for. You're a big one, aren't you?"

After untying her hands, he moved to her feet, while she rubbed her wrists.

"Where are you from, ma'am?"

"Well, I'll be, you can talk, can't you? I know you can fight. My goodness, I never seen the like. Quick as a wink you appear from behind that boulder and blast those two heathens. I just knew you were a goner when that third one jumped you. He did it so fast I didn't have time to yell. Just wait until I take you to Mr. Tate. That's my husband, Morgan Tate. Owns a ranch, some distance from here. He'll be mighty glad to see you, yes, he will."

Clay had untied the woman's feet and was rubbing her ankles.

"I'm sure glad you came along. They grabbed me a couple of days ago. Thought they were gonna kill me. But Mr. Tate is well known in this country. I think they were planning on selling me back. In fact, I'm sure that was their plan until that feller that jumped you decided he wanted my hair. It might have something to do with me slapping him. He tried to get fresh with me. I'll have no man touching me. Except for Mr. Tate, of course."

"Mrs. Tate, do you think you can stand?"

"I can stand. I don't see how you can. You took quite a kick in the family jewels."

The brightening sky of the new day reflected off Clay's red cheeks. He'd never heard a woman talk like this.

"No need to be embarrassed, young feller. I've seen many a man hit down there, and I know it can hurt. You'll be sore for a few days, but you'll get over it. What's your name?"

While the woman continued to talk, Clay went to calm the three horses. At the white man and blood smell, they stepped back, pulling on their lead ropes. He laid a calming hand on one's neck and started talking. Gradually they calmed. One stretched his neck around to smell of him, the blood not bothering him. Clay scratched that one behind the ears. Now that they were quieted, he moved to examine the dead Apaches. Two of them had 1873 model Winchesters in 44-40 caliber. The weapons were worn from heavy use. He picked one up and worked the action, smooth. Examining the open chamber and barrel, he found both clean with signs of wear.

"Name's Clay Barlow, Mrs. Tate."

"You the Del Rio Kid?"

Turning back to the woman, Clay's forehead wrinkled,

eyebrows drawn together. "That name wasn't my idea, ma'am, and I don't like it! I'd be obliged if you didn't use it."

"Don't cloud up on me, sonny. How was I to know you was so touchy?"

"You know now," Clay said, and turned back to the Indians. He removed the belted bandolier one carried and laid it next to the weapons he was collecting. One of the two Apaches he had shot had an old Remington Army conversion. The dead man had it hanging over his shoulder with the gun across his chest. The gunbelt was loaded with the .46-caliber metallic cartridges. He swung around to the woman.

"Can you shoot?"

Out of one of the folds of her dress, she pulled a small tin of snuff, took a pinch between her lip and gums, then stuck it back into the pocket. "Been shootin' since I was knee high to a short grasshopper. Folks came out in '32, and I was born six years later, kinda in the middle of the pack. Them Comanches was right pesky, so my pa learned all us kids to shoot as soon as we was big enough to stay on our feet when we pulled the trigger. So yeah, I can shoot."

He carried one of the rifles over to her. She was on her feet now, scrounging around the camp. She had taken the knife of the warrior who had jumped Clay, along with the leather scabbard he had around his waist. Blood didn't seem to bother her.

"What you planning on doing with that Remington?"

"I was planning on giving it to you, if you can shoot it."

"Clay Barlow," Nora said, stopping to take a spit. "I can shoot anything a man can, and mostly better. Now gimme that Remington."

He handed the Remington and the gunbelt to her. She popped open the loading gate, checked the loads, and swung the belt around her waist. Once fastened, she slid the holster back and forth until she had it in the right place. "There, now, let's get outta here."

Clay had lain the bodies side by side. He had nothing to dig with, and it probably wouldn't have made any difference if he had, the ground was so hard. He started collecting rocks to cover the bodies.

"What in blue blazes are you doing?"

Clay stopped, raised to his full height, placed both hands to his waist, and bent back, stretching. Then he picked up another rock and continued his effort. "I'm burying these men as best I can. At least this should keep the coyotes away from them."

"Those are Injuns, boy. If'n they had killed you, which they almost did, they woulda ripped off your scalp, and if you was lucky, left you to die in the desert. You're wasting your time, and mine. We need to get outta here now."

She is right, Clay thought. *As much as I hate to admit it, we need to get away from this place as fast as we can.* He finished laying the last of the stones on the communal grave.

"Then let's go. I didn't see any saddles. You need some help getting on?"

She looked at him like he was a crazy man, walked over to one of the horses, and started talking to him. She spent only a moment talking, then, with one hand full of reins, she grabbed the horse's mane with the other, and with a grace that belied her age, leaped on the animal's back, straddling him perfectly.

"Nope," she said, grinning, "guess I don't need any help."

Clay stepped behind the boulder, picked up his pack, and slipped it on. Then, following her example, but a tad more carefully, he leaped to the back of his horse, leaned over, and picked up the lead rope of the remaining animal. "I'm following you, Mrs. Tate."

The woman gave a short nod and headed for the trail. Once on it, she kicked her horse in the ribs and, without a look back, her rifle across her legs, she loped in the direction Clay needed to go.

Since the trail was narrow, they couldn't ride side by side.

That quieted her down quite a bit. She had tried turning to talk several times, but the bouncing and talking must have been too uncomfortable for her. She hadn't said a word for over an hour. She rode down into a shallow valley and stopped. Clay pulled out of the trail, and halted his mount next to her.

"There's a spring that way," Nora said, and pointed to their left. "It'll be good for the horses if we got 'em some water. That'll also give you a chance to wash off that blood. You look a sight."

"Good idea," Clay said. "Lead the way."

This time he moved up, about ten or fifteen feet to her left side. She stayed quiet, but he noticed her hand rested on the Winchester with her thumb on the hammer. She obviously knew guns and how to use them. They came around the low hill and could see several cottonwood trees and green grass. He pulled up the buckskin he was riding, and Nora followed suit. They sat for a few moments checking the spring and the surrounding hills— nothing. He bumped the buckskin, and they started forward again.

Arriving at the spring, he slipped off his horse and started around to help her. Before he was halfway around, she came walking to the front.

"I told you, I ain't a woman what needs help. Why, when Mr. Tate and I was young, he'd leave me and the kids for days on end, nothin' but a rifle, a shotgun, and a six-gun. I took care of whatever problem might arise."

He started to reply when a group of riders topped a rise heading straight for the spring—and them.

7

They weren't Indians. As they drew closer, Clay counted eight. A few more moments passed and Nora started waving frantically. The big man in the middle of the group jerked his hat off, stood in the saddle, and waved enthusiastically.

When the men pulled up, the big man who had been waving leaped from the saddle and wrapped the woman in his arms. They held the embrace long enough for Clay and the other men to start getting embarrassed. Finally, they separated.

"Nora, you scared the hell out of me!"

"Well, excuse me! Those blasted Indians had me pretty scared, too."

At her statement, the big man grabbed his wife again in a big bear hug. After a few moments, she pushed away and said, "Yep. If it wasn't for this young feller,"—she tossed her head of brown and gray hair toward Clay—"I'd be dead."

Morgan Tate handed his reins to one of his men and strode over to Clay, his hand extended. Clay took the hand and had his shaken vigorously. "I'm much obliged, young feller."

Clay could see the man's blue eyes tear up. "Glad I was there, Mr. Tate."

"I'm mighty glad you was, too. Reckon I don't know what I'd do without my Peach."

The cowhands who were with Tate took the horses to water leaving only the Tate's and Clay.

Nora walked over and put her arm around the big man's waist. "Clay, this is my husband, Morgan Tate. We've been married for over thirty-five years. It'd be mighty hard for either one of us to have to go on without the other."

Morgan Tate pulled his wife to him and gave her another long kiss. She finally broke away from him and slapped him on the chest. "Here now, that's enough of that. You're gonna embarrass this here young feller." She grinned and continued, "If he ain't already embarrassed in those fancy pants, I'm bettin' there's a story behind them fine trousers."

Clay looked down at his sun-browned legs jutting out of the ends of the sheared canvas pants. "There definitely is."

"Well then, you need to tell that to us, but first, we both owe you mighty big. You and Morgan being about the same size, I bet he wouldn't mind giving you a pair of his britches."

Clay laughed. "You're sure not wrong. I'd be much obliged, if it's all right with Mr. Tate."

"Boy, you brought my Peach back to me. You can have anything I've got, and to you I ain't Mr. Tate. Call me Morgan."

Clay watched the older couple hug each other again. *They may be a little rougher around the edges than Miguel,* he thought, *but they seem mighty happy together.* His mind immediately went to Dee.

The cowhands had obviously lived in the Chihuahuan Desert for a while. The first thing they did was fill their canteens and water bags, then they led the horses up to the pond. The horses drank greedily from the cool water. Several of the men had moved away from the camp, setting up lookouts. A couple of them were busy cleaning out a pit and gathering wood. Before long, they had a fire going.

Morgan insisted on hearing what had happened, so Nora began her tale. Clay found out she had been out checking calves. She had ridden out with one of the cowhands and had been headed toward an old cow and her calf when the Apaches jumped the two of them, appearing almost under their feet. They shot the cowboy with an arrow through his chest and before he could fall, he was yanked from his horse by one of the men and scalped. Both her horse and her companion's spooked and returned to the ranch. The Indians had loaded her behind one of the braves and headed for the Chisos Mountains, leaving her guardian dying in the hot desert sand.

Morgan took over for a moment. He had been working cattle and didn't get in until late in the afternoon. When neither she nor the cowhand had returned, he rode out to look for her, finding not her but the scalped man, who was dying but still alive. The man explained what had happened, and the direction they had taken. They got him back to the ranch, loaded up, and headed in pursuit.

Clay shook his head and, speaking to Morgan, said, "She didn't mention this, but your wife slapped one of the Apaches."

Nora's eyes fired daggers at Clay.

Morgan turned to look at his wife and started laughing. "Danged if that ain't my Peach."

She had her hands on her hips. "Honey, he tried gettin' fresh, and I wasn't having none of it."

Morgan waved the cowhands over to him. "Boys, listen to this." He turned to Clay. "Tell 'em, young feller."

Clay grinned and then told them what Nora had done. The cowboys erupted in laughter. Comments like, "I believe it," and "That's Mrs. Tate, for sure," echoed around the camp.

Nora was still standing with her hands on her hips. She laid her evil eye on each of the cowboys. "Every one of you boys have worked here for a passel of years. I'd hate to see you lookin' for a job, and that's what's gonna happen if I hear that story repeated. Does everybody understand me?"

Amidst chuckles and grins, "Yes, ma'ams," followed quickly.

The group broke up, still laughing. A short time later, "Coffee's ready," was called from the fire.

A few large cottonwood limbs had been pulled up around the blaze, far enough away so as not to get roasted in the late afternoon heat. Morgan and Nora sat down next to Clay.

"Now tell me, Clay. How'd you end up saving my Peach?" Morgan said.

"It's a long story, Morgan."

"We've got the whole evening."

Clay nodded and started from the beginning. The cowhands who weren't on guard gathered round, and before only a few minutes had passed, everyone was enthralled with the story. At the mention of his name, looks were passed among the crew. Then he added that he was a ranger. Several heads nodded, as if they already knew.

When he mentioned Shifty Joe Beck, Earl Griffin, and the red ant bed, Morgan spoke up. "I know that whole gang. They are a rotten, low-down bunch. But I'm thinking there's more than four. There's at least six in that bunch now. And not the lot of 'em's worth the powder it'd take to send 'em to hell. We've lost cattle— not many—but a few, and I know that gang is at the bottom of it. If I ever get my hands on any one of 'em they'll be swingin' from the nearest tree."

Clay spoke of getting out of the river bottom just ahead of the flash flood. All of the cowboys nodded. One of them spoke up. "Back in '52 I was up the hill from our house. Pa had built next to a creek, just above the cut bank, figgered we'd be safe there. Big rain come along and washed the house, Ma, and two brothers and a sister down the creek. Pa and I found 'em the next day, near five miles away, hung up in some brush."

Everyone was quiet, drinking their coffee. Finally, in a soft voice, Morgan spoke up. "Never heard that story, Joe Bob. We're mighty sorry. Flash floods can be bothersome things. I was over Austin way in '69, when it rained so much, we was thinking about buildin' an ark. The Colorado River got so high, it clean washed Bastrop and LaGrange away. Mighty sad—lot of folks died."

Morgan took another sip and said, "Go on, Clay, tell us how you ended up over here on this side of the mountains, and about those fancy britches you got there."

The crack about Clay's britches lightened the mood, and everyone chuckled. Clay continued, telling them about his feet, and using a sharp rock to cut his britches. When he reached the part about Miguel finding him, Morgan spoke up again.

"I'm not much on sheep. They're filthy little animals, but I've got to tell you, Miguel Lopez is quite a man. If he ranged on my land, I'd let him. He's always helpin' other folks."

Nora spoke up. "He's had four wives. They've all died, except the current one, and a very pretty girl she is. I've heard he's had over thirty kids. Can you imagine raising thirty kids? You'd think he'd be worn out, but he just keeps having 'em. I think he's had four or five with Alicia."

Clay grinned. "Make that six, and when I was leaving, he said she'd be arriving anytime."

One of the cowboys rolled his eyes. "Look for number seven a little past the new year."

Laughter rang out around the campfire. Morgan asked, "Does anyone know how old he is?"

There was no answer.

"Well," Morgan said, "in all seriousness. If that old Mexican ever needed help from me, he'd get it."

Murmurs of agreement traveled around the group. Before Clay could start again on his tale, Morgan said to Emmett Westin, "Why don't you whip us up some grub? We want to get an early start tomorrow."

"Yes, sir, Mr. Tate. Be glad to." The man stood and walked back to the pack horse.

"Go ahead, Clay. No more interruptions," Morgan said.

Clay picked up where he had left off. He glossed over the rescue of Nora, but she didn't let that pass.

"If you won't tell it, Clay, I danged sure will." She turned to her husband. "So I'm figurin' I'm dead or worse. Those Apaches finally stopped at a right nice camping spot, although I'm guessing there won't be any other Indians camping there now. We had pretty much settled down. I managed to get a little sleep, when, in the morning, they wake me up arguing. It's still dark, so they've got the fire going. I figure they're arguing about me, because the feller I had slapped keeps pointing at me and yelling at the other two. They was arguing back, shaking their heads. I figured the one wanted to take my hair and kill me."

Clay spoke up. "I speak a little Apache. The other two wanted to sell Nora back to you." He indicated Morgan. "One of them said they would never be able to rest if Nora was killed. Said that no Apache would be safe, man, woman, or child."

Morgan shook his head. "I ain't never killed a woman or child, and I wouldn't start. But if something happened to my Peach, I'd lay waste to the varmints that did it."

Nora patted her husband on the knee. "I'm just fine, honey. You ain't got to worry. Anyway, as I was saying, they was arguing, when they suddenly spun around toward one of them big boulders. The one anxious to kill me disappeared, and the other two started bringing their Winchesters up, but they was too late. Clay boy, here, steps out and starts blasting. Two shots, and both those Apaches were on the ground, dying. Neither one got off a single shot."

She paused for a moment, looking around the campfire at the cowhands. Each of them was leaning forward, nodding their heads. Again, they tossed knowing looks at each other.

"Then," she continued, "if it hadn't already, all hell broke loose. This here Injun that had disappeared leaped from the top of that boulder onto Clay's back. It looked like the tables turned. He had this big knife in his left hand, and when he hit Clay's back, they both fell. Somehow Clay's gun got loose, and he grabbed the Apache's wrist, the one holding the knife, just as that sharp blade was about to be drawn across his throat."

Silence covered the camp. Even Emmett had stopped banging pots and stirring chili, caught in the drama of the story.

"I didn't tell you, Clay had a big Bowie knife in his right hand. When he grabbed that feller's wrist, he stabbed back over his shoulder, darned near scalping that Apache. But the Indian threw himself off Clay's back. That broke the grip on his wrist, but he ended up on his back with Clay bringing his own knife to that Injun's throat. Now, I'm tellin' you, I ain't never seen nobody fight so hard to keep from gettin' stuck. That Apache drew his legs up and kicked Clay where it hurts the most, throwing Clay off him."

She again stopped and looked at the cowhands, all of whom had pained expressions on their faces.

"I know, I imagine everyone of you boys been hit or kicked there at least once in your life. So, I figure we are done for now. Clay has doubled over, somehow still holding his knife. I could see that Apache's face. Blood was streaming from his head. It was everywhere, but he had this grin, the ugliest thing I ever seen. Reckon he was busy countin' his chickens. He rushed in, quick as a wink, and drove that knife right at Clay's neck. Only this young feller, at the last minute, knocks it aside and drives that big Bowie right through that man's chest. I swear, it was sticking out his back. He was in the happy hunting ground before he ever hit the rocks. Yes, sir, this big feller saved my bacon."

All heads turned to Clay. He felt himself turning red, thankful it was dark. "I was lucky."

"Whatever it was," Morgan said, "I'm glad you was there."

Emmett yelled from the fire, "Come and get it before I throw it out!"

One of the cowhands said, "The way he cooks, we might be safer if he did."

Everyone stood, moving over to the pot. Emmett had stacked metal plates and utensils on a stump he had pulled up next to the big chili pot. He had also whipped up a huge stack of biscuits.

"No more'n two biscuits, boys. We want enough to go around." The men held back until Nora stepped up to the pot. She loaded up her plate and took a taste. "Emmett, that's pretty good. You been takin' lessons?"

He grinned back at her. "No, ma'am, but you can call me Chef Emmett."

"Humph," she said, while the rest of the cowboys roared and made comments about Emmett's cooking.

"Clay," Morgan said, "come over here and sit with me and Peach."

With plates full, the three moved to the end of one log, the cowhands leaving space where they could have some privacy.

Clay and Nora wolfed down their chili and biscuits. Clay leaned back and stretched. "That was mighty good."

"Yeah," Morgan said, "but don't tell Emmett. He might want a raise. He's gotten so good, I'm thinking of making him cook on our next drive.

"So, Clay, you never mentioned why you're headed to Presidio."

Clay thought about the statement for a moment. Normally he wouldn't talk about ranger business, but he might eventually need help. It wouldn't hurt to confide in this rancher.

"I got a message almost six weeks ago from a fellow ranger. It was only four words. Need help in Presidio. So I've been trying to get there—had a few delays."

"I'd say. Mind my askin' who the ranger is?"

One of the cowhands stepped over and took their plates. Clay looked up and said, "Thanks."

"De nada."

He turned back to Morgan. "Jake Coleman."

The ranch owner nodded his head. "I saw Jake." He closed one eye, thinking. "Maybe . . . three, four weeks ago. I've known Jake since the war. He was asking if we'd seen any strangers around. He also wondered if we'd had anyone ambushed." Morgan shook his head. "He didn't say much more. That was the last time we saw him." He looked to Nora for confirmation, and she nodded in agreement.

Clay shook his head, mystified. "Up until the time I left, he hadn't mentioned investigating anything over here. That sounds more like something that would fall in the sheriff's bailiwick."

Morgan gave a harsh laugh. "Sheriff? He might as well be marshal. The county seat is Fort Davis, and the sheriff doesn't venture out of sight of town."

"Morgan," Nora said, "don't be unfair. Presidio is a huge county. It would be impossible for any one man, or even an army, to cover it. At least Gordon has put a deputy in Presidio."

This time Morgan snorted. "Boone? You call him a deputy? About all that feller does is prop his feet on his desk and read the paper. The only decent law officer we have around here, besides Jake, is Butch Ironside, the town marshal. Now there's a lawman. Don't mess with his town. He came here from California. Butch was headin' through when he met himself a little señorita in Presidio, elected to stay, and the town's the better for it."

Nora poked Morgan in the arm with her index finger. "You know there's more to it than that." She turned to Clay. "I heard this from the mayor's wife."

Morgan turned his head slightly away from Nora and rolled his eyes. This time Nora hit him in the arm with a substantial fist.

Morgan turned back to her, a frown on his face. "Why'd you do that?"

"I know you rolled your eyes at me. Every time you make that little half-turn with your head, you roll your eyes, and I don't like it!"

"Instead of beating me up, why don't you just go ahead with your story?"

She turned back to Clay. "Yes, well, as I was saying, Marshal Ironside—of course he wasn't a marshal then—was just passing through Presidio. One of the prominent families in town is the Garcia family." Nora leaned forward to Clay and lowered her voice as if this was some kind of a secret. "Marshal Ironside saw one of the Garcia daughters at the market, Eva Garcia. She is quite a lovely girl, thick, shiny, black hair, dark, entrancing eyes, and beautifully long eyelashes. I don't know how she gets them—"

"Good gosh, Peach, he don't care about what this girl looks like. Tell your story and be done with it."

Nora whipped around to Morgan. "You listen to me, *Mister* Tate. I let you tell your awful, long, and boring stories without interruption. Would you allow me the same courtesy?"

Morgan shook his head at Clay. "She ain't never allowed me to tell a whole story since we've been married."

Nora's eyes narrowed. "You best quit while you're ahead, *Mister.* You know what I'm like when you upset me. And you're about to upset me!"

At her last statement, several of the cowhands decided they had things to do and wandered over to the horses. Clay watched them go. *Evidently,* he thought, *they know what Peach is like when she's upset.*

She stared at her husband for a moment longer. When he had no response, she turned back to Clay. "As I was saying, she is a very attractive girl, maybe seventeen when they met. She was very taken with Butch. I think it must have been his red hair, or maybe his wide shoulders." She stopped and looked at her husband, but receiving no response, she turned back to Clay. "At first her father wasn't happy, but she eventually convinced him. I think he was just glad this daughter was not marrying an eighty-year-old man. Alicia, Miguel's wife, is Eva's sister. Anyway, they were married, Butch stayed in Presidio, and they have presented Señor Garcia with two healthy grandsons."

She turned back to her husband. "I'm done."

"Thank you, Peach." To Clay he said, "Butch is a good man. You can trust him, and he'll back you. He's not one of those marshals that won't step out of his town. He chased one man across the river into Mexico and dragged him back. The Mexican authorities said not a thing. They like him, too."

Clay nodded. He was tired. The long walk yesterday, the early wake up, and the fight had really taken it out of him, and his feet were hurting. The moccasins were comfortable, but the fight had irritated them.

"Thank you, both. That's a lot of good information—a lot of help." A yawn escaped Clay.

"You're lookin' mighty whipped," Morgan said. "We've got some extra blankets. Why don't you find a place and stretch out? Don't worry about keeping watch. We'll take care of it. We'll pull out in the morning when you wake up."

"Thanks," Clay said.

Morgan led him over to the pack horse and gave him two blankets. Clay thanked him again and found himself a spot under the stars. He lay down, tossing the warm wool blanket over his tired body. *Tomorrow or the next day,* Clay thought, *I'll be in Presidio.* Clay's eyes closed, and he was sound asleep.

8

Clay woke early. The camp was coming to life. The morning meal was jerky and leftover biscuits, thanks to Emmett. Evidently he had wanted to save enough for breakfast, and no one complained. Cold biscuits were always good.

Clay stayed on the buckskin, riding it on to the ranch. The terrain was constant. Prickly pear, short bunchgrass in patches, ocotillo, and some types of cactus he was unfamiliar with. Joe Bob rode next to him.

"See that cactus?" Joe Bob pointed out.

Clay looked where the cowboy was pointing. The cactus he saw was maybe four or five feet high with a central brown and fuzzy trunk. The limbs were light green, with thick, oblong shoots coming from the main branches. They all looked fuzzy and soft. As they rode nearer, he could see the many spines, comprising the cactus' body and limbs.

"We call it Jumping Cholla. It's Cholla, and I guess it don't jump, but it sure seems like it. If it just touches you, those sections will break off and cling to you with thorns barbed like a fish hook. Unless you have gloves, there's no place to grip it. It'll just dig deeper. That stuff drives horses crazy. Me, too. I can't stand it."

As they rode by, Clay got a closer look. The thorns were close together and looked like they were just waiting for some unsuspecting animal to brush against them. One of the first things he was going to do when he got to Presidio was get some new boots and chaps. They were needed everywhere in Texas, but some of the cacti here were the worst he had ever seen.

Early afternoon, they topped a rise, that provided a magnificent view of the ranch. Morgan pulled up, the others following. He had built quite a home. It was all earth-tone adobe with a Mexican red tile roof surrounded by a tall adobe fence that circled the ranch headquarters.

"Mighty impressive, Morgan," Clay said.

"Yep, it sure is. I'd like to take credit for it, but I saw several rancheros across the border done like this to protect from the Indians. When we settled out here the Apaches and—mostly during the summer—the Comanches, were relentless. We must've been attacked four or five times the first year. Now, not so much. The rangers and the army, mostly the rangers, persuaded them Indians that peaceful was a much better way to go."

The big rancher swung his arm from right to left along the horizon. "As far as you can see is Bar Seven range. I've bought the land around the water sources. Without water, this land ain't worth a plugged nickel."

Clay nodded. He understood the importance of water on any land, but this country in particular. He could see longhorns scattered to the horizon. Near the ranch were a few Hereford. "How's the Herefords working out?"

"Too soon to tell. Just got 'em last year. They seemed to winter well, and they danged sure got more beef on their bones than them stringy longhorns, but I ain't seen a cow yet as tough as a longhorn—or as mean."

"It don't matter how many times I see it," Nora said, riding next to Morgan. "This ranch is beautiful. I love living here."

"Me, too, Peach, me, too." Morgan bumped his horse in the flanks, leading on to the ranch.

Cowhands waved as they rode into the yard. There was a separate white picket fence surrounding the main house with a multitude of different-colored roses growing inside the fence. They pulled up at the corral.

"Come on in, Clay," Morgan said. "Get some rest and put the feed bag on. We've got a great cook. She would've had word we were arriving, and by now has us a big meal prepared."

Clay heard his stomach growl, but shook his head. "Jake's in trouble, Morgan. I've dawdled way too long. I've got to get moving."

Nora had already stepped down from her horse. "I know you're in a hurry, Clay, but let us fit you out with some clothes, and you can't put clean clothes on without a bath. So come on in. While you're getting cleaned up, we'll have Maria pack you up a big lunch, and you can be on your way."

Clay thought for a moment. It would be stupid for him to refuse this kindness. A bath would feel glorious. "I'd be obliged. You folks can have the other two Apache horses, but I'd like to keep this buckskin."

"Thanks, Clay," Morgan said. "When you come back through, they're yours if you want 'em."

"Won't be needing them, but thanks." He joined Morgan and Nora as they walked to the house.

LATER, Clay tied the saddlebags on behind the saddle and turned to face Nora and Morgan. She was the first to speak. "I owe you my life. If you hadn't showed up, my hair would be hangin' on that Apache's belt. You stop by here anytime."

The woman gave him a big hug.

Clay grinned. "Glad I could help. I don't know when I'll be back this way, but thank you for the clothes and gear, and the bath. I feel like a new man."

His buckskin shirt was rolled up and stuffed inside the saddlebags. He was fully dressed in Morgan's clothes, except for the hat. He had elected to keep the sombrero. It was a gift from Miguel, and he wasn't ready to get rid of it. The boots fit perfectly. In fact, everything fit as if he'd picked them out from the store himself. The shirt was a red-and-blue checked wool that, though a little scratchy, protected him from the searing Texas sun.

"Morgan, I can't tell you how much I appreciate the loan of all this gear." He patted the saddle and then shifted the gunbelt as he spoke. "I'll get it back to you, somehow."

"Clay, look around you. I ain't gonna miss a little tack. That was an old gun rig I ain't used in years. Besides, I could give you everything on this ranch and still be in debt to you for bringing Peach back." He reached over and pulled Nora to him.

Clay swung up into the saddle and leaned down, extending his hand. "I'm much obliged, anyway."

The two big men shook hands, and Clay, turned the buckskin. "*Adios, amigos.*" He lifted his hand in salute as he rode out of the ranch yard, turning onto the trail to Presidio.

This was the best he'd felt since before he was jumped by Griffin's gang. He rocked in the saddle as the buckskin, after his short rest and water, stretched his long legs. It seemed both horse and man were happy to be on their way. Clay felt the boot where the Winchester '73 rested, handy if needed. The Colt rode solid in the new holster, not rubbing against his belly. He wiggled his toes in the boots. Thank goodness they were a pair of older boots, broken in. After all his feet had been through, and having felt nothing but the moccasins for the past few weeks, he'd hate to have to break in a new pair.

Middle of the afternoon and a full belly, Clay laughed to

himself. He should've known he wouldn't get out of the house without Nora sitting him down to a fine dinner. Maria had put on quite a spread. When he felt he couldn't eat another bite, she had laid out bear sign. He couldn't believe it. It'd been years since he'd tasted his ma's doughnuts, and he'd have to say Maria's were darn near as good.

Clay kept a sharp lookout as he rode down the trail. He didn't want anyone, whether Indian or white man, to get close enough to do him harm again. He had a lot of life to live, and he aimed to live it to the fullest. But first, he had to locate Jake and find out what the urgent note was about. Movement on a far ridgeline caught his attention. He pulled the buckskin up and reached into the saddlebags for his binoculars. His hand was feeling around inside when he remembered. All of his equipment had been stolen. He took his hand out, fastened the outside flap, and scanned the ridgeline. He could make out nothing, but keeping an eye on the area, he moved the horse off at a walk.

He felt frustration rising. How could he have been so stupid? He'd had to watch those chuckleheads ride off with Blue. But there was nothing he could have done.

He had lowered his guard, thinking of Dee, relaxed his constant vigilance for only a few seconds. The bandits were elated with their good fortune, catching a ranger. Shifty Joe hadn't said much, but he had kept eyeing Clay like a bobcat eyes a mouse. The only good thing Clay could remember that came out of it was the half-breed getting bitten by a couple of ants. He didn't flick them off like most people, though. He pulled them from his leg individually and smashed them between his thumb and forefinger. Then he had found that rock and shoved it under Clay's back. Griffin had a good laugh over that move.

The buckskin had covered quite a bit of ground. Clay reached for his pocket watch resting in his left vest pocket. He stopped his hand before it reached the nonexistent watch in his nonexistent vest. He'd bought that watch in Brackett from Mr. Brennan when he was on the trail of his folks' killers. It was hard to believe eight years had already passed since he had been there. In fact, he had to stop thinking of it as Brackett, since they had changed the name in '75 to Brackettville.

As his eyes swept the Chihuahuan Desert, his mind continued to wander. His grandpa wasn't doing well. He had never completely recovered from the back-shooting. Last Clay heard, the man who had shot his grandpa, Washington Jefferson Blessing, had died in prison. He didn't shed a tear over that old reprobate.

His mind went back to his grandpa. *I hope he's still alive when I get back.* He had no idea how long he would be out here. Heck, he had no idea what he was doing out here, besides looking for Jake. What kind of trouble was he in that he needed help? Hopefully, the answer would be in Presidio.

The countryside had gotten rougher. He had crossed several ridges and rocky canyons, following the trail. Morgan said that coming to the sixth ridge, he should turn right and parallel it for about half a mile, then look for a black volcanic outcropping. He rode steadily on, eyes straining in the dimming light.

Sure enough, he found the outcropping. Just past it, he weaved his way around several boulders, until he could see green brush. By now, the buckskin's head was up. Clay gave him his head, and the horse led them to the spring Morgan had talked about. It gurgled into a small pond that had been formed when someone had dammed up the spring, but it trickled no farther. It must disappear beneath the pond and continue its flow underground.

In the stark desert landscape, green grass fought its way through the sand and rock, surrounding the welcome spring. Clay stepped from the saddle. He let the horse drink while he filled his canteen and got himself a long, cold drink from the spring. Stripping his gear from the buckskin, he tossed a loop over the horse's neck, led him away from the waterhole, and staked him out to feed on the grass. Clay went back, hefted his gear, and moved away from the water where he dropped the saddle and blanket. When he was young, his pa had taught him to never block a waterhole with his camp. Water was a life-giving nectar, but animals would stay away, no matter how thirsty they were, if man was too near.

No fire tonight. He cleaned the ground around his tack, sat, and, after pulling his Winchester from the scabbard and propping it within reach, leaned back against the worn saddle. The leather had carried cowhands many a mile, but still had a lot of miles in it. The great thing about the old saddle was that it had worn out most of its squeaks. Something he had learned was that a new one talked too much, and those squeaks would carry farther than the sound of a walking horse.

Clay pushed the wide black sombrero to the back of his head, and scanned the darkening sky. Stars were beginning to slip out from behind their curtains, showing their pale glow in the early twilight. He surveyed his surroundings. A pair of coyotes were tuning up, not far from his camp, and the nearby quail were fussing as they settled into their roost.

He noticed movement near the waterhole and sat motionless as a doe and twin fawns slipped cautiously to the water. She froze, looked in his direction, and waited a few seconds. After accepting he was far enough away and no threat, she led her fawns in to drink. She'd start to lower her head, then jerk it up to look around. Deer had many enemies in this harsh country. Relaxing her vigil, even just for a moment, could mean the death of one of her fawns or herself. The deer drank quickly, then slipped quietly back into a draw, disappearing from sight.

Clay reached into his saddlebags and pulled out the food Maria had prepared. It was wrapped tight to keep the flies out, but no amount of wrapping could trap the aroma of fried chicken. With his mouth watering, he unwrapped the delectable treat and went to work. Even after all of the riding, wrapped and stuffed in the saddlebags, the crust was still crispy. He took a bite of fried chicken and a then bite of biscuit.

A smile drifted across the ranger's broad face, lifting the drooping corners of his thick, black mustache. This was a lonely life, but these quiet moments underlined the joy he felt in the wild country.

Would he ever settle down? It was looking a lot more promising since he'd seen Dee. He was pretty sure she felt the same way. He was beginning to believe Dee was a lot like Nora but more refined. Even though Nora was rough around the edges, she and Morgan made a fine pair. They fit well into this wild, hard life. As he chewed, he thought about Miguel. Kind, hard, old Miguel. He'd outlived three wives. Losing a wife, now that must be hard, but losing three? It would take a strong man to continue on as Miguel had, but, like Pa told him when he was young, a man takes what life throws at him, and presses on. Clay nodded agreement with his thoughts.

He slid the gunbelt around where the holster was more comfortable, making sure the Colt was loose and ready. He had eaten all of the chicken. You couldn't let chicken go too long. Clay tossed the wool blanket over himself and stretched out, his head against the saddle.

Tomorrow should find him in Presidio. It had taken a long time for him to reach his friend. Tomorrow he'd find out about Jake's note. Tomorrow . . .

CLAY LAY on his side facing east, the blanket pulled tight around his neck. The early-morning chill searched the blanket for an opening and found it where the blanket lifted from his back when he rolled over. The cool air gradually pushed sleep from his mind. The rising sun finished the job. After finding a space between two boulders, it sent a beam of light straight into Clay's eyes. He opened one eye and, without moving, scanned the area. He could hear the comforting sound of the buckskin chewing on the tender grass. Grasping the blanket, he threw it off, then stretched. His long arms reached out to each side almost as far as he was tall.

The buckskin looked up and stared at him, as if saying he'd slept too long and it was time to be on the road. Clay stood and surveyed the camp. Aside from the horse and a jackrabbit sitting at the water hole, he was alone. *Good thing*, he thought. *I must of been tired, but I can't let myself sleep that sound. I could wind up on another ant bed.*

Clay led the buckskin to water and while the animal quenched his thirst, Clay surveyed the morning countryside. The hills, blood-red in the early sun, were free of any movement. With the recent monsoon rains, the yellow prickly pear flowers joined the bright green of the long, straight stalks of the ocotillo that shot for the sky, their brilliant red flowers bright in the sunlight. Even the creosote bush was getting in on the color with its soft yellow blossoms. It was amazing what a little water did for this land.

After the buckskin finished drinking, Clay saddled up, slipped his rifle into the boot, tied his gear on, and mounted. Initially guiding the horse away from the waterhole, he gave him his head, allowing the animal to pick his way through the rough volcanic landscape. Once out of it, Clay reined the horse toward the trail. Clay felt an anxious tremor run through the horse's body. "Hang on, boy," he said and patting him on the neck. "We'll be on the trail shortly, and I'll let you stretch out."

9

The towns of Presidio and Ojinaga, facing each other on opposite sides of the river, appeared suddenly. He had been riding south down a sparse narrow valley with tall bluffs rising to the west and a tapering ridgeline decreasing in height from north to south, to the east. Though the ridge was low, it restricted his view to the southeast. Nearing the end of the valley, the land flattened out and, in the distance, he could make out fields with the Rio Grande cutting between them.

He followed the trail around the end of the ridge, and there it was. A sleepy little village no more than a half-mile away. He reined in his horse and sat watching the small town. A small barge pulled away from the United States side of the river, moving slowly to the Mexico side. Looking upstream, he could see the Rio Conchos funneling out of Mexico into the Rio Grande.

Clay nudged the buckskin forward, and puffs of dust flew up like tiny dust devils with each of the horse's steps. He turned down the north end of Main Street and pulled up again. Several buildings lined the street: a general store, bank, two saloons, two hash houses, barber shop, sheriff's office, and the marshal's office.

Following Morgan's advice, he stopped in front of the marshal's office. Clay swung down from the buckskin and tied it to the hitching rail. Opening the door to the office, he stepped inside. No one there. He walked to the door in the back wall, near the marshal's desk, opened it and examined the jail. In the cell at the end, a husky man, maybe five feet eight inches, raised up from the hard wood framed bunk bed.

"Can I help you?"

"I'm looking for the marshal."

The man swung his legs over the side. As he turned, Clay could see the badge on the man's left shirt pocket. "You found him," he said. "Gettin' a little siesta. Not much goin' on around here today."

When the man stood, his shoulders were so wide his body looked top-heavy. Carryin' his hat in his left hand, the man opened the unlocked cell door. Closing it after his passage, he walked past Clay and seated himself in the chair behind the wooden desk.

Clay watched silently as the marshal sized him up. "Have a seat, and tell me what I can do for you. Name's Butch Ironside."

Clay examined the three chairs sitting in front of the marshal's desk and sat in the only one that looked capable of supporting his weight.

"Marshal Ironside, I'm Clay Barlow, Texas Ranger. I'm here to meet up with Ranger Jake Coleman."

"Yep, you fit the description Jake gave me. Been a while since he sent for help. What took so long?"

"You wouldn't believe me if I told you. I'm here now, and I'm ready to help. Can you point me on my way?"

"I'd like to, believe me, I would." The marshal leaned back in his chair and steepled his fingers, looking at them. Then he looked up. "But I don't know where he is. Last time I saw him he was headin' upriver. There's a shallow crossing above where the Rio Conchos joins the Rio Grande. This time of year, with the monsoons, the Conchos adds a lot of water down here. At Presidio, the river gets pretty deep and fast."

"How long ago did he leave?"

"Three weeks."

"Do you know where he was headed?"

Marshal Ironside stared out the front window at a dust devil spinning, picking up tumbleweeds and tossing them out of its vortex. It turned and twisted until disappearing out of the frame of the window. He let out a long breath and turned sad eyes toward Clay.

"I do."

Though impatient for news, Clay waited, giving the marshal time to collect his thoughts.

"He's south of the border."

Clay struggled to keep the surprise from his face. *What the blue-blazes is he doing in Mexico?*

After gazing out the window again, the marshal continued. "I wasn't here then, but somewhere around ten years ago, Jake and several other rangers rode into town. They were patrolling the area for Apaches. There was still plenty of Apache activity back then. They'd come over from Mexico, raid, then head back across the border. Well, the rangers garrisoned here and sent out patrols for several months—had more luck than the army."

The chair creaked as Clay leaned forward. "That's all interesting, Marshal, but I've already taken too long getting here. Jake needs my help. If you know what's going on, could you get to the point?"

"Relax, Clay. Mind if I call you Clay? This marshal and ranger stuff gets old fast."

Clay waved his hand. "Sure, just get to the point."

Butch Ironside leaned forward and placed his forearms on the desk, clasping his sizable hands together. "The short of it is, Jake saw a girl. Not just any girl, but a daughter of one of the most prominent Mexican families in Presidio. The Garcia family."

"Wait, how many daughters does Señor Garcia have?"

Butch smiled. "So you've heard my story?"

"Yes," Clay said, "and Miguel Lopez's."

"Really? You'll have to tell me how you learned about Miguel." Butch watched Clay squirm in the small chair and start to speak. The marshal held up his hand. "But not now. Let me tell you what happened."

Clay tried to relax, but the exasperation came out in his one-word response. "Please."

"All right, I'll make this short. First, to answer your question, Señor Garcia has six daughters, no sons. They are all beautiful, kind, sweet women, and they all love their father, but he raised them to think for themselves, and they certainly do."

Clay considered himself a patient man, but his patience was wearing thin. He was weeks late getting to Jake. All he knew was that his friend was in Mexico. He had no idea what or whom Jake was after, and this marshal just prattled on.

"Marshal, I just need to know where Jake went, so I can lend him a hand. Can you get to the point?" Clay enunciated each word of his question with emphasis.

The marshal nodded. "Jake's married and has a seven-year-old son."

Clay couldn't have been more surprised if the marshal had pulled out his gun and shot him. "He's what?"

"Married. With a son that's been kidnapped!"

Clay felt all the frustration disappear. That explained Jake's long disappearances and why he was always willing to volunteer for duty in this part of the country. But it didn't explain why anyone would kidnap a ranger's son. Didn't they know this would bring down the wrath of the rangers on whoever did it? But wait, no one knew about Jake even being married. Why had he kept it a secret?

"Why would anyone kidnap Jake Coleman's son? As far as I

know he's not wealthy, and I wouldn't want to be in any man's boots that brought harm to that boy."

"You're right. As far as the kidnappers were concerned, they didn't kidnap Jake Coleman's son, they kidnapped Señor Garcia's grandson. He is a very wealthy man and would pay a hefty ransom for the boy's return. Which he has. That's what Jake is doing. At least, that's what we hope he's doing. As long as he's been gone, we're getting concerned about him and the boy."

Clay contemplated what the marshal had told him. Then said, "How many riders went with him?"

Butch shook his head. "No one. Jake figured he could do it better by himself."

Clay nodded at that. "I understand. Any idea who did it?"

Wrinkles suddenly coursed across Butch's forehead, and his jaw muscles clenched and released. "There's a Mexican bandit. He often raids on the north side of the Rio Grande, that way he keeps the *federales* off his back, most of the time. The rest, he just pays off. His name is Hugo Medrano. There is very bad blood between him and Señor Garcia. They grew up together. At least, until Medrano killed another boy and headed south. But one thing that can be said for him, he's not a stupid man."

"So Jake is after him? How does he know he's the one? What if, Heaven forbid, Jake's son is already dead?"

"Rumors have it that Medrano is having a hard time. The Yankee army and the rangers have clamped down on the southern border of Texas. That's where Medrano likes to raid. He does come up here to occasionally rustle cattle, but mostly he takes his bandits east. He needs money to keep paying the trash that work for him. That's my guess, and Jake agrees.

"It's getting near lunch. Why don't you come with me and meet the family. We'll have lunch and I'll tell you more."

"That'll work for me, but I need to swap horses and head out as soon as possible."

"Eat first," Butch said, pushing back his chair and rising.

As the man stood, Clay looked him over. Wide shoulders, hands calloused and scarred, made it clear that the marshal wasn't afraid of hard work or a fight. At the same time, his bowed legs bore testament to the fact that he had spent a lot of his years in a saddle.

Clay stood. "Lead the way. I need to get this buckskin to water."

Butch headed out the door and said, "Bring your horse. I'll get him taken care of." He then turned right, headed down the boardwalk toward the river, then cut across the dusty street. The dust, pulverized from constant horse and wagon traffic, was fine like powder. There was no breeze, which allowed the dust to leap up around their knees before settling back in place. The marshal turned left on a cross street. At the end of the street was a large adobe home, surrounded by a perimeter fence with a guard standing at the gate.

"Nice place," Clay said. "Marshal's pay must be a lot better than rangers'."

Butch laughed. "Nope, it ain't much. But this isn't mine, anyway. This is my father-in-law's. When Jake got here, he suggested we should all live together until he gets Medrano taken care of. I didn't much like it, but I want Eva safe."

"Yep, smart move," Clay said.

Stepping through the gate, Butch asked the guard to take care of Clay's horse.

"He just needs water. Gracias," Clay said.

"De nada." Taking the reins from Clay, the man led the horse to the water trough just outside the barn.

The two men took three steps to the veranda, and Butch opened the door, entering the huge room. Two large leather couches, with seating for at least five people each, sat near the fireplace, positioned so their occupants could receive heat from the massive fireplace and still talk with one another. On the floor, between the couches and near the fireplace, was a longhorn cowhide, tanned with the hair on. On the cowhide were two little boys, wrestling, while two more watched.

Farther away from and facing the fireplace at the end of the couches, were two oversize, dark leather armchairs. An occupant in either chair could see everyone seated on the couches and still receive heat from the fire. The couches and chairs were filled with people. Clay hadn't seen anything like this since his folks used to take him to visit his French grandparents in D'Hanis during Thanksgiving or Christmas.

Butch leaned over to Clay and said as quietly as possible, "Hold onto your hat."

All of the adults' heads turned, and their conversation ended abruptly. The older gentleman rose from his leather armchair and advanced on Clay and Butch.

"Señor Garcia, I would like to present Clay Barlow, Texas Ranger."

Butch turned to Clay. "Ranger Barlow, it is my pleasure to introduce you to the patriarch of this family and the jefe of Garcia Rancho, Señor Cesar Garcia."

The older man extended his hand. "Ranger Barlow, even without the introduction, if I had met you on the street, I would have known you. Jake described you so perfectly, and there are very few men of your stature."

Clay had removed his sombrero upon entering the home. He gave a shallow bow as he took Señor Garcia's hand. "*Buenos tardes,* Señor Garcia. *Cómo está usted?*"

Garcia replied, "I am fine, Clay. Do come in and meet the family. I feel I have known you for years. Please call me Cesar."

Clay met all of the daughters, except for Alicia who was with Miguel, and Sophia who was in her room. They were all attractive and very pleasant women. Two were still unmarried, Zoe and Nicole, and both intriguing, but, Dee filled his mind, leaving no room for other women.

"I am sorry," Cesar said, "that I cannot introduce you to my sweet wife, Antonella. She passed away three years ago from the cancer."

"My heartfelt condolences, Cesar," Clay said.

The young boys jumped up from the rug and gathered around their *abuelo.*

"And these are my grandsons. I'm sure you can tell which ones belong to Eva and Butch," Cesar said as he rumpled each of the boys red hair. "This is Luke and Bret, and the other two are Jessie's and Vanessa's, Flint and Jeb. Say hello to Ranger Barlow, boys."

"Hello, boys," Clay said, as their tiny hands disappeared in his. They turned and dashed outside.

"Stay in the compound," Butch yelled as they disappeared around the corner of the house.

"Sorry," Butch said. "I'm gonna check on 'em." He was quickly out the door.

"Please, Clay, join me at the table," Cesar said.

Clay moved over to the huge table that paralleled the wall across from the fireplace. It could seat at least twenty-five people. Cesar sat at the end opposite the front door, and motioned Clay to sit on his left.

Once seated, Cesar said, "Thank you for coming. Jake said you would, although he was surprised you hadn't arrived by the time he left."

Clay shook his head. "I had a bit of a delay, but I did get to meet your older son-in-law. He saved my life."

"Miguel. He is a good man. I wouldn't have chosen him for my Alicia, but he has been good for her and treats her like gold."

"I like him." Clay changed the subject. "Señor Garcia, it is imperative I find out exactly what happened, and then get on my way to help Jake."

"Ahh." The grandfather sighed. "Our little Rory. My sweet Sophia is beside herself. It has been six weeks since little Rory was taken, and three weeks since Jake left. We've had no word. I wish he would have let me send my vaqueros. We would have wiped out that child-stealing Medrano."

"You did the right thing. Jake knows what he's doing. He'll find your grandson."

"Yes, I suppose you are right."

The older man pulled a piece of paper from his vest pocket. "This is a copy of the note we received. The boys described the men that took Rory. The leader was Medrano. They came out of the hills while the boys were playing by the river. One of them got down, grabbed Rory, and handed him to Medrano. Luke told us Rory fought hard, until Medrano told him he'd cut his throat if he didn't settle down."

Clay took the note and read it. There wasn't much, just a demand for fifty thousand dollars in gold to be delivered to the town of Santiago de Coyame in one month. Clay looked up from the note to see Cesar watching him.

"Yes, it is past time now. But it is a long way to Coyame, and Jake may have already traded for little Rory and be on his way back."

"You could be right," Clay said, knowing that the odds were well against a trade happening. Both the boy and Jake would be killed as soon as Medrano got the gold.

Butch had come back in and taken the chair across from Clay. "When I interviewed the boys, right after this happened, they didn't think that Rory was targeted. They said that when the men pulled up, the leader yelled 'grab one,' and Rory was the closest. I don't think he had any idea he was taking a Texas Ranger's son. All he wanted was a Garcia."

"I agree," Cesar said. "It was just bad luck for Jake and Sophia."

Clay looked at the older man. "And bad luck for Medrano. I know Jake. Medrano's a dead man. He just doesn't know it yet."

Cesar shook his head. "As much as I want to see that murdering scum dead, the important thing is getting little Rory home safely." He looked around in surprise. The rest of the family had gathered quietly around the table while the three men were talking.

Camila, the cook, had come in from the adjoining kitchen. "Señor Cesar, it is past time for dinner."

Cesar nodded. "Yes, thank you. Daughters, would you get Sophia and help Camila?"

The daughters rushed to do their father's bidding. In a few moments, a lovely but sad young woman came into the room holding Vanessa's hand. Her large brown eyes were red and puffy. Though she must have tried to brush out her hair, it was still disheveled, and her lovely soft yellow dress was severely wrinkled.

Cesar held out his hand. "Sophia, please come. We have a guest."

Clay stood as she padded softly over to her father and took his hand. "This is the man Jake spoke of, Ranger Clay Barlow."

She cast a melancholy smile toward Clay and said softly, "Will you find my son and my husband, Señor Clay?"

Clay could feel his heart shudder at her pain. He knew that kind of ache, and wanted it for no one. "I'll do my very best, ma'am."

Her smile was a little broader. "From what Jake tells me, your very best will be more than enough."

10

Daylight was breaking as Clay swung up onto the big black stallion. Cesar had provided him with two additional Colt revolvers, all in .44-40 caliber, the same as his Winchester. Behind his saddle, he carried a ten gauge, sawed-off, double-barrel shotgun. He'd gotten used to having one. Though this shotgun was not a repeater, it offered two deadly rounds.

Butch handed Clay the lead ropes for the two geldings, a big bay and the pack horse, a red roan, that carried not only supplies, but an extra fifty thousand in gold that Señor Garcia had included, just in case something had happened to Jake. Sophia stepped up and placed her hand on Clay's knee.

"*Por favor,* Clay, bring my men back to me."

"Yes, ma'am. That's what I aim to do."

"Good luck," Butch said. "I wish I was going with you."

"You're needed here. This is what I do."

Butch nodded and stepped back as Cesar moved up to the tall man on the black horse. The older man's eyes were fierce. "I, too, wish I was able to go with you. I would like to settle my debt with Medrano."

"Don't you worry, Señor Garcia. It'll be settled, but first we want to rescue your grandson. I'll find Jake out there, and we'll get it done."

The man fixed his dark eyes on Clay, then stepped back, out of the way of the horses. "I believe you will."

The rest of the family stood around the hacienda as Clay wheeled the black and touched the flanks of the big horse. "Adios," he said as the family waved their goodbyes.

He rode through town and turned upstream. Here, the Rio Grande flowed deep and strong. He was glad there was a better place to cross upstream. Of course, he could take the ferry and ride through Ojinaga, but he didn't care for everyone knowing his business. Along with all the ammunition and food he carried, he had an additional fifty thousand dollars in gold on the pack horse. He'd get his throat slit in no time if the wrong element had that piece of information.

His first goal was to get above the Rio Conchos, which wouldn't take long. It was only a short ride to where the river flowed into the Rio Grande. But after talking to Butch and Cesar, he had determined that he should ride well past the juncture of the two rivers. He'd go far enough to be completely out of sight of anyone who might be watching from town.

The water boiled where the two rivers came together. However, above the junction, while the cut banks were at least fifty feet or more apart, the water was only about twenty feet wide, and though running fast, no more than four feet deep at the deepest point. After riding for half an hour, Clay stopped. He looked back, determining that no one had followed him and, having found a sloping bank, rode into the Rio Grande. The horse's shoes clanked against the rocky riverbed. He was thankful when they went into the water, and the sound was reduced to minimal splashing.

He stopped the horses and allowed them a drink. They hadn't been gone long, but the day was already starting to heat up.

When they had finished, he moved them across and up the opposite bank. He was in Mexico, and neither the federales nor the
locals had a soft spot in their hearts for the rangers. His badge
would do him no good here. He pulled it from his shirt, turned,
and dropped it into his saddlebag.

Riding out of the riverbed, Clay continued for several hours.
The landscape remained the same. In the distance, to his left
toward the Rio Conchos, farmers were busy working their small
plots of land, the grains ripening and turning brown in the hot
sun. To his right were draws, hills, and ravines, covered with tall
yucca and the green, sharp-leafed sotol plant, which, with the
serrated edge of its long leaves, created its own protection. In the
distance, hazy blue mountains rose out of the dry desert.

Cesar had told him the trail would keep him near the river
until he entered the mountains.

Butch had loaned him a fine pair of binoculars. He rode
into the shade of some boulders, pulled the glasses out, and
scanned the country. The binoculars brought the massiveness
of the blue mountains close. He first checked along the trail
he was following and then did a wide scan. It wouldn't do to
have some banditos surprise him like Griffin and his bunch
had. The mountains ahead were vertical. *I'm sure glad Cesar
put me onto this trail, Clay thought.* He could see what the
older man had been talking about. Cesar had told him this
trail would take him through the mountains, but to stick to it.
If he took off up one of the deep side canyons, he could get
lost or, with all the blind canyons and drop-offs, maybe even
worse.

Clay hung the binoculars on his saddle horn and bumped the
black, the big horse moved forward in a long, ground-eating gait.
After crossing the river, Clay had run the horses for a short
distance to take the edge off. Now, the black, though obviously an
independent horse that would control the rider if he could, was
settled down and covering ground fast. The bay and roan were

both steady and strong. They weren't flashy horses, but Clay could tell they both had real bottom.

His mind shifted back to Blue, as it had done so many times since the horse had been stolen. He remembered the day the horse had arrived. Pa and Ma had gone to Uvalde. Ma needed to do some shopping. Of course they always stopped at the Hewitt's on the way and on the return. Pa had taken the buckboard even though he preferred his horse. He was always thinking of Ma.

Clay had stayed behind to help Slim whitewash the barn. He had wanted to see his good friend Sarah Hewitt but really didn't mind staying. He liked ranch work, especially when he was doing it with either Pa or Slim. The past few weeks, he had been thinking it was about time he had his own horse. But everyone listened to him, nodded their heads, and said something like, "Relax, boy, it'll happen when the time is right." He felt the time was right now and couldn't help feeling let down.

Clay laughed to himself as he thought about how he had been chewing Slim's ear with every reason he could think of to have his own horse. Slim just kept painting and nodding. Finally, the tall cowboy straightened up and looked down at him.

"Boy, do you trust your pa?"

Clay had thought about it, then said, "Sure, I trust, Pa, Slim. Why wouldn't I?"

"Do you think your pa is a smart man?"

"About the smartest I know."

"Then don't you think your pa knows the right time to get you a horse?"

That stopped him. He continued painting and thinking. After a while, he looked up at Slim. "I hadn't thought of it like that," he'd said, and went back to painting.

It was less than an hour later when Ma and Pa pulled up in the buckboard, with Blue tied to the back. Pa helped Ma down, and she went up to the porch and turned to watch Clay. He had run over to the horse and was rubbing its neck. The young blue roan liked it and turned his head to the boy. Clay rubbed his cheek.

"Give me a hand here," Pa had said. "This here wagon needs unloading."

Clay grabbed some things and started up the stairs to the porch, behind Pa.

"Give your ma a kiss, Clay."

He stopped and gave her a quick peck.

She smiled at him, and he said, "Hi, Ma," then rushed into the house to drop his load on the table.

When they came back out, Slim had climbed down from the ladder and was standing by Ma, grinning at her. Clay noticed but figured it was one of those grownup things thirteen-year-old boys weren't supposed to hear. Pa had stopped at the wagon and was looking at the horse.

"What do you think of him, son?"

Clay looked at the colt as the young horse watched him. He walked over and pushed the horses gums back. He looked at the teeth, while the colt stood still and calm. "Pa, corners of the temporary teeth are starting to round. I'd say he must be about two years old."

His pa said nothing as Clay continued to examine the young roan. The horse's face was darker than his gray body, and the mane was almost black, as well as the legs. Clay picked up each hoof, feeling them first to make sure they weren't hot, looking them over. He felt the tendons and joints, then placed the foot back on the ground. He did this with each hoof, then, placing his hand on the horse's rump, walked as close as possible around the rear of the horse to ensure he couldn't be kicked. Walking from back to front he laid his hand on the roan and followed the spine to the neck. It was even. Then he stepped to the withers and, starting at the hoof, measured up the leg to the top. After measuring the roan, he turned to his pa.

"Pa, I reckon you got yourself a good horse. No heat in the

hoofs. The legs feel great, level spine, and he's gonna be pretty big. He's at least sixteen hands now. I'll bet he'll be seventeen next year."

"You're mostly right, son."

Clay quickly thought back over his exam and calculations. What did he miss? He ticked each item off, but could think of nothing. Puzzled, he looked back at his pa.

"He's not my horse," Pa said. "He's yours."

As much as he had been lobbying for a horse, he hadn't expected one, so this was a complete surprise. He stood stock-still, shocked at the revelation. After a few seconds, his face broke into a wide grin. He dashed to his pa, and just before he hugged him, he stopped, sticking out his hand. Gravely, his pa took Clay's hand in his. Even now, at thirteen, Clay's hands were almost as big as his pa's, and he towered over his ma.

"Thanks, Pa."

"You're welcome, son, but you better thank your ma and Slim. They're the ones that convinced me you're ready."

Clay jumped up the steps in one leap, wrapped his long arms around his ma's slim waist, and swung her in circles on the porch. "Thank you, Ma. Thank you, thank you, thank you."

His ma's musical laughter echoed through the hills surrounding the ranch house.

When Clay carefully placed her back on the porch, she pushed several shiny strands of brown hair back under her bonnet and said, "My, my, if I had known I would've gotten that kind of reaction, I would have talked your pa into it a lot sooner." She gazed up at her son's pitch-black hair, and his startling gray eyes. Eyes that could be happy, or soft and tender, or, even at the young age of thirteen, turn hard as granite. "You are most welcome, my dear son." This time she grabbed him and hugged him to her. She smiled at him when she let him go.

Clay turned to his pa's good friend and his. "Thanks, Slim."

The tall man placed his hand on the boy's shoulder. "Yore

shore welcome, Clay. I know you'll take good care of that blue boy."

Clay turned to his pa. "Have you named him?"

"Nope. I reckon that's up to the owner."

Clay grinned. "There ain't no better name for a blue roan than Blue."

Clay knew he had tossed an ain't into his statement and fully expected his ma to reprimand him, but she said nothing. Slim nodded, and Pa said, "You're exactly right, son."

Nearby, movement pulled him from his pleasant memories. A covey of Gambel's quail burst from a draw less than a hundred yards in front of him, followed by a coyote leaping into the air. One of the quail wasn't quite quick enough, and the coyote caught the bird in its initial flight. Feathers flew. The song dog came down on the side of the draw in full view of Clay. He pulled the black up to see what the coyote would do. With a mouthful of fluttering quail, the animal stood watching man and horse, then spun and disappeared into the draw.

Clay bumped the black to get him moving, stood in his saddle, and looked around. If there were quail around, there was water not too far. He saw nothing. Continuing on the trail, he stopped on the next rise and picked up the binoculars. Past the draw and to his right and to the west, he spotted a patch of green. It was getting late, and rather than riding to the river that was off to his left a couple of miles, he felt the tank might be safer.

Riding west, leaving the trail, he was forced to cross several deep draws. Once in the bottom of each, he was at least six or seven feet below the top of the bank. With each one he had to find a trail that was sufficiently sloped on each side. That took time. The sun was close to disappearing behind the nearby fifty-foot-high bluffs, when he finally reached the tank. Just as he rode up, a bass inhaled a large bug on the surface. Clay had packed the new saddlebags with similar equipment to what his old bags had held.

After finding an opening through the cattails, he let the horses drink. The animals were thirsty and would drink much more water than was good for them, so he monitored them carefully. When he deemed they'd had enough, he carefully pulled them from the water's edge, leading them to a suitable area that would provide ample grazing. He took ropes from the pack horse, looped them over the horses' necks, and staked them out in the grass. Before he could remove the tack, they had started feeding on the bunchgrass.

After looking around for a level area, away from the water, Clay dropped the packs and saddle. Immediately, he went to the saddlebags and pulled out a stick with twine wrapped around it and a fishhook on the end. He was looking for a big, juicy grasshopper when he heard another bass strike. Light was dwindling quickly. He caught three grasshoppers in close succession and threaded one on the hook. With the only weight on the line being the hook and the grasshopper, he twirled it around his head until there was enough line out and released it onto the water.

The grasshopper settled on the water and started kicking frantically. The hopper had been on the water less than a minute when a hungry bass that had been patrolling his domain, violently struck the hook. Though he had been hoping for just such a result, the fish surprised Clay. He yanked hard, setting the hook, and pulled the fighting fish to the bank. He looked at it, guessed its weight at about two pounds, and decided he needed one more. He pulled another grasshopper from his vest pocket, slipped it on the hook, and repeated the process.

This time, a bass leaped into the air, taking the hook and grasshopper before they could hit the water. Clay pulled that one in and figured it for three pounds. That would be enough. He released the last grasshopper, carried the bass over to his camp, and started making a small fire. *It's sure a lot easier with matches,* he thought as the fire quickly grew. Once the fire was low and steady, he pulled his new Barlow knife from his other vest pocket, took the two bass back near the bank, and cleaned them.

Finished, he examined the meat of the two fish, almost three pounds. That should be enough for supper and breakfast. He washed the tender flesh, his hands, and his knife in the water, tossed the carcasses farther away from the camp, and moved back to the fire.

The white meat of the bass glistened in the firelight. He laid them both on his saddlebags, then stepped to a mesquite tree and cut off two limbs, about three feet long, each forming a fork at one end. After trimming the branches and sharpening the ends, he was satisfied with the two fairly straight sticks that formed a wide v at one end. Back at the fire, he shoved both ends of the v into each fish and propped them on some large rocks so that they were suspended over the coals.

While the fish were cooking, he untied his bedroll from the saddle and spread it on the ground, moving whatever rocks and debris that could poke him through the groundsheet, then stepped over to the cattails, searching for some young shoots. Finding them, he pulled up four, cut the lower white portion off, washed them in the pond, and by the time he got back to the fish, it was curling, the stage just before it would start coming apart.

Clay removed both bass from the fire and laid one on a rock near his bedding. He sat on his groundcloth and took his revolver out of the holster. Laying his weapon next to him, he leaned back against his saddle. Clay had always loved fish, and this was no different. He took a bite of fish, then cattail, and went back to the fish. The cattail tasted a lot like the cucumbers his ma had grown in her garden. They were just right. A full-grown cattail would be tough, but these were tasty and tender.

Coyotes started howling nearby. It was funny how two could sound like ten. An armadillo shuffled in the night, hunting for grubs. He enjoyed his fish probably just as much as the coyote enjoyed his quail. Moments later, he heard snuffling around the fish remains. A raccoon's yellow eyes reflected in the firelight as it enjoyed a free meal.

Clay laid his head back on the saddle. Gazing at the stars, he thought about Jake. He understood why his friend hadn't waited for him. When Jake had been notified, he'd been in Brownsville. He must have ridden hard, to make it to Presidio near the time Clay arrived in Fort Davis. Clay couldn't have waited, just like Jake didn't, but now it was up to Clay to find his friend. He raised up and took one last look around. The horses were calmly munching grass. They were a lot better watchmen than he could ever be. Lying back, he held the Colt loosely in his right hand and closed his eyes, a picture of Dee's warm smile forming before he drifted off to sleep.

11

Clay watered the horses one last time, mounted the bay, and headed east. It was at least an hour before daylight, and a chill lay over the Mexican countryside. Once headed toward the trail, he gave the thick, muscular horse his head, letting him pick his way down, into, and across the several draws he had to transit. Like all men who survived in the wild country, he had noted the location of the waterhole. It would forever be imprinted in his memory for ready use, should he ever again need the life-giving elixir.

Reaching the trail, he turned south, hoping to find some sign or message from Jake today. He didn't know if his friend had accomplished his mission or was dead. He'd have to be careful here, for even though he was just across the border, he rode in a different country, with different laws. He felt better than ever about his decision to keep the old black sombrero. It helped him blend in. Miguel's serape, which he wore on this cool morning, also helped. Times like this made him appreciate the fact that, though his ma was the teacher, his pa had made sure he learned and was fluent in Spanish. "You want the Mexicans to accept you?" Pa had said. "You've got to speak their lingo." Pa was never one to tell another to do something he wouldn't do himself. When he spoke, he sounded Mexican.

Clay had been fortunate with languages. Because his ma and his grandparents were French, he picked up French quickly. His family had always wanted him to become a lawyer, and Ma believed any lawyer worth his salt should speak Latin, therefore she taught him Latin. He caught on to languages easily. He also spoke German, having learned it from the many German communities in the hill country, and Running Wolf and his family had helped him learn Tonkawa.

He laughed to himself as he thought, *I guess if I ever get tired of rangering, and don't want to be a lawyer, I can find me a schoolhouse and teach.* Clay tried to picture himself as a teacher. Somehow, the image just didn't fit. But you never knew what life would throw at you next.

Dawn was slowly breaking. His trail had turned into a road that looked heavily used. A jackrabbit dashed across in front of him, almost under the bay's feet. The startled horse reared, then, when its front feet hit the ground, started crow-hopping. Clay, as surprised as the horse was, leaned forward to maintain balance as the horse came up. After the initial surprise, Clay grinned, enjoying the jolts, a touch of safe excitement. The other two animals milled around behind them on a long lead, but remained calm.

Once the bay settled down, Clay patted the horse on the neck. "Easy, boy. Don't let those long-eared jacks scare you."

The surprise gone, and at the sound of his voice, the horse calmed down and returned to an easy ground-eating walk. On a nearby slope, Clay could make out a herd of mule deer. They got their name from their ears which were long like a mule's. The deer were feeding beneath the top of the ridge, eating for a few moments, then jerking their heads up in case something might be trying to slip up on them. They never all had their heads down at one time. He watched the animals as he passed. They were all bucks, their horns were growing tall and wide but still in velvet. It wouldn't be long before the antlers started to harden, and they began rubbing them on anything they could find to scrape off the velvet. Just a short time after that, this bachelor herd would break up in search of does, and so life would continue.

He passed the deer and continued south. The river was still to his left, but the country had grown rougher. There were only a few farms, scattered in what little level, fertile land could be found. The bay continued its steady walk, up one hill, down the other side, over and over. Just before topping the next hill, he heard voices coming from the other side. One voice was pleading and Clay could hear loud, humorless laughter. He removed the leather loop holding his Colt in place and, reaching behind him, pulled the shotgun from his bedroll. It wasn't his Roper, but it would do. As the bay continued moving up the hill, he released the catch on the back of the double-barrel ten-gauge and checked that two shells nestled in their chambers, ready for action. Snapping the shotgun closed, he cleared the top of the hill.

In front of him were four men, either vaqueros or banditos, but no matter which, they were rough-looking characters. All four sported thick, drooping mustaches that gave them a sinister appearance, even when they laughed. And they were laughing when Clay topped the rise. The laughter ceased immediately when he rode into view. The four men had stopped a man who had been walking beside a two-wheeled cart that carried his wife and a heavy load of vegetables. Several pots that had contained tomatoes were lying shattered on the side of the road, the tomatoes smashed. A bandit was eating one, the juice and a few seeds spread across his mustache and chin.

Clay pulled up about twenty feet from the group. He shoved his sombrero to the back of his head with his left forefinger. "Howdy," he said.

It was obvious that the man and woman were both frightened, but the husband was doing his best to stay between the men and his pregnant wife. The only weapon he had was a staff the thickness of a man's wrist and almost six feet long.

The ugliest of the four spoke in Spanish. Clay just stared at him with a vacant look, which the men interpreted to mean he didn't speak the language. The man talking, who seemed to be the leader, said in Spanish, "This stupid gringo does not speak our language, but he has some fine horses, and the pack horse is loaded. This is our lucky day."

With a vacant smile on his lips, Clay said, "Sorry, no comprende, amigos." He"d made sure to use an exaggerated Texas drawl.

The ugly one spoke again. "You no understand the Spanish, Señor?"

Clay shook his head and grinned. "No, sir. I ain't had much learnin'. Just a poor cowboy lookin' for work."

With that, the ugly one flung back his head and roared. When he stopped laughing, he spit and said to the young couple in Spanish, "Leave now. You are lucky this gringo came along. Go!"

The husband looked back at Clay and shrugged his shoulders. Clay waved to them like he didn't have a care in the world. The four mounted men opened a space for the cart to go through. As they passed, one of the men leered suggestively at the woman and moved his horse toward her. The young man immediately stepped between his wife and the bandit and lifted his staff. His sudden move startled the bandit's horse and it shied away from the couple, sidestepping. The threatening move by the young husband angered the bandit.

Clay watched the whole thing play out. He saw the anger slide across the bandit's face and his hand start for his gun. Before the six-gun had cleared leather, Clay had drawn and fired twice, driving the man from his saddle and into the dirt. At the same time he drew his Colt, Clay swung the ten-gauge like a pistol. The bandits had been split, two on each side of the cart.

The two to Clay's right were completely clear of the couple, giving Clay an open shot with the shotgun.

He knew the power of the ten-gauge, both in front and in back. The sawed-off barrels reduced the weight, thereby increasing the recoil. For an average-sized man to try to fire the weapon like a pistol was insane. The recoil would either drive the gun out of the shooter's hand or could feasibly break his wrist. Clay, however, was a different matter. At twenty-five, he was physically in his prime. At six feet two inches, he was a tall man, but not just tall. He had been working since he was a button. All the corral posts, the logs, the cattle he'd manhandled, came into play here. His wrists, like the rest of his body, were huge. Would he feel the recoil? Of course. But he could handle it.

Knowing his own strength, Clay swung the shotgun on one of the men who even now was bringing his Winchester's muzzle up. Clay had no desire to get shot again, now or ever. He pulled the trigger of the ten-gauge. Being far enough away from the bandits allowed the shot to begin spreading. The man he shot was driven from the saddle, throwing his hands up and tossing his Winchester high into the air. But since the shot spread, the man's companion, who was also drawing, collected four of the eighteen, thirty-caliber lead balls. Three of them hit him in the chest, wounds that, on their own, would have eventually killed him, but the fourth ball struck him just above his right eyebrow, penetrating his skull. He collapsed from the saddle.

With three of them down, the only bandit Clay had to be concerned with was the ugly one who had been doing all the talking, but he needn't have worried. The man was racing away from them, down the road. He was spurring his horse hard, over and over, his legs flying out to the side, as he raced away from the gun battle. His sombrero had blown off his head and was flying in the wind, held only by the string under his chin.

Clay reached for his Winchester. He had never shot anyone in the back in all of his years as a ranger, but if this man spread the word about him it might ruin their chance to get Rory back alive. His stomach turned at what he was about to do, but he settled the front sight of the Winchester into the buckhorns of the rear, holding slightly above and in front of the rapidly disappearing rider's right shoulder, tracked for just a moment, and squeezed the trigger. The Winchester '73 roared, sending a two-hundred-grain slug downrange. A moment passed. Finally, the man threw up his arms and tumbled from the saddle. The couple had stood first watching the bandit, then looking back at Clay, then at the bandit.

When the man threw up his hands, the young woman's hands flew to her mouth. Clay's heart was heavy, but he told himself that he'd had to do it. He took a deep breath and forced himself to put it out of his mind. He turned back to the other three killers. The two hit by the shotgun were dead. It looked like the man shot with the Colt was still alive. Clay climbed down from the bay, patting the horse's neck as he did. "You did real good," he said to the animal.

Evidently all of the horses were trained with firearms. None had panicked, all still standing in place. Clay was thankful for that. One of the things so great about Blue was that Clay could discharge a cannon from that horse's back, and Blue wouldn't twitch. He moved quickly to the dying bandit's side, now able to see he was a younger man. The couple had tied their donkey and came hurrying back.

Kneeling down beside the bandit, Clay asked him in Spanish, "Do you know Medrano?"

The young man looked up at him, eyes filled with surprise, blood now wetting his drooping mustache. "Am I dying, Señor?"

Clay nodded. "Fraid so. Do you know Medrano?"

The man coughed, more blood running down the side of his mouth. "Sí, he is my *jefe*."

"Where is he keeping the young boy he took?"

The dark brown eyes stared up at Clay. The man's mouth

opened, as if to say something, then the jaw relaxed, the mouth stayed open, and the man's eyes lost focus.

The young woman had walked up. In Spanish, she asked, "Is there anything we can do, Señor?"

"No," Clay replied in Spanish. "He's gone." Clay stood and turned to her. "Are you all right?"

"Yes," the woman replied, "we are fine."

The young man stepped up and spoke in Spanish. "Thank you, Señor." He put his arm around his wife's waist. "If you had not been here, I am afraid they might have harmed my sweet wife."

His wife looked up into the young man's face, and said, "Yes, I am afraid so, and they would have killed my husband, for as long as he took a breath, he would have fought for me."

Clay looked at the young couple. It was obvious the man was a farmer, and probably the two of them lived in a one-room adobe hut with a dirt floor. But he could see the love, admiration, and trust in the eyes of the wife, and the adoration of her in the husband's eyes.

He looked back down at the bandit who was someone's little boy, and probably grew up in a home like the expectant mother and father would provide. Even with death all around, his mind was beginning to nourish a tiny thought. Maybe a woman helps provide stability. He shook his head. No time for that thinking, he had to find Jake.

In his boots, he towered over the couple. Clay, realizing how intimidating he must look, smiled at the young woman. "I'm just glad I was here. Do you know these men?"

The husband spoke up. "We do not know them, personally, but we have seen them before. They work for Medrano. He is an evil man. He supplies his ranch with the food grown by the poor, with no thought of how those he steals from will survive. I know for the fact, he takes his gang of cutthroats to the United States and steals from the Americanos. I have seen him pass by."

"You have seen him? When was the last time?"

The man bowed slightly and said, "I am sorry for my rudeness, Señor. This lovely lady, who is my wife, is Julieta Ortiz, and my name is Mateo."

"Thanks," Clay said, "I'm Clay Barlow."

The two of them looked at one another, and Mateo asked. "Have you ever been in Del Rio, Señor?"

I can't get away from that, Clay thought. "Yes, Mateo, I have been there, several years ago."

The two young people looked at each other and nodded, then turned back to Clay. Mateo again spoke. "Señor, we are deeply in your debt. Would you do us the honor of accompanying us to our village? It is only a couple of miles up the road. I will apologize now. Our village is very small, and our family is very large. They are a good part of the village. But if you would be so kind, I'm sure there will be a fine dinner."

Clay thought about the opportunity to question a large group of people who might be friendly toward him, and a delicious meal. He didn't think long. "I would be honored, but first I must bury these men."

The young man nodded his head. "Yes, even the greatest sinner should not have his body mutilated. I will help you."

"Thanks. Let's drag these fellas over by the depression behind the sage and ocotillo. First, though, we need to get their guns and whatever money they might have."

At the word money, the young man recoiled.

"Relax," Clay said. "They won't need it, and it might allow them to do some good for the first time in their lives."

At Clay's words, Mateo relaxed and began stripping the guns and emptying their pockets. All of the men had quite a few pesos in their vest pockets. Once he had emptied the pockets from one man, he waited for Clay to finish the ones shot with the shotgun. When Clay stood, Mateo handed him the money. Clay had a few dollars in a pouch in his vest. He pulled it out, stuffed the pesos in it, and handed it back to Mateo.

"Señor?"

"Look, Mateo. I have enough money with me. You take this. It might help you, especially since Julieta is pregnant."

Julieta had gone back to the cart which was parked at least fifty yards down the road. Mateo looked toward Julieta, and she waved. He waved back to her, then faced Clay, extending his hand. "Thank you, Señor."

"Don't thank me, thank these fine gentlemen."

Clay thought nothing of his remark until he saw the disgusted look that came over the other man's face. His face hardened as he stared at Mateo. Then he went back to work.

After a moment, Mateo relaxed. "I must apologize, Señor. I was born into a *very* Catholic family. I almost became a priest, but then I met Julieta. I am, perhaps, too sensitive."

"Never apologize for being a good man." Clay reached down to the body he was standing by and stripped the gunbelt from the dead man. "Check that man for weapons." He pointed toward the man who had been shot with the Colt. He was less gruesome. "Be sure and check in his boots and between his shoulders. Take anything you can find, be it gun or knife."

While Mateo moved back to the other man, Clay continued to check, just as he had instructed Mateo. He found a knife in one boot and another knife tied to his back, but no hidden guns. He stripped the gunbelt and laid it to the side with the knives, reached down, and picked up the Winchester '73 that the man had attempted to kill Clay with. He laid the rifle with the growing stack of weapons and checked the other man. This search only yielded the revolver on his gunbelt, a Colt, and a big knife similar to a Bowie.

He gathered the weapons and took them to Mateo's pile. The three men's horses were still standing nearby. "You want those horses?"

"As much as I would like to have them, Señor, I am afraid they would be identified. If Medrano found out, he would personally come down from his hacienda in the mountains and kill us both." Mateo looked back at Julieta before continuing. "And probably our families. No, Clay, I do not want them."

"I'm sure you could use some of these weapons," Clay said. "I imagine there's at least two more rifles on the horses. Take one horse and catch the other one." He nodded down the road. "Put the bandito on his horse, and bring him back. I'll get started digging." Clay noticed the hesitancy in the man as he gazed toward his wife.

"Your wife will be safe, Mateo I promise." The smaller man looked up at Clay for a moment.

"Yes, I believe she will. I will be back as soon as I can."

12

_____

B y the time Mateo returned, Clay had finished digging the hole. It was only about three feet deep. The ground was hard. *Deep enough for this bunch,* Clay thought. He glanced up at the sound of horses and could see Mateo returning. *Good. We need to get these fellas buried and be on our way. We've been lucky no one has come along.*

Clay dragged the three men to the edge of the hole and rolled them in. Mateo rode straight to the hole, dismounted, and led the ugly bandit's horse to the other side. The man was laid over the saddle. Mateo grabbed his feet and flipped him into the hole with his compadres, then Clay jumped into the hole and spread them out. The morning was warming up. He reached for his watch. Gone, stolen, and he had forgotten to get another one in Presidio. Glancing at the sun, he figured it was pushing ten o'clock. He reached for the shovel and started filling the hole. It was a good thing Butch had convinced him to bring a shovel.

"Señor Clay, I can help," Mateo said, reaching for the shovel.

"Obliged." Clay handed the man the shovel, then reached up and pulled his bandanna from around his neck. After taking off his sombrero, he wiped the bandanna around the inside hat band

and then across his face and neck. It was hot work. He walked back to the bay, and pulled his canteen from the saddle, taking a long swig. It made it a lot easier to drink from his canteen with the river in sight, knowing there was plenty of water to refill it.

"A drink?" he said to Mateo. The man shook his head, steadily working. "How about your wife?"

Mateo stopped and looked at his wife in the cart. "We have a goat skin in the cart. She can drink anytime she wants." Then he grinned. "With the baby, she wants all the time, but must visit the bushes often."

Clay smiled, thinking that was way more information than he needed. He watched Mateo make quick work of the communal grave. Clay had pulled a bush from the other side of the road. Now he smoothed out the dirt and sprinkled topsoil lightly over the grave, adding a few random stones. "All right, let's move back to the road."

Mateo led the horse back with Clay following, brushing, and dropping leaves and gravel. When he made it back to the road, he checked his handiwork.

"It looks good, Señor Clay. Where did you learn to do that?"

"An old Indian trick I learned from a not-so-old Indian. It'll fool the casual passerby, but it won't fool a tracker. There's no reason for Medrano or any of his men to come by here looking specifically for a grave. Of course, once it starts settling, it'll be easy to spot, but for now it should be fine."

Clay walked back to his horse. "You got all of the weapons?"

"Yes. They are in the wagon and covered with vegetables."

"Good idea. How far is it to your village?"

Mateo pointed up the road. "A short distance to the turnoff, then maybe an hour. We will get there in time for eating."

"Good," Clay said. "Shoveling makes me hungry. Mateo, do you mind tying these horses to your cart until we get to your village? Then I'll take care of them."

Mateo shook his head. "No, Señor Clay. That is no problem. I was only worried about having them around my house. That would not be good."

"Great, let's be on our way."

Clay swung back onto his horse. It felt good to be sitting in the saddle. There was a warm breeze blowing from the southeast, and with them moving south, it increased the breeze across his sweaty body, providing much-needed cooling. His sombrero was positioned on the back of his head, and he felt pretty good.

He had just killed four more men. Though they were bad ones and it had needed doing, he did wonder why it didn't bother him more. He had never wanted to kill anyone. The sidewinder had started drawing down on Mateo, and he'd had to protect those folks. *That's what I do*, he thought. *Some people are good at farming, some at ranching, and some at lawyering, but I'm good at killing.*

He rode on behind the cart. Now Julieta and Mateo were riding two of the horses. *I'm glad I came along. If I hadn't, no telling what they would have done to Julieta, and for sure they would have killed Mateo. That would have been the end of their new family. If I just hadn't had to shoot that fella in the back.*

MATEO HAD BEEN off on his time estimate. It was more like two hours before they pulled into the village. Clay could see why it had no name. It was made up of a few small adobe homes, scattered fields on the sides of the foothills, and large gardens. Entering the village, they were surrounded by excited children, chattering away about the pretty horses, the silver inlaid saddles and bridles, and the tall gringo. They stared up at Clay with awe. They had probably never seen anyone as tall, and sitting on his horse, he seemed gigantic. One of the little ones, probably eight years old, was braver than the others. She ran to Clay, looking up at him as they trotted into the village. She rested one hand on his boot, as if to say, "he is mine," and ran alongside, holding his boot all the way to Mateo's family's home.

When they stopped, all of the villagers converged on the young couple, immersing them in questions about the big man behind them, and the horses, and even the guns, when they saw them. From Clay's viewpoint it looked and sounded like the young couple was holding their own, like the kids, chattering away. Clay remained in his saddle.

An older gentleman broke away from the group and strode back to Clay. In rapid Spanish, he invited him to step down. Clay, equally comfortable in either Spanish or English, replied in the man's language. "Thank you, Señor." He dismounted. That was something he liked about riding. It always felt good when you climbed up on a horse, and it also felt good when you climbed down.

"I am Mateo's father, Fernando Ortiz. I want to thank you from the bottom of my heart, for saving my son and his family. I know what would have happened if you had not come along. There are too many banditos in this country. A man must be very careful.

"I am sure you are hungry. Please, come with me."

"First, I must take care of the horses," Clay said.

Fernando called to several of the young men who were walking around the side of the house with the others. They turned and headed quickly back.

"Take Mateo's donkey and these horses to water, and give them a good rubdown. When you are finished, turn them into the corral."

"*Si, Padre,*" the four boys said.

Clay walked to the pack horse and pulled out a sack of oats. "Give them some of this, too. Thanks for your help."

The boys nodded and took the horses. Clay thought for a moment about the gold at the bottom of the pack. He dismissed the thought. After these past years as a ranger, he felt he knew people, and he was sure these family members would not go through his packs. He followed Fernando to the back of the largest home. There, in a spacious courtyard, tables were arranged with big pots of beans, peppers, tortillas, chicken, and beef.

Fernando showed Clay to a place at one of the tables, near the end. He was seated next to the patriarch, across from Mateo and Julieta. He waited for the ladies to sit. There was much giggling. Fernando's wife said to her son Mateo, "Your gringo is polite as well as good-looking."

Before Mateo could answer, Fernando laughed. Addressing his wife, Teresa, he said, "Yes, he is, and his Spanish is also very good."

Teresa hastily turned to Clay. "I am sorry, Señor Clay. Please forgive my rudeness."

Clay tossed a grin her way. "Thank you for your hospitality. I heard no offense, only compliments."

She smiled back, seating herself at the other end of the table. "Thank you."

They blessed the food and started eating. Fernando turned to his guest.

"You wear a sombrero. That is unusual."

Clay finished chewing the bite of bean and pico-filled tortilla he had just put in his mouth. "My hat was stolen. A friend loaned me this one."

"Stolen?" one of the younger boys said. "I would think that would be difficult since it is so far from the ground."

The comment garnered laughter from all of the tables and a frowning glare toward the boy from Fernando.

Clay joined in the laughter, then explained, "Normally, I'd have to agree with you, but these banditos waylaid me in Texas, and stole all of my gear, including my horse."

From all tables there were words of compassion, and the boy stared at his plate.

"Don't feel bad for me. I'll catch the men who did it and ensure they are punished."

Fernando nodded. "We have the bad ones in our country, too. Some you have already met. They can make life hard."

Clay stopped eating and turned to Fernando. "I understand you are familiar with Hugo Medrano?"

"Sí," Fernando said. "Medrano takes from us our food that we eat, and the grain we use to feed our animals and grow our crops. What is worse, he threatens to kill us should we complain. He is a devil."

"Do you know where his rancho is located?"

"Yes, I know it well. At one time it belonged to a friend, until Medrano killed him and his family and took the rancho for himself."

All of the people around the tables were silent now, listening to Clay and Fernando's conversation. The solemn faces reflected their fear and concern.

"Señor Ortiz, do you have someone in your village that knows the way well enough to guide me? It would have to be a brave man, for this trip will be dangerous. In truth, we may not survive."

Fernando leaned forward and asked softly. "Why do you need to go there?"

Clay explained Jake's letter, and what he found out when he reached Presidio.

"I know Cesar Garcia very well. I also know that one of his daughters married a Texas Ranger and has a son." Fernando looked at Clay, eyebrows raised.

"Yes, that is my friend, Jake Coleman. He is a Texas Ranger, as am I."

The declaration was met with a sudden intake of breath, followed by silence—no talking and no eating, even the children falling quiet. The mothers present wrapped their arms around their little ones. Everyone stared at Clay.

"You know that Texas Rangers have invaded our land and killed our people."

"Señor Fernando, I know that Texas Rangers have chased rustlers and thieves, just like Medrano, back into Mexico. Yes, sometimes innocent people get killed. But that happens on both sides of the border. If you've a mind to help, I'm here to put an end to Medrano and his shiftless bunch. When that happens, it will be good for you, your family, and your village. If not, I thank you for your hospitality." Clay stopped and looked around the tables.

Cold, hard, and angry looks, mixed with a few sympathetic gazes, were aimed at him. Placing his hands on the table, he started to rise. "Much obliged for this fine dinner."

"No, Clay," Fernando said. He placed a restraining hand on Clay's arm. "Please stay." Fernando gazed around the tables. "Do not forget, this man saved Mateo and Julieta. If not for him, they would be dead now."

Clay slowly eased himself back down.

Fernando leaned forward and looked Clay in the eyes. "I would not ask anyone else to go. I will guide you."

"Thank you, Fernando, but I could not ask you to do this. There will be fighting. I don't doubt your bravery, but it will take a younger man."

"Then I'll go," Mateo said. "I know the back way as well as you, Papa. You know that. I can shoot and I can ride. I can do this, but I will need Julieta looked after, and my farm tilled while I am gone."

"Mateo," Clay said, "this is going to be dangerous. I've got to find my friend, Jake Coleman, and his son, Rory."

Mateo nodded. "I understand, Clay. Do you understand that your friend could already be dead?"

Clay let out a long sigh. "Yes, I do. But that doesn't change my mission. First, I'm here to get the boy, and then, if there is any way I can, end Medrano's reign over this country."

Julieta clutched Mateo's upper arm and hugged him to her. "Are you sure, Mateo? Can you do this?"

"The young man patted his wife's belly. "Julieta, we are alive because of Clay. Our son will see a sunrise, smell a honeysuckle, and hopefully even know love, because of Clay Barlow. How can I not do this?"

Mateo turned back to Clay. "We should leave at dusk. The fewer people that see us, the better off we will be. Medrano has spies all over the land. If they spot us, they will report to him, and we will be finished."

"You mentioned a back way?" Clay said.

"Yes, Señor. It will take us through some very rugged country. We will pass along the eastern edge of the canyon of copper."

"I heard of it. In the states, it is called Copper Canyon."

"Yes, it is called that because of the green cast to all of the earth. It looks like copper. But we must move through it, and stay off the regular trails. No one will travel where we go. Are your horses sure-footed?"

"I don't rightly know. Those horses belong to Señor Garcia. He loaned them to me since mine were stolen."

Fernando spoke up. "Knowing Cesar, he would sell any horse that wasn't. He has ridden this country since a boy."

A somber tone had fallen over the dinner participants. Clay couldn't blame them. Mateo, a family member, was leaving with Clay to attack Medrano's rancho. Few probably thought either man would survive.

They had finished the meal, and Clay now lay under the big oak tree, escaping from the heat and resting for the evening departure. Many of the others had returned home after taking a few moments to thank the Texas Ranger for saving Mateo and Julieta. Those two had retired to the house. The last Clay had seen Julieta, she was clinging to Mateo's arm as if she would never let it go.

The big sombrero lay over Clay's face, keeping most of the

afternoon sunlight from his eyes. He had planned on taking a siesta before their departure, but his mind wouldn't slow down. Thoughts raced through it. *Where is Jake? Will I be able to find him before the rescue attempt? Is Rory still alive?* So many unanswered questions. Fortunately, Fernando was sending several of the men, under the auspices of going to market, to search for Jake. They would meet with him and Mateo on the other side of Copper Canyon. His thoughts finally slowed, and he drifted off to a restless sleep.

"Señor Clay . . . Señor Clay."

The voice slowly brought him back to consciousness. He lifted the sombrero to see Mateo leaning over him.

"It is time."

Clay sat up and looked around. The sun had disappeared behind heavy clouds hanging over the mountains. He stood, slipped the sombrero back on, and checked his gun. Satisfied, he dropped the Colt back into its resting place in the holster and looked over at Mateo.

Mateo wore crisscrossed bandoliers over his chest, loaded with ammunition, and now carried one Remington slung on his right hip, and another, butt forward, behind his waistband. Clay nodded.

"Looks like you're ready."

"I am. The horses have been fed and watered. We will take all of the bandits' animals. That way if we need to ride like the wind, we can. Also, once we have the boy, he will have something to ride."

Clay nodded agreement.

The family had put together additional food and supplies for the two men. Those were now loaded on one of the bandit's horses. The remaining two and Clay's animals had been saddled and were ready, held by the boys who had fed and watered them.

"We will eat on the way," Mateo said.

The two men strode to the waiting family members. This time, there was no laughing, no smiles, only hugs and tears. After telling Mateo goodbye, Fernando and his wife, Teresa, came over to Clay.

Fernando spoke first. "Mateo is a brave man. He owes you a debt and will fulfill it."

"I appreciate the sacrifice you folks are making," Clay said. "I'll do my best to bring him back in one piece."

Teresa's eyes were full when she looked up at Clay. "Please do your best, Señor. Save the little boy, and protect my brave son." She stood on her toes, placed her hands on his shoulders and pulled him down, so she could kiss him on each cheek.

"Yes ma'am, I sure will. Thanks."

Mateo and Julieta had finished their goodbyes and walked over to Clay.

"Goodbye, Julieta," Clay said.

"Señor." She bowed her head, then looked up into his eyes. "Bring my Mateo back to me."

He nodded, then turned and mounted the bay. Mateo embraced his wife one last time and swung up onto a big buckskin. Without another word, the two men rode out of the village. This time the children hung back, held in the arms of their parents.

13

Mateo was in the lead as the men rode from the silent village, each leading two horses. Mateo looked back once, rose up in the saddle and waved to his wife and family. His goodbyes said, he faced forward as the village disappeared behind huge boulders. They rode in silence.

The sun slipped from beneath the clouds and momentarily rested on the mountain's peak before sliding from view. Dropping out of sight, its remaining presence was marked by the brilliance of the clouds. First gold, then pink, and finally, a somber blue-gray as light retreated from the countryside.

"With all those clouds, it's gonna be mighty dark," Clay said.

"Sí, but I could travel this road with the eyes closed. Trust me, Señor Clay. It is better that we cross the bridge in the dark. There will be no travelers on a night like this. Once across, we will leave the road to follow a trail known only by my family."

In the remaining twilight, Clay could see they were continuing to climb. They had been climbing since leaving Mateo's village. He moved closer to the younger man. "How much farther to the bridge?"

"Another hour. It will be dark when we get there. Keep me in sight, and follow closely."

His eyes constantly scanning the broken countryside, Clay eased the bay slightly back from Mateo. Though he was anxious to find Jake and Rory, he felt apprehensive about traveling this country at night.

He found himself again depending on a complete stranger. He had been lucky so far. Would that luck hold? Did this young man know the trails as well as he said? The edge of the road, if it could be called that, dropped sharply to the left, falling away into a deep canyon, but Mateo rode confidently forward in the fading light.

It had been almost an hour since they had last spoken. Clay had been listening to an increasing roar as they rode. He could faintly see Mateo motion him forward.

In a voice pitched louder than normal so he could be heard, Mateo said, "It is just around this bend. The river will be very loud as we cross the narrow bridge. It is short, only wide enough for one wagon. Keep tight hold to your horses, but be ready to release them if they go off the bridge. The rails on the sides are low, so if a horse starts fighting you, he could easily go over the side."

"All right, amigo. Lead the way."

Rounding the bend, the roar of the river was deafening. The ears of the bay Clay was riding pricked forward. He glanced at the other two horses. Though he had pulled them close, he could barely see them, but he could make out the wide eyes and lifted necks. Neither appeared happy about the noise or the spray.

Clay felt the dampness from thousands of tiny droplets of water escaping from the raging maelstrom beneath the bridge as they approached. He strained to keep Mateo in sight while holding tight to the lead ropes of the frightened horses.

The thick clouds above devoured all light from the moon and stars. The first hollow step the bay made onto the bridge startled both Clay and the horse. It tossed its head and paused. Clay leaned over the horse's neck and spoke to it, rubbing the tensed muscles. The horse calmed enough to continue forward. Clay held to the lead ropes of the black and the roan. He could feel the black tossing its head, but both horses moved forward.

They crossed the bridge quickly, enjoying the feel of the solid ground as the roar receded behind them. No more than a mile down the road, Mateo turned off, following a trail that he could only be navigating from memory, for it was impossible to see in this darkness. They continued into the night. Hours passed.

Finally, Mateo pulled up, climbed down, and walked back to Clay. The ranger swung down, enjoying the feel of solid earth beneath his feet.

"We will rest for the night," Mateo said. "There is some grass for the horses and a small spring where they can water."

"Dark night," Clay said. "I think I'll hobble the horses. I want 'em kept close. I don't know this country, so if we light a fire, can it be seen?"

"No, not from any direction that might bring us harm. I'll gather wood."

Mateo returned to his horses, and the two men led them to water, then removed saddles and packs, and finally hobbled them. The Mexican lad moved confidently through the darkness gathering wood. Moments later he was back and went to work building a small fire. In the faint light, Clay could make out some of the surroundings. They were in a shallow decline, too small to be a valley and too large for a gulch.

Mateo pulled out a portion of the food that his mother had sent, warmed the beans and meat for a few minutes, then, using a wooden ladle, scooped up the mixture and dropped it into a corn tortilla. He rolled it and, after handing it to Clay, fixed one for himself.

Clay took a bite of the tortilla, enjoying the spicy taste of the beans and meat. "Good," he said.

"Sí, *mi madre* makes the food very well."

Clay finished the tortilla, walked to the fire and picked up the empty skillet. He moved to the pond and washed it. Then, off a ways to his left, he stretched out on his belly, and took a long, satisfying drink from the sweet water. Shaking the moisture from the skillet, he returned and set it on a rock near the fire, moved to his bedroll, and rolled it out next to his saddle. Pulling his Winchester from the saddle scabbard he laid it next to the shotgun, sat, and leaned back against the saddle, angling slightly away from the fire.

"I'll take the first watch, Mateo. You get some sleep."

"Gracias."

Within minutes, Clay could hear Mateo's breathing grow steady. Overhead, the clouds were starting to break, letting light from the moon stalk across the broken land. He gazed at what he could make out in the welcome moonlight. The land had changed drastically, since leaving the village.

From where he sat, it looked like the edge of the valley he was sitting in ended abruptly no more than seventy-five yards away. He could barely make out the edge and glanced quickly at the horses to ensure they were well clear. They were pulling contentedly on the bunchgrass, now calm and relaxed, the canyon crossing leaving no aftereffect.

His mind wandered to his grandfather. *I sure hope he's doing well,* he thought. *I'd like to see him again.* His grandfather had been instrumental in his decision to go to New York and get his law degree. The older man had hoped that he would join him in the firm in Austin, but unfortunately for him, Clay's call was to the rangers.

Dee was never far from his thoughts. It was hard to accept such a lovely young woman could care about him. She was perfect—those pretty hands didn't get that way by babying or manicures. He had felt the callouses from using the rope and branding iron alongside her pa. A grin slipped across his face.

She was definitely no shrinking violet. That blow she'd thrown broke the buffalo hunter's nose. That was a woman who could stand with a man, side by side, and meet whatever troubles came their way. His mind moved from Dee to the rangers.

The past few years had gone by quickly. He had gone from feuds to renegades to rustlers, always busy, always using his gun. He was good with the gun and had one thing many men didn't. He could overcome his fears and face men who were set on killing him, with cold, calculating precision. Also, his size didn't hurt. Broad-shouldered, and standing six-feet-two inches in his stocking feet, he intimidated many criminals, making it easier to arrest them. He had brought in several men he might've had to kill had he been smaller..

The clouds were gone, the moon lighting the land with a pale glow. He glanced at the stars, figuring it must be about two in the morning. Standing, Clay walked to Mateo and tapped his boot with his rifle barrel.

"I'm awake, Señor."

"All quiet."

Clay moved back to his saddle, lay down on his groundsheet, and pulled his blanket over him. He glanced at the horses one last time before laying his rifle next to him. Settling in, he laid his head on his saddle, his hat over his face, and was quickly asleep.

He awoke, to his mouth watering. The smell of beans and chorizo tantalized him to the point that his stomach growled. He adjusted his hat and sat up. "Howdy, Mateo."

"*Buenos Días, Señor.* It is time for the breakfast."

"Is there time to water the horses?"

"Sí."

Clay stood, gathered the horses, and led them to the pond. Once they were satisfied, he moved them back to the grass and let them continue grazing. When he glanced at the fire, the skillet Mateo was working over held a number of eggs.

"Eggs?"

Mateo squatted at the fire. He turned to Clay and grinned. "Sí, mi madre packed some eggs for us."

"Well, that was mighty nice."

Clay went back to his saddle bag and pulled out his plate and fork, taking it back to the fire. Mateo piled beans, chorizo, and six eggs on Clay's plate. Then, he produced salt and pepper, offering them to Clay.

"Now this is special. I feel like I'm in a restaurant in Austin." He sprinkled salt and then pepper over his eggs and handed them back to Mateo.

"Food is never as good as it can be without salt and pepper," Mateo said.

The two men, both squatting on their heels, quickly devoured the big breakfast. Clay had been taking in the new country since he woke up. He knew they had been climbing since leaving the Rio Grande, but he had never seen anything like this. This had to be the roughest country he had ever traveled. There were canyons he could see that must be easily several thousand feet deep. On the top of the rim, he could make out tall fir and pine trees, but here, where the trail led, wind-hammered juniper and scrub oak made up the majority of trees.

Once finished, they cleaned up. Using the two skillets to pour water across the remaining coals, they put out the fire and saddled the horses. Clay swung up on the black, keeping his Winchester handy, the shotgun in the boot. Leading the bay and the roan pack horse, he followed Mateo. In the beginning, the trail was wide and protected, the edge of the canyons well away from them, but as they continued along the winding path, the trail narrowed. In spots, his left stirrup dragged against the sheer canyon wall, while his right hung over the edge. There was nothing but space for a long way down. The horses proved their mettle on the trail. All of them took to the narrow, precipitous path with calm and steadiness.

Clay occasionally allowed himself a look over the edge to the bottom, many thousands of feet beneath them. When he made that mistake, he could feel the crawlies work up his thighs and back. His hope was that they wouldn't meet anything or anyone on this narrow trail. There was no room for travelers to turn around. He laughed to himself. *That would be a true Mexican standoff.*

The trail dropped lower, and Clay felt the sweat popping out all over. When they reached a wide point, Mateo pulled up and stepped down.

"Time for a break, Señor. We must let the horses rest. In about an hour, we will be at a stream. The horses can water then."

Clay swung down. "Is it my imagination, or is it getting hotter?"

"Sí, it is hotter. We will not go all the way to the bottom of the canyon, but if we did, you would find it much hotter. We must keep our eyes out for the jaguar. They like horse meat."

"Great," Clay said. "Anything else?"

"The mountain lion and bear, also. And there are many skunks. I would not like to meet a skunk when the trail is narrow. They are always unfriendly and often have the rabies."

In silence, the two men rested the horses for a few more minutes. Mateo nodded and they swung back up and headed down the trail. This time Mateo's estimate was close. After little more than an hour, the narrow trail opened up to a wide, grassy meadow, through which a wide stream, lined with poplar, oak, and alder, flowed. Well before reaching it, the horses had tried to pick up their pace, obviously smelling water. Though not on the canyon floor, and now blocked from the sun by the high walls, the meadow was hot.

Clay walked the black into the stream alongside Mateo. All of the horses drank deeply.

"Spending the night here?" Clay asked.

"Yes. This is the best place to stop. Tomorrow the trail will climb out of the canyon."

"How long to our meetup with the folks that rode ahead?"

Mateo thought for a moment. "Four days, maybe three, depending on how long we travel tomorrow."

Clay nodded. "I'd like to make it three."

They rode their horses from the stream and swung down, unsaddling their mounts. Clay removed the pack from the roan and then rubbed both horses down with the long grass around the stream. When he stopped, the black and the roan took the opportunity to roll in the grass.

Using long ropes, Clay staked his horses out on the good grass, close enough to the stream to get a drink when they wanted it. Mateo did the same.

"We should sit watch tonight," Mateo said."

"Expectin' someone?" Clay asked. "I'd think we would be pretty safe down here."

"We will, Señor. But the horses may not. One of the big cats or a bear could come along. There are many throughout this canyon. We must be ready."

Clay nodded. "Makes sense. Choose your watch."

"If it is all right with you, I will go first."

"Sounds good. Let's hope it's a quiet night."

The men made camp, and when Mateo started building a large fire, Clay said, "That's mighty big. What about Indians and bandits?"

Mateo shook his head. "They will not bother us here. This is a dangerous place to make an ambush. The single trail is the only way in or out. The Tarahumara are friendly and reclusive. The Apache will not put themselves in such an ambush spot. They are too smart."

They ate, and Clay stretched out to sleep. Dee had been on his mind a lot recently. *Too much,* he thought, thinking back to being captured by the bandits. *Yet she's still on my mind. How could*

I feel this strong about someone I just met? Even more important, how was it possible that a twelve-year-old girl could make up her mind like she had . . . and stick to it as a woman? I do have strong feelings for her. When we get Rory back, I'll stop by their ranch on the way to Austin. Comfort won't be that far out of the way. The next thing Clay knew was Mateo poking him with a rifle barrel.

"I'm up."

"All is quiet, Señor."

Clay had slept with his boots on. He stood, swung on his gunbelt, and picked up his Winchester. He strolled through the horses, petting and talking to each one. They were all calm and quickly went back to sleep. He moved to the fire and tossed a few more logs on it. Then he eased over to a large oak that sheltered him from the glare and settled down.

He had to move a couple of rocks that were poking him but finally stopped moving. Clay sat still, listening to the night sounds. Hours passed. The fire had died down, and his night vision was working well. There was a faint light reflecting on the western rim. He was about to rise and wake Mateo up when first the bay's and then the rest of the horses' heads jerked up. Each one turned to the trail they had come down, ears forward. Clay waited, seeing nothing.

The horses turned, facing the trail. In the faint light of the fire, Clay could see the whites of the wide eyes staring into the darkness. Whatever it was, it was moving. Then, in the still night, he heard it, a low, guttural rumble, like the sound of boiling water in a big iron wash pot.

A cat, he thought. He searched the darkness, looking for the intruder. The horses were starting to mill around, though they couldn't get far, being staked to the ground. The big black screamed a challenge, charged toward the cat, and stopped after a few feet. Mateo leaped up, grabbing his rifle, eyes wild.

Clay said nothing, searching, trying to see it. In the growing light, he finally made it out, low, clinging to the ground, looking for an opening.

Clay's rifle leaped to his shoulder, and in one smooth motion the sight settled on the big cat's head. His finger squeezed the trigger immediately when the cat and the sights lined up. The roar of the Winchester echoed throughout the canyon. Birds called and wings beat in their fear and confusion. The cat lay dead, only its legs twitching.

The black, sensing the cat was injured, completed its charge. Rising high above, he slammed his forefeet down on the cat. Mateo raced over to the horse, calming him and pulled him away from what they could now see was a cougar.

"Good shot, Señor. I would like to save the hide to show my family."

Clay walked to the black while Mateo moved to the cougar. The big cat's ribs had been crushed by the horse. He grabbed it by the scruff of its neck and dragged it near the fire.

Squatting, Mateo examined the cat and held the head up. "Look, you hit him right above the left eye. How could you see him? I had not."

"Well, it was starting to get light, and I could just make him out. That's about the best I can tell you."

"You have good eyes. It was not light to me. We are fortunate he came so late. Earlier in the night he could have killed a horse."

"You're right about that," Clay said. "I'm thinking he must have crossed our trail a ways back and followed it, just now arriving. Why don't you skin him out, and I'll get us some grub? We need to be on our way."

14

L ate afternoon of the third day, after killing the cougar, Clay pushed the black through a wall of brush behind Mateo. Once through, the trail they followed was almost invisible.

Mateo turned around to Clay and, in a low voice said, "That is why we don't worry too much about someone knowing of our trail. When necessary, the family has used it for many years. The main road is less than a mile east of us." Mateo jumped down from his horse, motioned Clay to lead all of the horses forward, and, using a brushy mesquite limb, wiped the tracks from sight. A few days of wind, maybe a little rain, and any sign of a trail would disappear.

The two men rode around the south end of a ridge and jerked their horses to a halt. There, no more than fifty yards, was a small camp, completely concealed from the road. Four men stood to face them.

Clay slipped the loop from the Colt, freeing it in the holster. He rested his right hand on his thigh.

Mateo turned to him. "Three of those men are ours, the ones that my father sent to Coyame."

Clay didn't need any assistance recognizing the fourth. It was Jake. Approaching the camping spot, Clay evaluated the men's choice. Whether Jake or the men from the village, they had chosen their camp well. It was hidden from the road and near a small holding basin that had caught the last runoff, and at its deepest point was four or five feet deep.

Jake waited at the edge of the camp. As Clay swung down from his horse, Jake stepped forward, and the two men clasped hands. *He looks exhausted,* Clay thought. *I guess having a child kidnapped would make even a young man look tired.*

The horses pulled toward the water. "Good to see you, Jake," Clay said. "The horses are tired and thirsty. We'll take care of them and then talk."

After men and beasts had quenched their thirst, introductions were made all around, and the horses were led back to camp where they were relieved of their burdens. Using a handful of grass, Clay started rubbing down the black. Jake pitched in, taking care of the bay and unloading the pack horse. Mateo and two of the men who had been waiting for them also started working on the horses. In no time, all of the animals were rubbed down and staked out on the grass near the water with the other animals. One of the men remained in camp, cooking supper.

There was little talking while the men worked. Once finished, and as the horses rolled, they moved back to the small fire.

"You're a sight for these tired, old eyes, Clay," Jake said in Spanish. "I had near given up on you comin', until these fellers cornered me."

Hector, the cook, looked up. "It wasn't exactly like that, Señor Clay. When we finally located Señor Jake, he cornered us. We had to talk fast. We are thankful men that he speaks before shooting."

The other two, Bruno and Juan, nodded in agreement, while Clay laughed.

"He's not known for a lot of conversation. You were lucky."

"Reckon I was the lucky one," Jake said. "These fellers saved my bacon. The town magistrate was starting to eyeball me. I imagine I'd been asking too many questions about Medrano. The law probably gets paid to look the other way where that bandit's concerned."

Bruno spoke up. "It is true. The magistrate, he is a pig. Medrano pays him. It is not good for the small people with little or nothing." He thought for a moment, then shrugged. "But what can you do?"

"What have you found out about *your son*?" Clay asked.

At the question, Jake stared at Clay for a moment, then relaxed. "I reckon you've got a right to be upset about me not telling you. As much as we've rode together, I probably should've said something. I just didn't want to put Sophia and the boy in danger. There's a lot of bad men that would harm my family to get even." Jake spit a stream of tobacco juice into the fire. "I never realized that my son might be harmed because someone didn't know who he was."

Clay listened as Jake spoke. Then there was a long silence around the fire. Clay finally broke it. "I'll admit, I was a mite surprised when I found out. But when Señor Ortiz explained your reasoning, to protect his daughter and grandson, it made sense. Presidio is far enough away from anywhere, so that this is the one place you could probably maintain the secret. That's behind us. What have you found out about your boy?"

Jake shook his head. "I hate to say it, but he is well guarded. Medrano doesn't let Rory go anywhere without at least four guards. His rancho is located about twenty miles south of Coyame. If we follow the road, after we get Rory back, it'll take us right back through the town."

"No," Mateo said, "there is another way. Just like the trail we took from our village, there is one from down south. The only problem is that it will take us longer than the road will."

"Thanks, Mateo," Jake said. "We'll keep that in mind. I'm thinkin' that speed is going to be our best friend, at least until we get past Coyame. I'm not real sure if they will even chase us without a leader."

The four villagers looked up at Jake. Mateo spoke for them. "Why would Medrano not chase us?"

Jake looked west for a moment, watching as the sun drifted beneath the mountainous horizon. "'Cause I aim to kill him, and as many of his men as I can. I want to send a clear message: mess with my family and you ain't gonna be upright very long."

Mateo looked at the other three men from the village, then at Jake. "These men are not gunmen, Señor Jake. They are farmers. The land is what they know."

Jake looked at the four men. "I ain't askin' you to fight my battles. You got families of your own. In fact, it'd probably be best if all of you got mounted up and headed back to your families. I'm much obliged for what you've done already, and I'm gettin' almighty tired of señor. Just call me Jake."

Mateo nodded. "Jake, I will stay with you, for my father taught me somewhat of the gun, but these other three have no experience with firearms. They do not hunt, they plow. I think you are right. In the morning it will be time for them to go back home."

The three men started to argue, but Mateo held up his hand. "I did not say you lacked bravery, I said you did not have experience, and I'm sure Jake or Clay do not have the time to train you. It would be best for everyone if you went home."

"What Mateo's saying is true," Clay said. He looked at each of the men. "You have been brave in your quest for Jake. Now your job is done. As Jake is doing, you must think of your families. What would they do if you were killed? Who would take care of them?"

Jake chimed in. "If you hadn't found me, I might have ended up in the Coyame jail. I'm much obliged to each of you. If there's ever anything I can do for you, come looking for me. I'll be in Presidio."

Hector spoke up. "It is time to eat."

Each of the hungry men had their utensils with them. They held them out to Hector, while he dished up a thick brew of peppers, meat, beans, and more peppers. After filling their plate, each man reached into the skillet sitting by the fire and pulled out two corn tortillas.

The villagers started putting away the concoction like they were eating ice cream. Clay took his first bite, and then quickly took a bite of tortilla while glancing over at Jake. His friend was shoveling it down, but there were little beads of sweat on his forehead. Clay was used to hot food. He grew up not far from the Mexico border, but this had to be the hottest that had ever made it to his mouth. He figured he could eat anything after this because his taste buds were melted off.

He looked up, and found Hector watching him. The man had a little twinkle in his eye. "Is it good?"

Clay looked down at his plate and then back at Hector. "It sure smells good. I can't tell you much more than that, since my taster's done been seared off."

Everyone roared. Bruno spoke up. "It is dangerous to allow Hector to cook the meal. I think he could suck on a hot coal and find it refreshing. Even for us, it is very hot." Then the men went back to their eating.

Finally finished, and glad of it, Clay walked with Jake to the pond, knelt at the edge, and washed his metal utensils, then dipped and drank several cups of water.

Jake, next to him and doing the same thing, chuckled. "I swear, I ain't never et anything that hot in all my born days on the border."

The two men laughed. They checked on the horses, making sure they were secure and could reach the water should they want any.

"Where's Blue?" Jake asked.

"That's part of the story of why I took so long getting here."

On the way back to the fire, Clay told Jake about his kidnapping and near murder. By the time he finished, the villagers were enthralled and amazed at Clay's nonchalance in the telling.

Jake frowned. "I've come close to gettin' Earl Griffin in my sights. I think I winged him once, but I was never sure. I didn't realize that Shifty Joe Beck was riding with him. That's a mean pair, but Beck is in a class all his own. He's about the meanest no-good I've ever known of."

"After we get Rory back," Clay said, "I'm headin' out after them. I suspect they'll be surprised when they show up on the end of a rope, especially from me. I imagine they figure those ants did me in."

Darkness had covered the countryside. The moon was peeking over the eastern horizon, providing faint light. Clay looked at the sky and yawned. "Who takes the first watch?"

"Since I'm still on fire from those beans," Jake said, looking over at Hector, who grinned back at him, "I'll take the first watch."

"Fine," Clay said. "Wake me up when you need me." He laid the shotgun next to him and pulled the Colt from his gunbelt, laying it beside the shotgun before he pulled his blanket up to his throat. Nights were chilly. Thankfully, there was no wind. His mind drifted to Dee, and his heart jumped. The strong jaw, chiseled cheekbones, and cleft chin were emphasized by the flickering firelight but softened by the smile that slid across his face.

It was hard to believe that the little girl he rescued from the stagecoach robbery had grown into such a beautiful woman. What was even harder for him to accept was that this young woman loved him. He had listened to Miguel speak of his wives, and he could hear the love and admiration in his voice. Then there were the Tates, hard, crusty ranchers, but those two not only loved each other, but it looked like they enjoyed ranching together. That reminded him of the way Nancy had talked about Dee's riding and roping. Now, there was a woman who would fit on a ranch, and she had seen him shooting those men and didn't even flinch. In fact, her ma, Nancy, had shot one of the bandits as well.

Dee would make someone a fine wife—maybe him.

HE CAME AWAKE at the movement around him. Through the years he had developed the ability to wake with a clear mind. The noise he heard was Hector, Bruno, and Juan packing their burros.

Clay sat up and put his hat on. Next, he shook out his boots and pulled them on. He didn't need one of those big Mexican scorpions waiting for him inside his boot. He glanced across at Jake as he raised up and looked around. They nodded to each other. Clay stood and swung his gunbelt around his waist. He rolled his bedroll, watching the three men finish their packing.

Bruno turned to face him. "I am sorry we must leave. I only wish I knew how to handle a gun. I would come with you. We all would."

Clay towered over the three men. He placed his hand on Bruno's shoulder. "I know you would. I never thought you afraid, but it is important to think of your family first. I know you have men in your village who know their way around firearms. Have one of them teach you, so you can be ready the next time."

"Yes," Bruno said. "I think all three of us will learn."

Clay addressed the three men. "Thanks for finding Jake, and have a safe trip home."

They nodded and, after saying their goodbyes to Jake, turned toward the road. Mateo walked with them for a ways before turning back to join Clay and Jake.

"They're not taking the trail we took?" Clay asked.

"No, they are only three peons, and they have nothing except their donkeys. No one will bother them."

Clay watched for a moment longer, then saddled the bay,

sliding the shotgun inside his bedroll. He pulled the Winchester out and worked the lever slowly. After checking the action and removing the round that was in the chamber, he lowered the hammer, checked it, and slid it back into the loading gate. Then he shoved the rifle back into its boot, patted the bay, and loaded the pack horse. He rubbed the horse's neck for a moment, moved to the black and did the same, then stepped to the fire.

Jake had started brewing coffee while the other men were leaving. Hector had made some earlier but had to pack his cooking gear and pot. Jake looked over at Clay.

"You still don't drink it?"

"Nope. Never developed a taste for it."

"Mateo?" Jake pointed at the pot.

"Sí. I never pass an opportunity for coffee."

"You have a plan?" Clay asked.

"Yep," Jake said.

"Are you going to share it with us, or just stare at that pot?"

"Boy, relax. I'll tell you all about it just as soon as I can drizzle some of this fine brew down my throat." He picked up the pot and shook it toward Mateo.

The younger man hurried over with his cup and thrust it under the spout. Jake poured a cup of the steaming, black brew, picked up his cup, and filled it. After setting the pot on rocks at the edge of the hot coals, he sat on the log that had been pulled near the fire and took a sip from the cup.

A wide grin broke out on his wrinkled face. "Now that's a fine cup of coffee." He smoothed his mustache with the thumb and forefinger of his right hand, tracing the evenly trimmed ends at the edge of his mouth. Then his hand dropped down to his chin hair, wrapping around the goatee as he softly pulled the long hairs together to bring it to a point. The goatee and mustache were sprinkled with white, no longer the dark brown they had been when Clay first met him.

"Now can you share this plan of yours?"

"Why, I sure can, Ranger Barlow. We're going to ride in there and get my son back."

"That's it? That's your plan?"

Jake grinned at him. "Well, that may not be the complete plan, but that's the gist of it. Don't it sound fine to you?"

Clay knew that Jake was a planner. He also knew his friend was pulling his leg. He'd tell him when he was good and ready.

"Jake, that sounds like one of the best plans you've ever hatched. I'm going to enjoy watching you execute it."

While they had been arguing, Mateo had poured himself another cup of coffee and sat watching the two rangers apprehensively.

"Don't mind us, Mateo," Jake said. He stood, picked up the pot and poured the remainder over the coals, creating a big cloud of steam to rise.

The three men looked around as the steam disappeared quickly into the early morning. Daylight was slipping over the craggy land as Jake motioned for Clay to come over beside him. He knelt on the ground, picked up a stick, smoothed out the dirt, and started drawing the hacienda.

"Now, this Medrano ain't no slouch. He's fixed him up a mighty fine place."

"He didn't build it," Mateo said. "It was built by Señor Renaldo Flores, a fine man. Medrano went to work for him and then murdered him. He claimed that Señor Flores left him his rancho, and that he had the documents to prove it. I'm sure he tortured the family to get Señor Flores to sign it."

All of the humor that Jake and Clay had been feeling was driven out by Mateo's reminder of Medrano's character.

"The compound sits in the middle of a shallow, narrow valley. Medrano has an adobe fence that surrounds his place. The compound is square. The barn and corrals are on the south side adjoining each other and using the adobe fence as a wall. The corrals are right next to the main gate. The bunkhouse sits on the east side against the adobe fence, running north and south. The entrance is almost directly across from the main house gate. So the house is located in the northwest corner, facing southeast. That not only gives 'em morning sun in the winter, but allows them to keep an eye on the front gate, which is located in the south wall."

Jake looked up to make sure Clay was following his drawing. "The interesting part is the long low building along the inside of the north wall, between the main house and the bunkhouse. I've been watching them for the last few days. Men are constantly coming out of that building with weapons and what looks like ammunition. My guess is that Mr. Medrano has himself an armory, and *there's our distraction!*"

15

C lay examined the map Jake had drawn, noting the distance from the armory to the house and the bunkhouse. The armory was positioned between the two buildings, right next to the bunkhouse and close to the main house. If one of them could get inside from the back, the explosion would do severe damage, maybe even taking out most of Medrano's men, at least those who were there.

"How do we get inside?"

Jake stood up, leaned way back to relieve some of the pain in his old back, and said, "Dig."

"Dig? Through the walls?"

Jake shook his head. "Through the floor. The ground in that valley has a lot of sand in it. It should be easy digging. The only problem is, with all of that sand, It won't hold together. We stand a good chance of it collapsing."

Clay thought for a moment. "Then we need to shore it up. It shouldn't be more than four feet. That won't take much timber, just enough to hold it for an hour or so."

"Go through the wall," Mateo said.

Both Clay and Jake looked at him. "It'll make too much noise," Jake said.

"No, it won't. This house is old. The adobe is worn. The north side will be especially bad. The winters are hard here. Rain, snow, and sleet blow out of the north and the northwest and beat upon the wall. If any snow drifts against the wall, as it melts, it will soak into the adobe. Over the years, the adobe becomes thin and weak."

"Well, that sure beats digging a shaft in loose sand."

Clay nodded. "It better be right. I don't see us getting more than one chance."

Mateo pulled himself to his full height of five feet and six inches and placed his hands on his hips. He tilted his head back so he could stare directly into Clay's eyes. "I do not lie, Señor Clay. What I tell you is the truth."

Clay admired the younger man for standing up to him. He squeezed the man's shoulder and nodded. "I know you don't, Mateo, I was just thinking of our chances. We've got one shot, either way we go."

The men stood in silence, staring at the dirt map, all three thinking the same thing. How would they keep Rory from getting hurt in the blast and subsequent escape? Finally, Mateo broke the silence.

"There may be a way to get the boy out, at least away from the blast."

"Well, spill it," Jake said.

Clay felt sure Jake had been laboring over the possibility of getting his son away from Medrano unharmed. Now, at least there might be a fighting chance.

Mateo nodded. "My mother has a friend who has the misfortune of working for the evil man. She would like to leave him, but he will not let her go. She is a very good cook . . . and very pretty. He does not treat her well. She would kill him, but then she would die. If I can reach her, I believe she might help."

"Does she know you?" Jake asked.

"Sí, she comes from our little village. Four years ago, on one of Medrano's visits to collect his taxes from us, he noticed her when she was cooking for him and his pigs. He killed her husband and took her and her son."

"Mateo," Clay said, "if that's the case, then she's also a prisoner. He won't let her leave."

"Yes, he does let her take trips to Coyame to buy the produce. He knows she will always come back because he keeps her son."

"How old's the boy?" Clay asked.

"I am not sure, nine, maybe ten."

Clay looked at Mateo for a moment. "That's why you wanted to bring the extra horses, so you could make sure the two of them had something to ride. All along you have been planning on rescuing them."

Mateo did not flinch under Clay's hard gaze. "Sí, Señor Clay. That was my hope. I had no idea how it would be done, but I knew that we must have horses for them. I could not leave without them."

Clay considered what Mateo had just said. He couldn't be angry with him. The man had hoped to rescue this woman and her son from Medrano, mighty brave for a farmer with no fighting experience.

"You should have told me."

"I am telling you now. I did not know you when we left my village."

"You knew I rescued you and your wife."

"Yes, and I *thought* you were a good man. But I had to be sure. You must remember, Señor, you are a Texas Ranger. You do not have the best reputation in Mexico."

"He's got you there, Clay," Jake said. "Lot of folks in Mexico are either afraid of us or want to kill us, or both."

Mateo nodded. "Sí, but I have grown to know you, and I know

you are a good man." Mateo grinned and turned to Jake. "You too, Señor Jake. I think you both are good men."

Jake smoothed his mustache and pulled his goatee. "Well, Mateo, I reckon you're a good man too. But let's git back to planning this thing before we start slobbering all over each other."

Clay chuckled while the others grinned, and then all three grew serious. "How do we get a message to your ma's friend?"

"The only chance is the market," Mateo said. "Medrano's men do not watch her closely. They go to the cantinas for the drinks and the girls."

"How often do they come into town?" Jake asked.

"She must feed many men. It is a long trip, but she must make it at least once a week, or they will run out of the vegetables. No frijoles and peppers makes for very unhappy pigs."

Jake nodded. "We need to get you into town. Hopefully, she ain't come in yet this week."

"I am sure she hasn't. Market day is Sunday when all the people come into town for church and fiesta. We are lucky, today is Sunday."

"Then we best head for town right now," Jake said.

"Jake, we need to write her a note to explain when we're going to make our move. If we're going to do that, then we probably need to figure it out for ourselves."

Jake started kicking dirt over the few remaining hot coals in the fire pit.

Clay could see that his friend was impatient to be on the move. He turned to Mateo. "What's the lady's name?"

"She is Maria Gomez. Her son's name is Eduardo."

"Can she read?"

"Sí, the Spanish."

"Can you read, Mateo?"

"Sí. I can read and write."

Clay immediately moved over to the bay. He opened his saddlebags, hunted around a moment, and pulled out a pad, and a bunch of pencils held together by a leather string. He took a pencil from the group, pulled his knife from his belt scabbard, and quickly brought the wooden pencil to a point. After closing the saddlebags, he stepped back to Mateo and handed him the pad and pencil.

"When do we want to do this, Jake?"

Jake stopped what he was doing. "I think tonight, around one in the morning. That should give everyone time to get to sleep. Hopefully there's enough powder in that armory to make sure when they wake up, they'll be talking to the devil."

"Good," Clay said. "Write the note, Mateo. Tell her to come to the barn. We'll also dig a hole through the barn wall. That'll be your job. Once they're out of the compound, we'll blow it."

"How's that sound to you, Jake?"

Jake had the fire out by now. He straightened and said, "Sounds good. We git this place blown, and we'll head on down the road. There's an ambush spot between Medrano's place and Coyame. One man can do a lot of damage."

"Good," Clay said, watching as Mateo finished the note. He took the pad, read the note, then tore the paper out and handed it back to Mateo. "Let's be on our way."

The three men climbed into their saddles, all three leading additional horses.

They rode for an hour without incident. Clay had been looking over the rough country. The land was broken and cut with sharp cliffs and deep canyons, the primary colors red and brown, with splashes of green around small streams.

"You know this country, Mateo?"

"Sí, Clay. Very well. It is *intimidante*, no?"

"Very intimidating. I'm glad we've got you with us. I'd be lost up one of these canyons if I left the road, which we might have to do."

"Two trails, besides the road, will get us home. We will be fine."

Nearing Coyame, Mateo pulled up at a path that swung down toward the of the town and dismounted.

"I must leave you now."

"You'll be all right?" Clay asked.

"I will. No one will bother a poor peon. Follow this trail. It will take you around the town, far enough away no one will see you. I'll meet you on the other side. There is an old oak by a little stream. Do not stop there. Many people do. Go past the big oak and you will find a large patch of prickly pear. It will be higher than your horse. Wait for me there."

Mateo turned and started for town. Clay and Jake divided Mateo's horses and turned off the road, following the trail. They rode in silence, down into deep arroyos and up across a splintered land. It looked as if a huge explosion had driven parts of the land up while dropping others, creating deep canyons, and all the while pulverizing everything. The boulders were broken and jagged, their peaks pointing at the sky as if laying blame for their fractured state.

Occasionally, when they were on the tops of the ridges, they could faintly make out the town of Coyame, hidden under a thick curtain of dust and smoke.

Finally, just before they dropped into another draw, they spotted the big oak ahead and slightly to their right. The trail they were on continued, almost paralleling the road. They strained their vision for the cactus. After another twenty minutes, they saw it and pulled up.

Clay eased next to Jake. "We crossed a small stream about ten minutes back. What say we ride back and water the horses? This could be a long wait."

Jake nodded and they swung back down the trail, dropping into a shallow canyon. Reaching the bottom, the animals walked directly to the stream. The two men sat their saddles until the horses had their fill, then moved them out of the water, ground hitched, and snagged leads in some brush.

Moving a little upstream from where the horses drank, Clay bellied down and washed his face. He turned to Jake. "Not the best water in the world. A little alkali but drinkable." He then rolled back and drank his fill, washed his face again, and stood up.

Jake took his turn. He stretched out in the water so that his gunbelt was still on the bank, while above his waist was in the water. He blew and threw water all over his face.

Clay stepped back, laughing. "Now aren't you the sight. If we had a few pigs down here, you'd fit right in."

Jake ignored him. He pulled his hat off and filled it with water, then poured it over his long hair. He did that a couple more times before he stood up.

Using his fingers to comb his long hair back, he said, "I feel as young as you look, you big, tall drink of water. Why, I feel like I could take on all those bandits by myself."

Water streamed from his hair, running down the back of his vest and shirt.

"If that's the case," Clay said, "why don't I just turn around and head for Comfort? I've got me a fine gal waiting for me."

At this statement, Jake's eyebrows went up, and he pushed his hat to the back of his head, rolled his wad of tobacco around in his mouth, and spit, hitting a big bullfrog right between the eyes. The frog blinked for a second, and then took one long leap back into the water.

Clay laughed and shook his head. "It's dangerous to be within ten feet of you when you've got a wad of tobacco in your mouth."

"Don't try to change the subject, boy. Tell me about this girl."

"We need to be gettin' back to meet Mateo, don't you think?"

"No, we danged sure don't. That young feller'll be tied up in town for a while. Anyway, it won't hurt him if he has to wait a bit. I need to find out about this love life you got goin' on. Now, don't be shy. This is ole Jake, and you can confide in me."

A self-conscious grin slid across Clay's face. "You remember a few years ago, the stage I came upon being robbed?"

"I sure do. If I remember correctly, you saved a lady and her . . . daughter. Why, her daughter weren't no more than six or seven." Now a frown spread across Jake's face. "You ain't messin' around with a twelve-year-old are you, boy?"

"Jake, she wasn't six or seven, she was twelve years old."

"Well, I'll be durned. I'll bet that's the little gal that said she was agoin' to marry you."

"That's the one. Only, she's not twelve years old anymore. She's nineteen or twenty, and I don't think she's changed her mind."

"So, boy, how do you feel about her?"

"You know it's been tough with my folks killed like they were. I've got to admit to a little loneliness now and then. But I'm thinking Dee is about the most perfect woman I've met. She's smart, she can ride and rope, and she doesn't have a problem with what I do. Of course, it doesn't hurt that she's about as pretty as a newborn filly."

Jake nodded, looking at the big man wearing a silly grin. "Clay, I'm happy for you, son. I've been worried about you, the way things have gone. I've been afraid you might be gettin' a mite hard. It takes a woman's touch to help keep us soft inside, no matter what we have to do. I'm lookin' forward to meetin' this fine girl. I've gotta tell you, while you were gone to New York, I was almighty afraid you'd get tied up with one of them fancy city women."

The horses had started to wander over to a patch of grass up the creek. Clay looked around. "I guess we better be going. He could be there by now."

"Yessir, you're shore right."

They mounted and turned back toward the road, leading the horses. When the cactus became visible, they could see a man sitting in its shade. As they drew closer, they recognized Mateo.

Clay whistled, and Mateo looked around the cactus, saw them, and started walking toward them.

"It went well," he said upon reaching them. "She says there are no other innocents in the house, besides your son, her, and Eduardo." He took the reins to his horse and the lead. Once mounted, the three of them moved up onto the road and headed south.

They were edgy about being on the road, but the country was too rough to travel cross-country. After an hour, a wagon loaded with kids came out of a draw the road passed through. Clay pulled his sombrero low, hiding his eyes. He knew the family would talk once they arrived in town. Hopefully, the deed would be done long before any hint of them reached Medrano.

The wagon had passed only a short time before two riders rode into view. They looked like vaqueros headed to town for a bender. One of them wobbled in the saddle. The two vaqueros watched closely as they passed. "*Buenos tardes,* good afternoon," Clay said.

Both of the men took in Clay's size for a moment, answered him, and continued on toward Coyame. After the two had passed, they met no one else for the rest of the trip.

Early in the afternoon, Jake led them off the road. The trail was narrow and rough, but the horses were used to this type of terrain and never faltered. When they topped out, they were looking down into the highway where it narrowed to the point that only a single wagon could pass through.

"If we're chased, this spot will make an excellent ambush. You have a clear shot of the road. It's no more than a hundred yards, like shooting fish in a barrel."

Clay looked it over and made up his mind. If someone needed to stay behind it would be him, but he said nothing.

They rode down the other side of the hill to where it leveled and rejoined the highway. Mid-afternoon found them at the turnoff to Medrano's ranch, where they quickly moved off the highway and down the road.

At this point, Jake took the lead. He left the road and led them down into a shallow canyon. Slowing, he allowed Clay and Mateo to ride up on either side.

"We need to be quiet from here on. Medrano's place is just a short distance up this canyon. He keeps it pretty well guarded. The house sits in a little valley just over this ridge. We'll leave the horses here and ease up to the top—from there you'll be able to see the layout. If we kept going down this draw, we'd cross the road to the house. From where we cross it, the compound is only a couple of hundred yards to the right. Now, Mateo, tell us what happened with Maria."

"Fortunately, the bandits that were with her had gone to the cantina. She was surprised but very happy to see me. When she read the note, she began to cry, but quickly pulled herself together. She said she would be in the barn with Rory and Eduardo a little before one in the morning. She seemed confident she could do it."

"Good," Jake said. "Did she ask any questions?"

"Only how big the explosion will be. I told her it would be best for her and the boys if they were out of the compound when the explosion went off, because it would be very big. I explained to her that I would be in the barn to meet her."

"Sounds like she is a pretty steady woman," Clay said.

"She is. Maria is much younger than my mother but is very much like her. She is a strong woman. You do not want to get on her bad side. She has a long memory."

"That all sounds good," Jake said. "Why don't we dismount here, and ease up to the top of the ridge? I've got a place up there where we can look down into the compound, and there's enough brush to keep us hidden."

The men dismounted and tied their horses. Jake and Clay pulled binoculars from their saddlebags and hung them around their necks. With each man carrying a rifle, they carefully climbed the side of the hill. It was covered with loose rock just waiting to roll under a man's foot. *If all of the terrain is like this,* Clay thought, *we'll have to be very careful moving around. One false step and a man would roll all the way to the bottom.* He didn't like it, but he knew there was always a hitch. You just worked through it or around it.

They eased up to the top of the ridge, and after taking his hat off, Clay raised his head only high enough for his eyes to clear the rim, then brought up his binoculars.

16

The compound bustled with activity. Men constantly went in and out of the building Jake had designated as the armory. Clay fine-tuned the focus of the binoculars and examined the fence and buildings.

With the field glasses, he could clearly see the poor condition of the buildings. The barn looked as if it would fall at any moment. The adobe was chipped, bricks cracked and falling, and there were holes all the way through to the interior. The other structures were in like condition—even Medrano's house was a sorry sight.

Jake had eased up next to him and leaned close to his ear. "Looks like they're headed out, but they don't have any horses saddled, so they ain't gonna be leaving soon."

Clay examined the portion of the fence that made up the wall of the armory. It was in as bad a shape as the barn. He could see several areas where the adobe bricks had caved in, settling into the sand. It wouldn't take much to get into the armory or the barn. The valley floor was made of a sandy soil with ironwood trees and ocotillo providing some cover. There were a few brushy areas that ran along the dry creek bed that meandered through the valley, not far from the compound.

"Structure's in terrible shape," Clay said.

"The better for us. I'm betting we can be through the walls in less than an hour, maybe half that," Jake said.

"What do you think they're up to?"

"It's for sure they're headin' out. To where, I have no idea, but it looks like they ain't movin' until in the morning. By then, it'll be too late for 'em."

Clay studied the bunkhouse and the men in the yard. "It doesn't look like Medrano cares much about where he lives, nor is he worried about security. The gate is standing wide open, and there's not a single guard around. If he's not worried about the law, what about the Apaches?"

Mateo had been listening. "No one bothers him. He owns the town and works with the Apaches. He sells them guns and whiskey. They do not bother him."

Jake shook his head. "When we get the good folks out of there, I'm thinkin' we oughta blow this place to kingdom come. From the looks of 'em, they ain't got the right to breathe the same air as a decent person."

Clay nodded. "I agree. When I'm in the armory, I'll pack all the powder I can find together. If they've got enough, we should be able to send a few of those devils to their resting place, although I don't think they'll be doing much resting."

"Whoa, young feller. You ain't gonna be the one in that armory, that'll be me."

"Jake, that doesn't even make a little sense. You need to be up front when your son comes out."

"He'll be fine with you and Mateo. I'm blowing that armory."

Clay decided this was not the place to argue. He finished looking over the compound and handed Mateo the binoculars. The younger man put them up to his eyes and scanned the men, then he stopped abruptly, and pointed. "That's him! That's Medrano."

Clay reached out and grabbed Mateo's arm, slamming it to the ground. "Keep your arm down!" He held it to the ground, while Jake looked at the men. Fortunately, no one had seen them.

"Which one?" Jake whispered.

Clay released his arm, and Mateo drew it back slowly. Obviously chagrined that his excitement had caused him to make such a dangerous mistake, his voice was much more subdued when he answered. "He is the one with the silver inlaid sombrero hanging from his neck. He stands outside of the armory."

"I see him," Jake said. "Hand Clay those glasses and let him take a look."

Clay could see the man they were talking about, the silver glinting in the evening sun. Once he had the binoculars to his eyes, the evil face leaped into his vision.

The man was handsome, in a cruel way. Black hair hung down to his ears, ears that jutted wide from his head. He had a big nose framed by a full black mustache that drooped down the sides of his mouth, almost to his chin, giving him a perpetual frown. A scar ran down the left side of his face. It looked like someone had come close to snuffing out his lights. Thick, black eyebrows covered deep-set eyes. They were so deep, at this distance, it was almost like looking into empty sockets. *I'll never forget that face,* Clay thought. *If a man wanted to draw evil, Medrano would be the face for it.*

Clay looked at the other two. "I've seen enough."

Jake nodded and started slipping back down the ridge. Clay waited for Mateo and then slid in behind him. Much of the trip back down the ridge was done on their rears. It was so steep and gravelly they couldn't take the chance on falling and breaking something. Not this close.

About halfway down, the slope lessened, and they stood, carefully making their way to the horses. Once there, Mateo spoke first as he rubbed his wrist. "I am sorry for raising my arm. I know they might have spotted the movement. I just became excited."

Both of the rangers nodded.

Clay spoke up. "Don't worry about it. That could happen to anyone."

Mateo rubbed his wrist. "It won't happen again."

"Yep," Jake said, "that big fella can hurt you without even trying." He then turned to Clay. "I've been thinking about those horses in the barn and corral. We could have a lot of hurt and dying horses from that explosion."

Clay nodded. "I was thinking about that. I can't believe their security is so lax, but we should be able to use it to our advantage. If they leave the entrance to the compound open—"

"They do," Jake said. "I've been watchin' them for over a week, and they ain't closed it yet."

"Good," Clay continued. "When I get inside the armory, I'll open the door so that I can see the corral. As soon as I see Maria and the boys enter the barn, and the horses are through the gate, I'll light the powder."

Jake frowned. "We'll see who sets off the powder, but whoever chases the horses out is gonna be waking up those folks, so it's gotta be done quick, or they'll scatter, and the blast won't be near as effective."

"You're right. I'll set a short fuse, just long enough to let me get out and around the fence corner. The house should shelter me from the blast."

"It's time we discuss who's gonna be settin' fuses."

"Jake, I know you feel you should do this, but look at it logically. This is your son we're rescuing. You need to be up where he can see you. Also, I'm younger."

Clay held his hand up when Jake started to protest. "Now, wait. It's a fact, I'm younger and faster. I can be out of there and away from the blast radius much quicker than you can, which will make it safer for everyone."

Jake thought for a moment, then spit a long stream at a lizard and missed, which riled him more. "Dadgummit, boy, I know you're right, but I don't like it even a little bit. I'm here to tell ya, it's hell to get old!

"All right, Clay, you take the armory. Mateo, you take care of the barn. I'd recommend you dig on the west side, just north of the corner, and I'll get them horses out of there."

Clay nodded and Mateo said, "Sí, Señor Jake."

Jake continued, "Mateo, if you have time, and if there's horses in the barn, run 'em out, and I'll chase those broomtails out of that compound so fast they'll think the devil himself is after them."

Clay laughed. "When the powder goes off, they'll probably think he's nipping at their heels."

"Yessir, I reckon if any of Mr. Medrano's men come out of this alive, they'll have a tough time finding anything on four legs to straddle."

Mateo grinned at the two men, happy that their disagreement was over. "The sun is close to disappearing, and I don't know about you, but I am hungry. I have had nothing to eat since breakfast."

"Now that you mention it," Clay said, "I'm pretty hungry myself."

"Well now," Jake said, "my stomach swears my throat's cut. I'm shore ready to chew on a big hunk of that nice soft jerky."

Clay said, "We oughta give these horses some water. They're probably pretty dry."

He walked back to the pack horse and pulled one of the water bags from the packframe. Jake and Mateo stepped up with their hats in their hands, and Jake filled each one, then sat his hat on the ground and filled it. Two of the three water bags were emptied watering the horses, but they would need them ready to ride this evening.

It took half an hour to water the animals. In that time, the sun slipped behind stark western mountains, turning the few clouds in the sky pink and golden, finally deepening to purple before the light completely disappeared. Clay had pulled two medium-sized flour sacks from the pack saddle, one of biscuits and one of jerky. The three men found boulders suitable for sitting and sat in silence while they ate.

Darkness enveloped them. Clay could make out each man, but no details. Once finished eating, Jake and Clay slid down to the ground so they could lean back against the boulders. They began talking in hushed tones.

"What are your plans when you get Rory back to Presidio?" Clay asked.

"Well, ole son, I've been thinkin' on that. I've spent at least ten more years in the rangers than I thought I would. We come out of this all right, this'll be it for me. It's time my son sees me more'n once or twice a year."

"You mean you're going to hang it up?"

"I reckon. I've got a little money saved. I can buy a few cattle and enjoy my wife and son. I've missed that." Jake turned to Mateo. "How's married life treating you?"

Mateo's white teeth flashed in the darkness. "Very well. I have a good wife and a baby coming. I have at times wondered if I have missed the excitement of the world, but I am tasting of that excitement now. It is more than I ever wanted. I will be happy to be back with my family."

"I can understand that," Jake said. "I've spent too many years chasing Comanches and white men. I'm way past being ready to hang it up."

Clay turned to the yellow light growing on the eastern horizon. "Looks like our light is right on time."

"Yep, not a half-moon, but just about perfect. Enough light, but not too much. Think I'll catch a little nap." Jake repositioned his holster for comfort, used his hat for a pillow and was soon asleep.

Mateo started to say something but looked at Jake and stopped.

"Don't worry about him. We've been on many a trail together. Nothing bothers him except a strange noise, then he'll wake in a flash."

"If you don't mind my asking, Señor Clay, what will you do when this is over?"

Clay slid his hat to the back of his head and looked up at the moon. It had changed from deep yellow to white. He watched it for a while, then slid down a little to find a more comfortable position against the rock.

"Mateo, I think I've got a girl back in Texas."

"You think? You don't know?"

"Well, I'm pretty sure I do. It's a long story, but I was with her and her folks in Austin, just before I got Jake's message. If she feels as strong as I do, I imagine she and I'll tie the knot."

"What will you do after you are married? Will you continue to be a ranger?"

"Now that is a good question, one I've been thinking on quite a bit. I have a ranch near Uvalde, but I'm also an attorney."

"Señor! You are an attorney *and* ride for the . . . the rangers?"

"I know that seems kind of crazy. But there's still a great deal of lawlessness in Texas. It makes me feel good to help people by putting the killers and bandits in jail or in a noose."

Mateo was quiet for a few minutes. "May I ask what made you become a ranger?"

Clay thought about it. He, didn't normally talk to others about his parents, especially someone he had known for such a short time. But he and Mateo had already been through some trying times, and he felt a connection with the younger man.

"My folks were killed by outlaws. My pa had been a deputy

sheriff. These men hunted him up at our ranch and killed them both. While I was hunting them down, I met Jake, who had been a ranger. One thing led to another, and I joined up. I've been rangering for about six years now."

Mateo stared at the big man in the soft moonlight. "You are young to be a ranger."

Clay shook his head. "Not necessarily. They've had younger men than me join."

The two relaxed against the rocks, the only sound an occasional snuff from the horses or the swish of their tails. Time passed quickly.

Clay, noting the moon's position, nudged Jake.

The ranger woke instantly. He lay there for a moment listening to the night sounds. The smell of a skunk drifted by on the faint breeze. At the smell, the horses grew restless, but settled down quickly.

"That don't smell fine," Jake said. He pulled out his watch and tried to check the time in the moonlight. He cursed, which Clay very seldom heard him do, and then pulled out a small pair of half-glasses and hooked them over his ears. He glanced up at Clay. "Another problem with getting old. I've got to have these danged things if I want to read anything in low light. The doc says it'll get worse."

Once the glasses were aligned, he checked the watch again. "Time to go. We've just enough time to get around to a draw where we can leave the horses and get our work done." He looked at each of the two men. "We understand our job?"

Both men answered in the affirmative.

Jake pulled the glasses from his face, folded them, and tucked them back into his vest pocket. "This draw turns just before we hit the road. We'll tie the horses in the draw. You'll need to walk —it ain't far—and I'll ride slowly to the hacienda. Clay, you move down the west wall and follow it along the north side to the armory. Let's get moving."

Just before the draw turned to cross the road, the men stopped, tied the horses, and Jake remounted. With Clay trotting on one side and Mateo the other, Jake rode slowly out of the draw and around the end of the ridge. When they reached the front gate, it stood open. Jake pulled up where he could just see the house and barn. From his position, he would be able to see Maria and the boys when they ran from the house.

Clay and Mateo jogged past the entrance, each with a rifle in his hand. Mateo also carried his machete in a scabbard hanging from his right shoulder and across his back. They slipped to the wall, and Clay made his way to the back of the compound.

If any one of them failed to execute his part of the plan properly, they would all be dead. Clay didn't like complicated plans or depending on civilians, but sometimes it couldn't be helped. Easing along the west wall, he found the walking fairly easy. Though he tended to sink a little into the sand, there were no rolling rocks or boulders to trip on when he would be running, after setting the charges. He reached the back corner, stopped, and listened. It was eerily quiet inside the compound.

He made his way around the corner. Recognizing the bush he had marked from the ridge, he knelt, facing the wall. In the moonlight, he could make out where the big hole had been worn. Clay pulled his knife and went to work. The adobe was soft and crumbly. Within fifteen minutes, he had a hole dug all the way through and into the armory.

When his knife blade broke through, he stopped, stuck his ear to the wall, and listened. No sound came from within. He quickly went to work enlarging the hole. This was one of the times when being smaller would be an advantage. His wide shoulders and long legs would have to make it through the hole, so he had to dig a lot longer and make the opening much larger.

It seemed like he had worked for an hour, but realized it had only taken a few more minutes. He pushed through the hole into a pitch-black room. He could see no light except for the faint outline around the door and the two shuttered windows. He moved carefully toward the first window. Hopefully, Mateo had as easy a time as he had with the wall. He unlatched the window, slowly opening it, flinching at the final squeak as it butted against the thick adobe.

Thank goodness for light, he thought looking around the room. The moonlight, streaming in from one window, already made a huge difference. Now able to see his obstacles, he realized they were many boxes of ammunition and rifles, and can after can of powder. He slowly opened the door a crack and peered into the compound. There was no movement. He widened the opening so he could keep watch across the compound as he worked.

Looking around inside, he decided opening the second window wasn't necessary. He had plenty of light to prepare a bomb they would hear in Coyame. He started stacking cans of black powder. There was enough here for an army.

While he carefully stacked the powder, he tried to keep watch out the door. He didn't want to miss Maria and the boys as they dashed for the barn. If anyone came after them, they weren't going to get far. Clay stacked powder waist-high, forming a T. The base ran from the hole in the back to the middle of the room, with the top crossing the base, and extending several yards from the center.

Once he had most of the cans stacked, he picked one up and cut a large hole in the side at the bottom, making a small mound of powder at the base of the can, as it leaned against the others in the stack. Picking up another, he jabbed a hole in the top and poured a line from the mound of powder to the hole in the wall.

He felt his vest pocket to make sure the lucifers were still there. They were.

Now, it was time to wait.

Only a couple of minutes later, a brute of a man stepped out of the bunkhouse. The man yawned and stretched, looking around the compound. *Did I make too much noise?* Clay thought. *I just hope Maria doesn't bring the kids out until this character goes back inside.*

The thought had no sooner hit his mind than the bandit jerked his head toward the main house. Clay followed the man's eyes and saw Maria and the two boys burst from the hacienda. She turned and headed straight for the barn.

The big man started to yell, changed his mind, and leaped off the short porch in a dead run, intent on catching them himself. Clay couldn't wait. He knew a rifle shot would wake everyone, but he couldn't let the man catch them. He took two steps outside the armory. At that same instant, Jake came racing into the compound to cut off the bandit. The man slid to a halt and reached for the hogleg hanging on his hip.

The faint moonlight barely illuminated the front sight of Clay's rifle as it settled on the center of the big man's head. The man's revolver cleared the holster and was starting to level on Jake. The last thought Clay had before he pulled the trigger was, *I hope this shot doesn't set off all the loose black powder floating around.* Then he squeezed the trigger.

17

The Winchester bucked against his shoulder, the blast reverberating through the compound. The rifle flash momentarily blinded him, but Clay blinked twice and vision returned enough for him to see the man stretched out on the ground, not moving.

Maria and the boys had disappeared into the barn.

Jake spun his horse and raced toward the corral.

Clay whirled, raced into the armory, dashed to the back, picked up the can of black powder, and started backing and pouring along the outside edge of the fence. He knew the bandits would start boiling out of the buildings any second, but he had to get the line of powder far enough away from the kegs, or he'd be scattered all over the Mexican countryside.

Finally, he couldn't wait any longer. Even though it was still thirty yards to the corner of the wall, he dropped to one knee and yanked a match from his vest pocket. Jerking it across the butt of his Colt, the match head popped off. Their chance of escape was dependent on him. Time was ticking away. Clay grabbed another match, this time snapping it across the leather of his gunbelt. It flared in the darkness, and he dropped the flaming splinter of wood into the line of powder.

Clay waited only a moment to see the flashing powder race toward the hole he had just exited from. It was too fast!

He leaped to his feet, turned, and sprinted toward the corner. Clay prayed he wouldn't make a misstep in the faint light. Rounding the corner, he didn't slow. Arms swinging and long legs driving, he ate up distance.

Down the west wall he raced. He could hear horses, men yelling. *I just hope the kids made it*—and the world exploded.

Night turned to day. The pressure wave drove him into the ground, his face slamming into the sand and rocks. His ears felt as if they'd burst. Huge blocks of adobe throbbed and vibrated through the air, while small chunks shrieked as they passed overhead. He wrapped his hands over his sombrero, pulling it down tight against his head and across his neck. Debris began falling. Several small pieces struck his back. No damage. The bright light of the flash was gone now, replaced by several fires. Pieces of adobe wall lay across his legs and back. Clay lay dazed for a moment, then leaped back to his feet and started to race for the end of the wall.

But the wall was gone. He stopped and turned. There before him lay the interior of the compound and what was left of the buildings.

The armory had disappeared. The remaining ammunition that hadn't been set off in the explosion now cooked off in the fire, sending projectiles across the compound.

The bunkhouse was almost as bad. The south end, that portion farthest from the blast, had only a small section of one wall still standing. The rest was completely demolished.

The big house had been vaporized. All that remained was a tiny piece of the back wall. The the rest of the adobe had returned to dust.

Bodies lay in front of the bunkhouse and the armory. No one

moved. Clay was thankful that the house and wall were between him and the shock wave. If he had been open to it, he would be like all those men on the ground—dead.

He looked to the corral. Surprisingly, though the barn was gone, the corral stood almost completely intact. Thankfully, there were no horses. Jake and Mateo must have gotten them all out.

Still dazed, Clay took one more look around. The thought to look for Medrano came to him, but he quickly dismissed it. The house was gone. He turned and jogged across the open compound, out, and toward the draw. Halfway there, Jake, with his son sitting in front of him, trotted up and out of the draw.

"Did everyone make it?" Clay asked.

"All in fine shape."

Clay took the reins of the black from Jake and swung aboard. It felt good to be in the saddle. There were a few seconds he had figured he'd never sit a horse again.

"Mateo and Maria have the other horses. I sent 'em on down the trail. We'll catch up. By the way, there won't be any more worries about Medrano."

Clay nodded in the moonlight. "That's for sure. Did you see what that explosion did?"

"Not what I'm talking about. You know Mateo said that Maria was tough? When they slipped out, she went into Medrano's room. He woke when she came in. I guess he could make her out in the moonlight. Anyway, he invited her to his bed. She crawled into bed with him and, quick as a wink, cut his throat."

Clay shook his head. "I'll tell you, Jake. Some of these women are way tougher than we are. Can you imagine what she had to put up with all this time?"

"Yep, yore right. She was protectin' her son. I'd say she got her a double helping of payback. Now let's catch Mateo and get back to Texas."

The two men galloped into the night and before long, they spotted Mateo and the horses. Slowing to a walk, Clay called softly. He didn't feel like surviving a huge explosion only to be shot by an edgy farmer. The rangers pulled up when they reached the group. Mateo made introductions, and Maria immediately spoke.

"Señor Clay, Señor Jake, and you, my Mateo, from the bottom of my heart, I thank you. Medrano, he was an animal. He liked to hurt women. He will hurt no more women.

"Eduardo and I have been there much too long. I constantly lived in fear, waiting for the day we could escape. You gave me such a wonderful opportunity, and we are again free. Thank you."

The rangers tipped their hats, and Clay spoke. "Glad we could help, ma'am. Tell you the truth, we didn't know you and Eduardo were there until Mateo told us. From the time he was included in this plan, he always had it in his mind to rescue you. He's the hero here."

Mateo ducked his head in embarrassment and said, "Gracias, Clay."

Clay changed the subject. "Jake, why didn't we lose any horses? That explosion was way bigger than I expected. I was afraid the horses might tear loose and escape."

"You can thank Mateo for that, too," Jake said. "That young feller was chasing the horses out of the barn, and raced out behind 'em, grabbed Maria and Eduardo, and took off for the main gate. They made it through and had just gotten to the horses when you blew the whole world up. My gracious, I ain't never heard anything like that, and I heard a lot of cannon fire in the war. If I hadn't been out near the draw when it went off, I think it would've knocked me clean out of my saddle.

"Anyway, they got back to the horses and held on to 'em. If they hadn't of done that, some of that fine horseflesh would've joined all the rest of 'em that raced on down the valley."

Clay turned to the young man. "We are in your debt, again, Mateo. Thanks."

Mateo nodded. "It was nothing."

Clay continued, "I don't think we need to dash out of here. I looked over what remained, which was pretty much nothing. I don't know how many men died in there, but there was quite a few that turned in their chips tonight."

Maria had been watching Clay as he spoke. "If the explosion killed them all, I fed twenty-four men at supper last night, including the monster Medrano. It is a good thing you and Señor Jake did, for these men were bad. No, not bad, evil. It is good they are no longer with us!" When she finished, she made the sign of the cross.

Clay thought for a moment. *The numbers keep rising. How many more men will I kill before someone kills me or I quit? But everyone I've killed has been a dangerous man, and this country still has those sort around.* Then his mind switched to Dee and his mood lifted.

"We better move it on down the road. I'm sure there'll be someone looking to investigate the blast. I would just as soon not be here when they arrive."

Jake swung Rory into the saddle of the boy's horse, spoke to him for a moment, and moved up front, to lead off the little band.

MARIA, Eduardo, and Mateo led their entourage into the little village as the sun was setting. Using the road for their return reduced travel time to only two days.

A young girl was the first to spot them. She stopped, looked, and raced back to the largest adobe house. Mateo's father, Fernando Ortiz, stepped out of the opening that functioned as the front door. He stood there for a moment before his face broke into a wide smile. He turned back into the house and called, "Teresa, come quickly." Then he sent a little boy off to a smaller hut farther down the single street. The child raced down the dirt street, his feet kicking up little puffs of dust.

Fernando and Teresa ran to meet the riders. Maria slid from her horse and flung herself into the arms of Teresa. Tears flowed like rain. Mateo and Eduardo quickly followed Maria's example, but Eduardo raced toward the older man and woman who were running toward them. He leaped into the woman's arms. The man joined in, flourishing kisses and rubbing Eduardo's back and his black hair.

When Maria looked up and saw her son in the couple's arms, she cried, "Mami, Papi!" She broke away from Teresa, dashing to her parents.

Mateo had accepted the manly hug and handshake from his father and was now wrapped in his mother's arms.

"You are safe," she said. "Praise God."

Worry started to cloud Mateo's face. "Where is Julieta?"

Teresa, an astonished look on her face, said, "Oh! I had forgotten Julieta. She went back to your farm to work it while you were gone. Raymond went with her. She is coming back today. In fact, she should be arriving any time."

"To the farm?" Frustrated, he ran back to his horse, leaped into the saddle, and raced out of the yard.

"You think we need to go with him?" Clay asked Jake.

"Nope. That young feller can take care of himself."

Fernando watched his son disappear around the turn and shook his head. "Young people. They are so impatient. But I have forgotten my manners. Thank you for bringing Maria and Eduardo home," he said to the rangers. To Jake, he continued, "I am Fernando Ortiz, and who is this fine-looking young man riding with you?"

Jake nodded to Fernando. "Señor Ortiz, it is a pleasure to meet you. I am Jake Coleman, and this is Rory Clayton Coleman, my son."

Clay, when he heard his own name used as Rory's middle one, snapped his head around at a grinning Jake. "Never had a chance to tell you."

Rory, a miniature copy of his pa, said to Fernando, "I'm pleased to meet you, sir."

Fernando stepped forward to Rory and extended his hand. "I am pleased to meet you, Rory, and I am glad you are safe."

Rory shook Fernando's hand and then looked back up at Clay. "Pa's told me a lot about you. I thought he was foolin', but now I believe everything he said."

"Well, I guess I'm speechless."

Jake laughed. "A lawyer, speechless. This has got to be a red-letter day."

Fernando, not understanding the English, looked puzzled for a moment, then continued in Spanish. "Please, step down and rest yourselves."

While Jake and Clay swung down, and Rory slid out of the saddle, Fernando called to several of the boys standing around in the crowd. "Take the horses. Give them a good rubdown, and feed and water them, for these men will be staying the night."

Jake shook his head. "I'm right sorry, Señor Ortiz, but we can't stay. Rory has a mom who is sick with worry, so we've got to keep on going. I'm thinkin' we'll be there by mid-morning tomorrow. Your hospitality is greatly appreciated. We might impose on you for some feed and water for the horses and frijoles and tortillas for us, but then we've got to be makin' dust."

Disappointment was written on the older man's face, but he nodded and turned to his wife. "Please, a table and some food for our friends." Teresa spun around, waving to several women in the crowd as she ran into the house.

Fernando turned back to his guests. "It is sad that you must go, but we are in your debt for bringing Maria and Eduardo back from the devil Medrano. We will have food and drink ready for you very soon."

"Thank you," Clay said, "and I must tell you, all of those horses are yours. The bandits are dead and will not bother you now. We take back only those we brought with us."

"But," Fernando replied, "we cannot take them. They are yours."

Jake jumped into the conversation. "Consider it our way of thanking you for your son's help."

"You are most gracious. Thank you," Fernando said.

The horses had already disappeared, taken to the river by boys from the village. Quickly, the table was set. Frijoles, chicken, fresh-sliced tomatoes, and onions adorned the table, along with picante sauce, butter, and a tall stack of tortillas. Three big glasses of cool water waited for them.

"Please," Teresa said, "have a seat and begin eating. We will fix you a little something else."

"Ma'am," Clay said, "this is the best meal I've sat down to since I was here before. You don't need to fix us anything else."

She smiled and dashed off. The three of them sat in the rough-hewn chairs and started to fill their plates.

Maria stepped forward and took the plates from their hands. "Please, allow me." She filled all three plates and so it went. As soon as any one of them finished anything on his plate, Maria added more.

Clay ate until he thought he was going to pop. He held his hands up. "I give up! If I eat any more I'll explode like Medrano's compound."

Maria laughed and clapped her hands. While they had been eating, she told the story of the rescue. The villagers were in awe.

Clay had a tough time keeping a grin off his face as the description of each segment of the event was embellished. The first telling, there were at least thirty or forty men. He knew that number would grow. Jake rode in under heavy gunfire while Mateo raced out and individually fought off bandits.

This village would have a legend that would last longer than it did. *Oh well,* he thought, *these folks don't have much, why not give them something to talk about for years to come?*

"I truly can't eat any more," Clay said. "Thank you, Fernando,

Teresa, Maria." He looked around, including all of the villagers, when he added, "And all of you, for what you have done. Not only have you fed us, but you provided a fearless young man to go with us." Clay stood and looked at each of the villagers as he continued talking. "I am glad that Mateo is not here right now, because that allows me to tell you, without embarrassing him, about his bravery."

Teresa brought out sweet cakes. While Clay was talking, Jake gave one to Rory, took one for himself, and leaned back in his chair to listen. Clay talked for at least ten minutes, telling them about the strength of Mateo, his courage, and his willingness to stand up to the rangers for what he felt was right. As he was speaking, he glanced at Mateo's parents. Fernando was beaming, and tears flowed from the dark eyes of Teresa.

"Let me finish with this," Clay said. "Julieta, Fernando, Teresa, and this village can be proud of Mateo Ortiz. Jake and I consider ourselves most fortunate to have had Mateo alongside of us. He is a strong and trustworthy man."

When he finished, he sat down to a long applause.

"Thank you," Fernando said.

Clay nodded to him, glanced at Rory, who had finished eating, and looked at Jake. His friend gave him a nod. The men and boy stood. Clay addressed Fernando and Teresa. "I am sorry that we must be rude and leave your hospitality after you have fed us such delicious food, but we must get Rory home." He placed a hand on the boy's shoulder.

"Yes," Teresa replied, "I know how much his mami must be hurting. Get him home as quickly as possible. Thank you so much for all you have done."

Jake answered, "It's our pleasure."

The boys had brought the horses back. Surrounded by villagers thanking and congratulating them, they made their way to the animals. Clay swung into the saddle, as did Jake and Rory. He was about to wheel his horse around when a wagon came bouncing around the bend and into town. Mateo was driving the team with Julieta sitting on the wagon seat, close, clinging to his arm. Raymond was riding behind them on Mateo's horse.

Jake turned, leading one horse with Rory following, and Clay bringing up the rear. Each man stopped at the wagon and spoke to Julieta for a moment as she thanked them profusely.

"I will not see you again," Mateo said to Clay.

"You're probably right, but you carried your part of the load. You can be proud of your actions. Your village has arms now, and horses. You and your father know how to use them. If I was you, I'd teach the rest of the men, so you can be ready should another Medrano decide to take from you or your village."

Before they had mounted, Clay had moved back to the pack horse and taken out a thousand dollars of gold coins, and placed them in a small leather pouch he carried. Now he pulled it from his vest.

"Take this."

Mateo took it, opened it, and looked, then started to give it back. "I cannot take your money."

Jake had seen what Clay was doing. He eyed a mangy old cur that had gotten within range and let fly. The tobacco hit the dog right behind his ear. He jumped back, looked up at Jake, pulled his lips back exposing his canines, and growled. "You're an all right dog, pup," Jake said to the animal, then turned back to Mateo. "You danged sure can take it. This ain't payment of any kind. This is just a thank you. Now you can buy more ammunition and rifles and really protect your village. So keep it, and say no more."

Mateo weighed the sack in his hand a couple of times. Then he looked at both men. "I cannot begin to explain how much I appreciate riding with you. I have learned much."

Clay said, "You're a good man, Mateo. Never forget that. Now we've got to ride. Adios." He tipped his hat to Julieta, waved to the crowd, and followed Jake and Rory out of the village.

Silently they rode, letting the horses set the pace. As the road widened, Clay lengthened the leads and sidled up to Jake and Rory. They continued north, content with knowing the job was done and they were returning with Jake's son.

Jake broke the silence. "So what are you gonna do now?"

Clay rode on a ways before speaking. They topped a rise and he could see miles across the Chihuahuan Desert. *Beautiful country,* he thought. *Hard and demanding.*

The sun, low in the west, lit the desert floor turning it into gold and crimson as it flamed against the rocky spines. Jake spoke again. "Mighty pretty country."

"Just what I was thinking. Well . . . when we get back to Presidio, I imagine I'll get after Earl Griffin and his gang. They have my things and Blue. I miss that horse."

"I'll go with you."

Clay shook his head. "Not this time Jake. You've got a family, and I know that now. How would your wife feel if you made it back with Rory and then went gallivanting off after more bandits? I don't think so."

Jake changed the subject. "When do you git back to that little gal in Comfort?"

"Right after I find Griffin and get him to a sheriff. Then I'm cutting a beeline to Austin to see my grandpa. He's not doing too well, and I feel like I need to see him. Then I'll be on to Comfort."

Jake nodded his agreement and pointed out west of the road, past the scattered tarbush and creosote bushes, where the light green tops of a thick stand of mesquite trees could be seen. "Reckon that's water?"

"Worth checking."

The great orb in the west was disappearing, and shadows grew longer across the broken land. The men allowed the horses to carefully pick their way through the rocky landscape, finally reaching the mesquites. The trees and brush fought for existence around a small spring that bubbled up into the desert, flowed no more than a hundred yards, and disappeared beneath the surface.

"This'll do," Clay said. He looked around cautiously before stepping down from his horse.

Rory piped up. "Watch for snakes. They like to be around water."

Jake reached over and rubbed his son's neck while he grinned at Clay and said, "I reckon."

18

The rangers and the boy stayed west of the Rio Conchos as they made their way to the Rio Grande. In the distance they could see Ojinaga, just across the river from smaller Presidio.

"Pa," Rory said, "do you think Mami will be angry with me?"

Watching the trail his horse was taking, Jake said, "Son, there is no way your mami will be anything but happy to see you. It weren't your fault Medrano took you."

"But we were down by the river. It was a long way from the house."

Rory was following his pa. Clay eased the black up next to the boy and looked over at him. "Son, you haven't a thing to worry about. When I left your ma, all she wanted was to have you back. I guarantee, she'll be overjoyed to see you."

The seven-year-old turned big brown eyes now wide with hope, toward Clay. "You think so, Uncle Clay?"

"Positively," Clay said.

Rory looked relieved. Then his face broke into a big grin. "I bet Flint and Jeb will be glad to see me."

His pa turned in the saddle. "I just bet they will, boy."

ory jumped at the mention of a swim. "Can we, Pa? That'd
be a bunch of fun."

Jake shot Clay a dirty look, and said, "No, son. We've got to get
you home. Yore ma is worried sick."

"Aw, Pa. She won't mind."

Clay, receiving another look from Jake, chose that moment to
examine the geological structure of the mountains in the
distance.

"My last word on it, son."

Clay looked over at Rory. The boy looked disappointed but
evidently knew when to stop pushing his pa. Rory must've felt
Clay looking at him. He turned his head up to Clay and received
a conspiratorial wink. The disappointment disappeared, replaced
by a big grin.

"Let's get moving," Jake said and led off, crossing the Rio
Grande, and moving up the United States side of the river.

When they reached the top of the bank, as one, they pulled
up. They sat, looking back across the desert, each in his own
thoughts.

"Good to be back," Jake said.

Clay nodded, and they continued to Presidio, paralleling the
Rio Grande. They passed where the Rio Conchos poured into
the river separating Mexico and the United States, the water,

roiled and muddy, flowed quickly between Presidio and
Ojinaga.

They crossed the wide bed of Cibolo Creek, with the horses
barely getting their feet wet in the small stream.

Clay could see Rory fidgeting in the saddle. The boy was
getting excited. Several boys ran out from the town to greet them.
Recognizing Rory and Jake, they spun around and raced toward
the Garcia home.

Clay laughed. "There goes your surprise."

"Can I ride ahead, Pa? Can I?"

"Sure, just don't run over anyone."

Rory popped his horse with the reins and raced toward town.

"He'll be the hero around here for a while," Jake said. "It'll do
him some good. We haven't had much of a chance to talk about
what happened to him."

Clay watched the boy gallop toward the lavish welcome that
would be heaped on him. "The best thing he could know, Jake, is
that his pa is going to be around to protect him. I imagine it'll
take a while to get over it, but he knows Medrano's dead, and he's
young. I'd bet he'll recover pretty quick."

Jake stared after the boy, watching even after he disappeared.
Then he said, "I sure hope so."

They turned up Main Street. Word had quickly raced through
the town. Shop owners, bartenders, and their customers stood on
the boardwalk, cheering and waving. Jake tipped his hat, and
Clay nodded to a few people.

Ahead, set off to itself, was the Garcia home. All the family
had gathered and were taking turns hugging Rory. Each time one
of his aunts hugged him, he got kissed. Clay chuckled inside. He
could see the boy had put up with more than enough of the
kisses, but they wouldn't stop. He finally broke away and stood
next to his ma. She hugged him to her side as if she would never
let him go, and beamed at her husband as they pulled up.

They dismounted, and men appeared immediately to take the animals off their hands.

Jake stepped up to Sophia and gazed into her eyes, then clutched her to him. The two held each other for a long moment before breaking the embrace.

Sophia caressed his face with her hands. "You look so tired."

"I'm fine," Jake said. "You're the one I've been concerned about. I knew you'd worry yore pretty head off."

"And it is true that she has done that," her father said. "I understand that Medrano will no longer be raiding over here?"

Jake grinned. "I reckon Mr. Medrano ain't going to be raiding over here or over there. He is dead and blown into pieces too small to bury."

"Good," Cesar said. "He has caused much harm to this family and deserves the worst that can be delivered upon him."

Jake squeezed his wife, looked down at her, and gave her a short kiss. "I'll tell everyone about it when we can get the adults together. For now, I don't know about Clay, since he's such a picky eater, but I could eat the south end of a northbound mule."

Señor Garcia looked at his two single daughters and said, "Go inside and tell Camila." Each bent over and kissed Rory again, then dashed back into the house, while the boy wiped his cheeks with his shirt sleeve.

"Soon you will eat," the patriarch said. "Now let us go into the casa. It is hot in the sun."

As Clay stepped into the inner courtyard, Sophia threw both of her arms around him and hugged him close. "Thank you, Clay, for bringing both of my men safely back to me. Jake said you always accomplish your mission."

Clay returned the hug, stepped back, and swept his sombrero from his head, following it with a deep bow. "I am always at your service, madam."

Sophia curtsied with her reply. "Why, thank you, sir."

Jake, watching the show, said, "Careful of him, honey. He's got a girl waiting for him back in Comfort."

Clay heard the single sisters giggling at his bow, followed immediately by deep sighs at hearing Jake's statement.

Jake heard it, too. "I guess I ruined the dreams of some mighty pretty girls."

Sophia turned to Jake. "Hush yourself. Don't tease them. They both were taken with Clay."

Embarrassed, Clay said, "Didn't someone say something about food?"

"Forgive my rudeness," she said. "Come, let us eat." She linked arms with her husband on one side and Clay on the other and led them into the dining room.

"Señor Garcia?"

The happy grandfather turned to Clay.

"I gave a thousand dollars of your ransom money to the young man who guided me and helped us in Rory's rescue. I'll give you a note for it that you can take to the local bank. It might take a few days, but—"

Cesar Garcia held up his hand to Clay. "Please stop. Only a thousand dollars of all the money I sent with you? And you bring my grandson back alive? Please, you owe me nothing. I am forever indebted to you."

As he started to protest, Clay stopped. He realized that the equipment and money was the only way the older man could contribute to rescuing his grandson. To object would insult him. "Thank you."

The older man had to reach up to lay his hand on Clay's shoulder and usher him into his home. "Now, enough talk. Let us eat."

Stepping into the room, Clay and Jake immediately spotted Butch sitting on the couch, his legs resting on a padded cowhide ottoman covered with a blanket, and his arm in a sling. Eva sat on the couch with him, her arm across part of his wide shoulders.

"What happened?" Clay said.

"I hurt it, but it ain't as bad as it looks." Butch tried to hold up his injured arm to demonstrate his statement and winced from the pain.

Jake caught the expression. "Reckon it's exactly as bad as it looks."

"That's what I've tried to tell him, Jake," Eva said. "I don't understand why men have to be so stubborn!"

"What I meant was, it ain't broken. I'm about ready to start moving around."

Clay looked at Butch's pale complexion and shook his head. "You're not looking like you need to be moving much. What happened?"

The family was silent.

"Why don't we talk about this after dinner," Cesar said. "We can find out about Rory's rescue, and then we'll fill you in on what happened to Butch."

Clay and Jake looked at each other.

What's going on? Clay thought. *We've both been rangers long enough to know when someone is trying to pull the wool over our eyes.*

"I don't know about Jake, but I'd like to hear what happened to Butch first."

"I told you," Butch said, looking at his wife and Cesar.

Sophia spoke up. "Can't this wait? We are all hungry."

Now it was going too far. Clay turned to Cesar. "Señor Garcia, I apologize for my rudeness, but I need to know what's going on."

The older man looked at Sophia, and Clay saw her eyes starting to tear. Cesar sighed at the sight of his daughter's pain, and then said, "Yes, I suppose you do, but we were in fear that when you found out, both of you would rush off. Butch told us we wouldn't be able to hide this from you."

Butch immediately threw the blanket off, exposing a white leg. "Dang, this blanket is hot." The thigh was wrapped in bandages from the knee almost to the crotch. His trouser leg had been cut off to allow him to slide them on. "I got shot."

Clay and Jake waited. Finally, Butch continued.

"It was the bank. Some crazy bandits tried to rob it." He gave a short bark of a laugh. "That was a big mistake. Eight of them rode in as big as you please and tied their horses in front of the bank. I guess they figured there was enough of them, they'd just run roughshod over this town. They left two of their boys watching the horses.

"The shopkeeper in the general store, across from the bank, saw them ride up. He sent one of his sons to warn me, and another one to warn the other storekeepers. While those idiots were inside trying to take the hard-earned money of our citizens, we were closin' in."

Butch tried to move his leg to a better position, bringing beads of sweat to his forehead. He took a deep breath. Eva patted his good arm, and he continued.

"It took no time at all to get that bank covered. We have danged few milksops in this town. Most of 'em fought in a war on one side or the other of the border. Anyway, I came up around the side of the building, and when I stepped out, you should've seen the shocked look on those two boys."

Clay knew how Butch told a story. It would be forever before he got to the point of who it was and if any survived. "What gang was it?"

Butch shot him a hurt look. "I'm gittin' there. So I told them fellers to drop their guns. Now, there I was holding this big Greener on 'em, figurin' for sure they'd throw down their guns. But of all the stupid things, they drew. Now, is that about the craziest thing you ever heard of? Those boys woulda had to spend a few years in prison, and they'd a been out, free, but no sir, they went for them hoglegs. Well, I shot 'em both afore they could even clear leather. There weren't hardly enough left of them fellers to bury. Now I'm tellin' you, when that Greener went off, business picked up."

Butch turned to Eva and patted her on the thigh. "Could I get a glass of water, honey?" She smiled at him before she moved over to the table and filled a glass for him, then brought it back. He took a couple of long swallows.

Clay and Jake looked at each other. Jake gave a tiny shake of his head and a slight lift of his shoulders. Butch was a good man, but it took forever for him to tell a story.

"There must've been one of 'em at the window, cause only seconds after my last shot someone fired through the bank's window and knocked that left leg right out from under me, but I managed to crawl back behind the corner of the bank. Just as I got there, they come boilin' out like a mad nest of hornets."

Clay had been patient long enough. They had ridden all morning. The stress of the search and rescue had exhausted them, and now they were expected to stand and listen to Butch turn this into an hour-long tale. "Butch, what gang was it, and how many escaped?"

"I'm tellin' this, Clay. You need to relax. I'm just about done. So they come pouring out of the bank, racing for their horses. As soon as the first one's foot hit the boardwalk, guns roared. I don't rightly remember how many holes that feller had in him." Butch stopped for a minute, punching holes in the air in front of him, obviously counting bullet holes. Satisfied with his count, he continued.

"The only reason the second one didn't get shot was he stumbled over the first one who was full of lead. He made it to his horse and got blown out of the saddle."

Butch stopped for a moment and looked around the room. There wasn't a patient face in the group. Eva leaned over and whispered something in his ear. He looked at her, a surprised look across his face, and turned back.

"Well, out of those eight men, three were killed outright, and two shot up pretty bad. They're in jail. The doc looks in on 'em several times a day. Three of 'em made it out of town, and I don't think any one of those three took a bit of lead. That beats all. There for a little bit, there was so much lead flying, I was afraid to stick my head around the corner for fear it'd get blown off. Oh yeah, there was two horses killed. I think that's it." He looked around the room, appearing pleased with his story.

Jake asked, "Did you recognize any of them?"

"Only two of the three that got away. I haven't ever seen any of the others."

After waiting for a few more seconds, Jake said, "Well?"

Butch looked at him for another second or two, then said, "Oh, yeah. One was Earl Griffin, and the other was Shifty Joe Beck. I don't know the third one."

When Clay heard Griffin's name, he immediately asked, "What kind of horse was he riding?"

Butch didn't have to think about that. "A fine-lookin' blue roan. When Griffin laid the quirt to that roan, he took off like the devil was chewin' on his tail."

Quirt! Clay thought. *I'm coming for you Blue, and you won't have to put up with Griffin much longer.* "When did this happen?"

"Three days ago. No tellin' where they are now."

"Which way did they head?"

"Northeast," Cesar said. "I followed them a ways to see what direction they were truly going. It looks as if they are headed for Fort Stockton."

"Thank you, Cesar. I'm sorry, but I have to be going."

Everyone except Jake started protesting.

"You're exhausted."

"You need to eat."

"You'll never catch them."

Cesar called to the kitchen. "Camila."

The large cook came into the dining room. "Yes?"

"Pack food for Jake and Clay. They'll be going after the

bandits."

Clay interjected, "Only for one."

Sophia had been quietly crying. Now, she wiped her eyes and looked at Clay.

Jake gave Clay a solemn look. "Let's step out into the courtyard."

Clay nodded, and the two rangers moved into the courtyard, pulling the door closed behind them.

Just before the door closed, Clay heard Rory, in a small voice, ask Sophia, "Mami, is Papi leaving again?" He didn't hear the answer.

Jake had his arms crossed. He was watching a hummingbird working on a cactus flower. The little bird's wings moved so fast they were almost invisible. As it flitted from one flower to the next, the sun glinted on its purple then green feathers. "Pretty little bird," Jake said.

"You know it's time, Jake. You were already talking about it in Mexico."

Clay's friend turned to face the big man. Before going into the hacienda, he had spit out his plug of tobacco. Now he fished in his vest pocket, found the package, looked at it, then slid it back into the pocket.

"You might need help."

"I won't, and you know it. I made a big mistake getting caught before, but it won't happen again."

"You've got the girl on your mind."

"Yes, but there's a time and a place. Until I catch Griffin's crew and get Blue back, it will be neither the time nor the place."

"I've got to tell the captain."

"Write a letter. I'll deliver it. Your own personal pony express."

Jake grinned. "They didn't last long."

"I'll last long enough."

The men stood facing each other. Clay realized that Jake was looking older. He looked tired. This campaign had taken a lot out of him, but he was still a strong man. With luck, he would have many years to give to his family.

The hummingbird worked a small red flower near the bottom of the cactus. He was there only a few seconds. Then he hummed up and hovered between the two men, facing Jake. He held that position for a few seconds, then, in a flash of color, was gone.

"Always surprises me, how fast they can move," Jake said. "Guess I'll be able to watch 'em more now."

It was Clay's turn to laugh. "Somehow, I can't picture you sitting around watching hummingbirds."

"See, that's something you don't know about me. I really like to watch those fluttering little feathered scamps. Come on back inside, and I'll write that letter. We better get you outfitted with some fresh horses."

The rangers grasped each other's right hand and stood there immobile, each thinking of the past.

The moment slipped by. Jake opened the door and stepped in ahead of Clay. Rory's eyes were big, watching his father move toward him and his ma. Jake stopped in front of the boy and Sophia, rubbed his son's thick head of hair, and then grasped his wife's arms.

Sophia's dark eyes were wide and full, locked on his, when Jake said, "I'm not going. My days with the rangers are done."

It took her a few moments to fathom what her husband, who had been gone for so much of their married life, had just told her. Then she crossed herself and whispered, "Thank you, God."

19

Rory gave Jake's leg a tight hug, then said, "Can I go outside and play?"

The moment broken, everyone laughed, and Jake said, "Go on, but tell your Uncle Clay goodbye. He's got to be going."

Rory ran toward Clay, and the big man scooped the boy into his arms, lifting him toward the high ceiling. Rory broke out in laughter, then threw his arms around Clay's neck and squeezed.

"Thank you, Uncle Clay. I'll miss you." Then his young mind moved on to more important things, and he said, "Now let me down, Flint's waiting."

Sophia turned to watch her son dash for the door. She started to warn him to stay close, and Jake softly placed his hand over her mouth. "He's safe now, honey. Let him be a boy."

She gazed up at her husband and smiled. "Yes, he's safe. His papi is home." Eyes moist again, she clasped her husband tightly to her, released him, and turned to Clay. "What can we do to help you prepare for your trip?"

The mood lightened. Cesar chimed in. "You will need horses and more supplies."

"Cesar, I only need one horse. Once they realize they aren't being followed, they'll slow down to lick their wounds. I'm betting I'll catch them either before or not far past Fort Stockton."

"If you think they'll stop," Cesar said, "why not wait and leave in the morning?"

"Sorry, I need to get on the trail. I'll want to cut their tracks today, if I can. Waiting longer means one more day for the wind or monsoon to work on their trail."

"Yes, I see what you mean."

Clay took a few minutes to say his goodbyes to the family. Zoe and Nicole took this last opportunity to give Clay a big hug and kiss him on the cheek. Each took an arm and escorted him, behind their father, out of the home and back to the stables, with the rest of the family following.

Cesar turned. "Girls, act your age."

Both daughters smiled sweetly, their dark eyes dancing, and Zoe said, "But we are, Papi." Giggling, they both stood on tiptoe and kissed Clay again, one on each cheek.

"I've got to say," Clay said, "being escorted by two beautiful women makes this about the best sendoff a man could have."

The girls, laughing, stepped back at the look they received from their father. They joined their sisters, still laughing.

Cesar shook his head. "I wish their mother was still here. She could handle them much better than me. I'm at a loss what to do with so many lovely girls."

Sophia, on Jake's arm, smiled at her father. "You do very well, Papi, and we love you for it."

Now embarrassed, Cesar turned and placed his hand on the big lineback dun that carried Clay's saddle and gear. The horse swung his head as if to nip at the man, but instead nibbled with his big lips. Cesar rubbed the horse between the ears.

"This is *Hombre,* and he truly is a man. He is a child of this country. He will find water where there is none, and though he is not the fastest of horses, he will be on his feet when others have long given up. Señor Clay, please accept him as a gift from my heart to you."

Clay looked the dun over. The muscles rippled in the shoulders and hips of the big animal. "This is a fine horse, Cesar. I cannot accept such a gift as this. Please let me pay you for him."

Cesar drew himself up to his full five-feet-seven-inch height. "Do not insult me. I could give you all I have, and it would not be enough for my grandson. Take him, with my good wishes."

Clay stepped toward Cesar and extended his hand. "Thank you." Clay said as the two men shook hands, "I will take good care of him."

Camila hurried from the house with two sacks. "Señor Barlow, in these bags is food enough for several days. I have included smoked ham, along with the roasted beef, and turkey. You will eat well for a few days."

"Thank you, Camila," Clay said, as she stuffed the sacks into the already filled saddlebags. He looked at the bulging bags. "Cesar, those saddlebags look mighty full."

The older man gave a slight nod. "I took the liberty of having more ammunition included for you—and another twenty shotgun shells."

"Thank you," he said, turning to the large group. "Seems I'm saying that a lot. As much as I would like to stay, I've got to be on my way."

He swung up onto Hombre. The horse felt strong and solid.

Jake had brought his horse up. "I'll ride a ways with you."

Clay waved to them all. "Adios."

"Vaya con Dios, Clay," Sophia called. It was echoed by the others.

With Jake at his side, for the last time, he turned in the saddle and waved to the Garcia family then faced ahead and they disappeared behind the wall.

The rangers rode in silence, enjoying these final moments.

Outside of town, Clay turned toward the northeast and the waiting hills. Jake pulled up.

"Pardner," Jake said, "I guess this is where we part ways." He reached inside his vest, pulled out an unsealed envelope, and handed it to Clay. "I'd be obliged were you to make sure the captain gets it. He'll understand. When you have a chance, I'd appreciate you reading it."

Jake sized up the younger man next to him. He'd grown from a determined boy, to a steel-nerved Texas Ranger. "You've come a long way in these past years. You're a good ranger." He waited a moment, then added, "And a good man. There's no one else I was sure would respond to my note, but I knew you would. Take care of that little lady. She sounds like a real keeper." He started to swing his horse around and stopped.

"You watch out for Beck. That breed is quick with either a knife or gun."

"Thanks for everything, Jake." Clay scanned the hills ahead. "I'm gonna miss you."

They sat for a moment longer. "Adios, amigo," Jake said. He spun his horse around and galloped back to Presidio.

"Adios, Jake," Clay called. He watched his friend's back grow smaller. *It seems like the past eight years have vanished like mesquite smoke in the wind,* he thought. He clucked at Hombre, and the dun started walking forward, Clay studying the ground.

"We get a little farther down the trail, Hombre, we'll cast around for tracks. It'll be easier where it's less traveled." Clay had been talking to horses since he was a kid and wasn't going to stop now.

The large number of tracks had played out well before he reached Alamito Creek. He swung down from Hombre and started checking tracks. Three horses, all carrying weight. All three needed new shoes, one badly. If that one didn't throw a shoe soon, he'd be surprised. Shadows were lengthening, but he wanted to make it to the creek before he pitched camp.

It was almost dark when Hombre picked his way through the cut, low peaks on each side, and Clay looked down on Alamito Creek. The trees were dark, the mountains now blocking the light. The coyotes were already warming up their singing voices.

Clay rode down the hill and entered the stand of trees along the creek. It was so dark under the trees he let Hombre pick his way. The trail crossing was in front of them and they dropped down into the creek bed. With the monsoons, the creek was running but still low. He wanted to get across in case there were heavy rains in the mountains. Those rains could fill the creek, delaying his crossing for hours.

Hombre's shoes clicked loudly on the rocks. Clay allowed him to stop at the water, and while his horse drank, slid out of the saddle, moved upstream, filled his canteen, and had a drink for himself. The water was cool and refreshing. When he finished, he led Hombre up the opposite bank, and the two of them made their way through the trees.

Clay turned upstream, looking for any small clearing not covered with leaves. He had only gone a short distance when he walked into the perfect spot. There was a small circle of grass, where, for some reason, the foliage was thin, but the little area was surrounded with thick brush. He wouldn't have a fire tonight. Camila had packed food, plus a fire could bring unwanted guests.

He stripped his gear from Hombre, tossed a loop around the horse's neck, and staked the end next to where he had placed his saddle and bedroll. He then pulled some grass and gave the horse a rubdown. Once finished, he cleaned the sticks from under his bed, spread his groundsheet, and laid the blanket to the side, situating his shotgun and rifle to his left, saddlebags to his right. He checked again to make sure that he had removed the leather loop securing his Colt in the holster. He had, just before they rode into the trees.

Once everything was in place, he pulled one of Camila's sacks from his bags and sat on the groundsheet, leaning against his saddle. When he opened the bag, the tantalizing smells assaulted him. He grabbed the package of tortillas and another wrapped package that felt pliable. He folded the edges of the cloth back to expose the well-seasoned roast beef. He laid beef inside one of the tortillas and rolled it into a cylinder and took a bite. It was delicious. That lady sure could cook.

It was nice, relaxing along the creek on a quiet, clear night. There was no wind, which was unusual in this country. He leaned back and thought of what was ahead. Once he had the crooks either dead or in jail, he'd take off for either Austin or Comfort.

He wanted to see his grandpa before he died, but he also wanted to see Dee. He tried to picture what the ranch would be like with Dee there. What would she want to do? Would she want to stay home or get out and punch cows? It would be an interesting question, but he knew he would be happy with whatever she decided.

Her pa had said she was a good shot. That would definitely come in handy for the times he was gone, both for protection and food supply. Then, he smiled to himself. It sounded like he was pretty confident. He best be careful about being overconfident. It would be a real shot in the gut if he asked her to marry him and she said no.

He was thinking about that possibility when he stretched out on the groundcloth and pulled the blanket up. Lying on his left side, Colt held loosely in his right hand, Clay closed his eyes and fell into a deep sleep.

"Boys, you gotta hep me. I ain't joshin'."

Beck walked over to his partner who was lying on the ground, and pressed his boot into Cobb's bullet wound.

The wounded outlaw let out a chilling scream.

In a gravelly voice caused by an unsuccessful hanging, Beck

said, "Shut yore whiny mouth, Cobb, or I'll open you up like a smiling pumpkin."

Arlo Cobb tried to move his ravaged body where he could see Griffin. He couldn't quite get there. "Earl, don't let Joe treat me like this. I'm gut shot and might be dying."

"There ain't no might, Cobb," Beck cut in. "Yore dying one way or the other. I'm not listening to yore carrying on much longer. I'll gut you and take your worthless scalp. You oughta be ashamed of that dirty, old, stringy white hair. You ain't even got any on top—worthless."

"But it hurts so bad. Ohhh," he moaned.

"I ain't kiddin' you, you filthy old man. Now, shut up!"

Griffin had pulled Clay's short-barreled Smith and Wesson from the shoulder holster and was examining it. He looked up when Beck yelled at Cobb. "Leave him alone, Joe. He'll die here before long."

"You damned right he will. The next time he whines, I'm guttin' him, and don't you tell me what to do, Griffin. I might just take care of you next."

Griffin eared the hammer back on the Smith and Wesson, swinging the muzzle to align on Beck. "Don't threaten me, Joe. I won't stand for it."

Beck glared at Griffin and growled in his guttural voice, "You point that fancy gun at me, Griffin, you better pull the trigger, cause I'll gut you next, right after I take care of Cobb."

Griffin held the stare, the muzzle solid on Beck, then lowered the hammer and started admiring the gun again. He weighed it in his hand—well-balanced, like the other two. These were special guns. He wondered how a ranger could afford all of these. He knew he'd never find out, since the man was dead. Staked out in that creek bed, he had probably been smashed to death from the flash flood. He laughed at the thought. That was a real haul they took in from that dumb ranger.

He'd never caught a ranger so distracted. Why, the big feller had no idea they were anywhere around until they had him. Good riddance. The world needed fewer rangers.

Cobb moaned again.

Beck jumped to his feet, pulling out his big knife that looked like a cutdown machete. Griffin started to say something, but he recognized the look in Beck's eyes. If a man knew what was smart, he didn't interfere with the man when he was looking like that.

Cobb heard Beck jump to his feet and turned his head toward the approaching man. "Help me, Joe. I'm hurtin' real bad."

"I'm gonna help you, you dirty old man." With that, Beck plunged his knife into Cobb's belly and yanked it across his waist. The dying man loosed a blood-chilling scream. Then Beck grabbed a handful of Cobb's stringy white hair, pulled it up, cut a circle around the man's head, and yanked the scalp loose, swinging it to get the blood off.

Cobb, whimpering now, lay on the hard ground. Beck looked down at him and shook his head. "You still won't shut up." He grabbed Cobb's chin, pulled his head back, and, swung the big knife, slicing his throat almost to the bone.

"Humph. Now I get me some peace."

Griffin sat quietly watching the butchery of the man he had known for almost ten years. He kept the revolver in his hand, ready to swing and fire. He hated it when Beck got bloody. The man was so volatile. Right then, he made up his mind. He was leaving. He just couldn't be around Beck. They wouldn't have killed the ranger if it had been up to him, but Beck wanted some entertainment. Griffin was sure glad the flash flood came along. If the ranger had been found like they left him, those other rangers would have never stopped until they found and hanged the whole crew.

"Let's eat," Beck said. "Killin' makes me hungry."

∿

THE NEXT MORNING Clay was on his way early. He had risen, eaten, and watered Hombre while it was still dark. When there was enough light to follow tracks, he moved to the edge of the tree line and stopped his horse. While going through the saddlebags, he had found an engraved set of Cesar's binoculars. They were exquisitely made French glasses that had to have been left intentionally. He was glad to have them during this manhunt.

Hopefully he would capture the remaining members of the gang by the time he reached Fort Stockton. If so, he would send these field glasses back with the explanation he had regained his.

He strung the binoculars around his neck. Sitting under the trees, he had little concern about a reflection from the glass, even though he would be looking to the north and east. Clay examined every rock and bush that could hide a man. Nothing. He saw a small herd of mule deer moving across a slope several hundred yards along the trail he was taking. He watched them cross the open hillside to finally disappear into many massive boulders along the trail.

He carefully laid the glasses against his chest, thankful for the poncho Miguel had given him. Early mornings were cool in the mountains. It wouldn't be long before evenings would be chilly across Texas. If he stayed in this country much longer, he'd need to pick up a heavier coat.

Clay continued following the trail for the next few hours. A couple of times it became so dim that most white men would have lost sight of it, but with the skills he had learned from his Indian friends, the trail read like a map. He often wondered where his friend Running Wolf was. In all these years as a ranger, he had not run into him.

He came to a creek that had water in the deeper holes. Clay rode Hombre to the water, got off, and searched in his saddlebags. While the horse was drinking, he pulled the last of the ham from his sack, carefully rolled it on a couple of tortillas, and ate. When the horse finished, Clay led him up the other bank to let him graze for a while. Approaching the top of the bank, he noticed something on several leaves by the trail. He didn't need to get closer to recognize it—blood.

So, one of the three who had made it out of town had been shot after all. There wasn't a lot, which might indicate the bank robber was gut shot. That would explain why, after getting well away from Presidio, they had slacked off to a slow walk. He'd better keep a sharp lookout. Beck was half-Apache and could be maintaining a close watch on his back trail. *If I have anything to say about it,* Clay thought, *I'm not getting ambushed again.*

20

Earl Griffin opened his eyes. He was cold. Without moving his head, the outlaw examined the area in front of him. The fire was in his field of vision, and in the early-morning light, no coals glowed. He lay still, gripping his revolver. What was Beck up to?

Too quiet. Beck was usually up by now, stoking the fire and making coffee. The Apache loved his coffee. But there was no movement, no sound of the Indian breathing. Then his eyes grew wide. He had laid his rifle next to him when he went to sleep. It was gone!

The outlaw threw his blanket back and sat up. Nothing. Beck was gone. Everything was gone, except Cobb's gruesome remains. Beck had even stripped the valuables from the dead man's body, including his boots. Griffin slapped on his hat and jumped to his feet. He had slept in his boots, uncomfortable, but sometimes necessary when you rode the owlhoot trail. He looked toward where the horses had been tied—gone.

Beck had wanted that blue roan from day one and had tried to buy him from Griffin. When that didn't work, Beck tried to get him to gamble for the horse. Now Beck had stolen the animal.

How could he do that? They were partners. A man could be hanged for horse stealing. Of course, Griffin failed to consider how he had gotten Blue in the first place.

He stomped around camp, growing more desperate by the minute. The Indian hadn't even left him a canteen. What would he do once he left the creek? The closest water he knew about was at least twenty miles away on the El Paso to San Antonio road at the stage station. Maybe he could get a horse there. He *could* stay in the Apache Mountains and turn northwest, toward Fort Davis. Whatever he did, he needed to get out of this country. His best bet was the stage line.

Griffin sat down on a log to think. *That blamed Indian has left me high and dry. If I turn to Fort Davis, he'll be long gone. Maybe the stage station'll sell me a horse, or I could take the stage, but I ain't got much money.* He reached into his vest pocket and pulled out some coins. After counting them, he came up with thirty-two dollars and loose change. He sat for a few moments staring at the money. *Beck took my horse, my rifle, and my saddlebags. If I hadn't been sleepin' against my saddle, I bet he woulda took that. I ain't hardly got nothin' left. Those blamed town folks. Why'd they have to be so tight-fisted? They wouldn't even of missed a few dollars. We weren't gonna take it all, but then they had to go and start shootin'.*

He waited a while longer. The sun was rising, and the air was starting to warm. Finally making his mind up, he slapped his knees, stood, and turned to his bedroll. After rolling it up, he looked around the camp. He still couldn't believe he had slept through Beck cleaning him out. Everything was gone except his saddle and his bedroll. He went down to the little creek and drank his fill of water. Then he came back, made a pad using his bedroll for his shoulder, swung his saddle up onto the pad, and started northeast toward the stage station.

It was tough walking in the mountains. All he had were the boots on his feet, and they weren't built for walking. About to start down the eastern slopes, he stopped, dropped the saddle, and gazed out across the dry plains toward Fort Stockton. A faint cloud of dust moved away from him, in the direction he would go if he had a horse.

Must be that danged Indian, he thought. He stood, alone and without food, water, or horse, watching the dust and cursing his partner. Then he shook his head, replaced his pad, swung the saddle back in place, and started down the slope toward the stage station.

NEARING noon of his second day, Clay spotted ominous, black birds circling in the sky. The buzzards announced the outlaws' camp long before he reached it. The black, carrion-eating harbingers of death drifted lazily in the sky, stacked in several layers, at least fifteen or twenty. The lowest ones would set their wings and drop in to join the feast, followed by the ones just above them sailing lower.

Clay worked his way through the oaks, maple, and mesquite that grew along the stream bed, following one of the saddles through the Apache Mountains. The mountains were alive with wild game. Besides both mule and whitetail deer, he had seen antelope, buffalo, and turkey. If he wasn't chasing the thieves who had stolen his horse, he would've been roasting a fat turkey, but not today.

The stench of death assaulted him before he saw the camp. Hombre nodded his head and blew. Clay patted the horse's neck and spoke to him. "Easy, boy. Be happy it isn't us." He rode into the camp with his shotgun lying behind the bow of the saddle, resting against his upper thighs, the stock to his left. If necessary, he was prepared to one-hand the powerful weapon. Hombre's reins rested lightly in his left hand, and Clay's right lay on his thigh near his Colt. He could draw with either hand, but preferred his right.

The death camp was empty. He sat Hombre while scanning the remains. The buzzards were flocked around Cobb, pecking and pulling. There was enough of the man left that he could be sure he was neither Griffin nor Beck. With the shotgun in his left hand, he dismounted and dropped the reins to ground hitch Hombre.

He shooed the buzzards away from the body as he neared. Several, too heavy to fly, only hopped away a few feet and glared at him for interrupting their lunch. The man was in bad shape. The outlaw, brutally slashed across the throat and abdomen, had also been scalped. *That's the work of Joe Beck,* he thought. *That man doesn't have a kind bone in his body.* "Well, fella," Clay said to the corpse, "you chose the wrong bunch to run with."

Clay turned away from the body and scanned the camp. He moved to where each man had slept and examined the depressions. It was easy to tell which man slept where. Earl Griffin was a big man, while, in size, Shifty Joe Beck was average. Size was the only thing that was average about Beck. He was huge when it came to cruelty, and Clay had first-hand experience where Beck was concerned.

He squatted down by the coals of the dormant fire and felt for heat. None. The fire had been out for hours, well before daylight. That was unusual. With no one on their tail, as far as they knew, he figured they would have slept in and had their coffee before they pulled out. In such a case, the coals would still be warm.

Clay stood and started working toward where the horses had been tied. He saw something interesting. Beck's Apache moccasins' tracks made several trips to the horses, while Griffin's tracks wandered over and across the horse tracks. "Hombre, Beck has left Griffin afoot!" He followed Griffin's track, and within a few minutes, he figured out where the man was going—the stage station. *Of course. He needs a horse and supplies. It didn't look like Beck left him anything.*

Clay walked back to Hombre, gathered the reins, and led the

horse to the small creek. While the horse drank, Clay moved upstream a ways and filled his canteen and water bags, then took a long drink. He stepped back to Hombre, who was still drinking, swung the canteen and water bags up, and stood waiting until the horse finished. "You best drink up. We've got some hard riding to circle around Griffin and reach that stage station before he does." He swung up into the saddle and pointed the horse south.

He secured the shotgun, and, as the horse picked his way along the ridge, they gradually trailed down to the base of the mountains. Clay reached into his vest pocket. He hadn't worn it since he crossed into Mexico, but now he pulled out the Texas Ranger badge and pinned it on next to the left breast pocket. He may not get Blue back at the stage station, but he would be one step closer.

THREE HOURS LATER, Clay pulled up at the station, a barking dog sitting in the middle of the open door. A burly man stepped to the door, and, using his leg, gently shoved the cur out of his way.

"Howdy," he said, his eyes focusing on the badge. "Don't get many rangers this way, but yore mighty welcome to come in and set a spell. We've got a stage due in the next couple of hours, so my wife's fixed enough for a whole herd."

"Much obliged," Clay said. "I know feed can run tight out here, but would you be able to spare some for my horse? I'll be glad to pay you."

"You dadblasted right I can. It'd be a sorry day when ole Will Chambers can't take care of a ranger's horse."

"Thanks," Clay said. "I'll take him over and give him a rubdown if you've got a place for him."

"Don't worry your mind of that. Gimme that horse." Will reached out and took the reins. "I been takin' care of horses my whole life. I'll give him a good rubdown, water, hay, and a little corn. He'll be happy as a pig in slop. You go on in and tell the missus I said to give you some grub."

Clay watched the older man lead Hombre to the barn. The man favored his left leg, which gave him a bad limp, but it didn't seem to slow him down.

From inside, a woman's voice called out. "Come on in here. I heard Will jawin' at you. I imagine it's about time you put on the feedbag."

"Yes, ma'am," Clay said, stepping through the door, the dog right on his heels. He stopped and looked around. As you entered the stage station, to the right, a bar ran for about five feet, behind which was a big cook stove, a few shelves, containing metal plates and cups, and several bottles. To the left of the door were three rectangular rough-cut tables, each probably eight feet long, with a bench on each side. At the back of the room, behind the benches, was a door that opened into another room. Another door, behind the end of the bar opened into an additional space.

"Name's Bess, but everyone calls me Aunt Bessie. If you'd like to wash some of that trail dust off, young feller, there's a wash-basin on a stand outside the front door, towel with it, too."

"Thank you, Aunt Bessie, I think I would. I'm Clay Barlow." Clay stepped outside and looked to his left, spotting the wash stand. He washed his hands, face, then poured some of the water over his hair. It was cool, feeling good as it ran over his head and neck. He pushed his hair back, replacing his hat, and dried his hands and face on the towel. There was a hand pump near the stand, so he rinsed and refilled the basin.

By this time, Will was hobbling back, his injured leg slowing him very little. The two walked inside, and Clay sat at the third bench facing the door. Because he was farther into the building, the light didn't penetrate quite as well, making it difficult for anyone coming out of the bright, Texas afternoon to see him, at first.

As he sat, Aunt Bessie brought him a steak that covered two

thirds of the oversized plate. Included with it were beans and potatoes.

"We grow our own potatoes," Aunt Bessie said proudly. "Our well has more than enough water for what we need."

"Thank you, ma'am," Clay said. He looked up at Will, sitting across from him. "You folks need to know, I'm expecting a desperado here sometime this afternoon. I'm thinking within an hour or two."

"Well, sir. You want some help?" Will said.

Clay shook his head. "No, sir. I just want you to be aware of it. This man will be walking. He may still have his saddle with him, if he hasn't dropped it on the plains. All I ask is that you leave him to me. There very well could be some gunplay, so when this man comes walking in, don't get between me and him, or in the line of fire. That's about it. If you don't have any questions, I'm gonna see how much damage I can do to this steak."

Aunt Bessie cackled. "From the size of you, I'm expectin' you might need another plate."

Clay grinned at her. "Well, let me finish this one first, and we'll see."

"Yessir," Will said. "I'll just kinda keep a lookout here, but Skunk'll let us know when he shows up."

"Skunk?" Clay said around a mouthful of steak. "Can't say I've ever heard of a dog called Skunk."

"I think that dog would rather chase skunks than eat. I ain't never seen a dog like him. He must not be able to smell his own rear end 'cause he's been sprayed so many times. It don't stop him though. If he sees a skunk, that black-and-white is dead. Tears him to pieces and eats what's left. Dangedest thing I've ever seen." Will turned and yelled at Bess. "Gimme a couple of them biscuits, woman."

"Bess spun around, shaking a big ladle at her husband. "You dad-blamed ornery old man, you want biscuits, you git over here and git 'em yerself."

Will stood and limped to the bar, turning to Clay when he got there. "See what I put up with? I reckon I just don't whip her enough."

Aunt Bessie had placed a plate on the bar with a big stack of biscuits, a container of fresh butter, and a jar of honey. She popped Will on the head with the ladle, which he hardly seemed to feel through his hat. "You old gimp, you ever decide to whip me, you better bring a sack lunch, 'cause it'll be an all-day job, and I promise you, not one you'll forget."

Will grinned at Clay, picked up the platter of biscuits in one big hand, and enclosed the honey and butter in his other hand. He set them on the table, then turned back to his wife and winked at her.

She said, "Humph," turned, and went back to work.

"Now, where was I? Oh yeah, Skunk. He ain't good for nothin' for a week after he kills a skunk. We danged sure won't let him in the house or near the stage passengers. But he is right watchful. He won't let anyone or anything come near this house or barn without barkin' like crazy."

The biscuits were steaming. Clay picked up one and bounced it on his hand until he could get it to his plate where he dropped it, and then gingerly broke it open to let it cool.

Skunk was sitting next to the table, his eyes on Will. The older man moved his hand slowly toward the biscuits, and Skunk's eyes tracked the hand. "He likes hot biscuits. Watch this." Will picked up a biscuit and tossed it to the dog. Skunk grabbed it and fiercely shook it, scattering pieces all around himself. Then he started licking them up.

Bess was working at the stove with her back to them. "Will Chambers, don't you give that filthy dog any of my biscuits!"

Will replied, as sweetly as he could muster, "I sure won't, honey." Then he grinned at Clay.

Clay finished his meal while the entertainment was going on. He leaned back and smiled. "Aunt Bessie? That was Texas good."

The lady turned to him and smiled. "You ain't seen nothin' yet." She spooned up a big bowl of cobbler and started around the bar.

Skunk growled.

Clay motioned her back and signaled for Will to move out of the way. He stood, moved to the bar, and leaned against it, his left elbow resting lightly on the bar's surface.

They could hear the slow steps of a man outside, then the sound of a saddle dropping and faster steps to the pump. It squeaked a few times, then squeaked again. Clay checked to make sure both guns were free, then leaned back against the bar. A moment later, Earl Griffin stepped through the door.

He stopped when he stepped inside. After coming from the bright sunlight, the darker room made it difficult to see until his eyes adjusted.

Clay could see the man blinking, trying to adjust.

"Hello, Earl," Clay said.

Griffin straightened, squinting, trying to see who it was and place the voice.

"You may not remember me. The last time you saw me, you had me almost completely stripped, and I was staked over an ant bed."

Recognition and disbelief flooded the man's face. "You? You're dead . . . the flood."

"Well," Clay said, drawing the word out, "sometimes things just don't work out the way you plan, do they? For instance, those Presidio townsfolk? Did you expect them to be that tough? And here Beck kills your partner and leaves you to face the consequences all by your lonesome."

Griffin's eyes had adjusted to the darkness of the way station. He could see Clay clearly. He stood in the doorway, the sun illuminating one side of his face. When he had first walked in his face was red from the heat and exertion. But now, with the realization of who he faced, it was white as a newborn sheep.

Clay watched the man. Griffin was known as a fast gun, and he had killed several men face-to-face. He could see the gunman start to go into his crouch.

"I wouldn't do that, Griffin. You see, if you go for your gun, I'll kill you, and I'll tell you why. I could be the slowest gun in Texas and still beat you, because you have a little piece of leather over your revolver's hammer. A hammer thong works great, except when you need to get your gun out, and it's still doing its job. There's no telling how many shots I could pump into you before you manage to get that Colt unhitched and out of your holster."

Griffin's hand stopped, then slowly started to ease forward toward the hammer thong.

21

The ruse at least has him thinking, Clay thought. But Griffin's hand moved closer to his gun. Clay felt the cool wave of confidence drift over him, relaxing his body. His arms felt loose and ready. His eyes were glued to Griffin's face, yet picking up everything in the room, including the movement to the man's right. A smile drifted across his face.

Two loud clicks echoed through the room, and a long barrel was thrust across the bar, stopping only a foot from Griffin's face.

"Sonny," Aunt Bessie said, "I've shot all sorts of game with this here shotgun, and even a few Injuns. What do you think my chances are of blowing your head clean off from this distance?"

Griffin froze.

Clay chuckled. "Aunt Bessie, if Will hadn't already staked his claim on you, I'd marry you right now."

"Why, Ranger Barlow, that's about the nicest thing anybody has said to me today."

"All right, Griffin, drop your guns," Clay said, then walked up to the ashen-faced outlaw.

The man's hands were shaking as he unfastened his gunbelt and handed it to Clay. "Can . . . can she move that shotgun?"

"Not until you hand me my Smith and Wesson and that shoulder holster—easy."

Griffin pulled the Smith from its holster and handed it to Clay. He shoved it behind his gunbelt. "Now the holster."

Once he had the harness in his right hand, with the other gunbelt containing his two full-size Smiths, he said, "Aunt Bessie, I think we're fine now. Could you tilt those barrels out of the way?"

The hammers clicked as they were lowered, then the barrel tilted up and away from the two men.

"Ain't she a tear?" Will said. "We been married thirty-nine years, and there ain't ever a boring moment with that woman."

This time Bess winked at her husband, set the shotgun against the wall, and went back to work in the kitchen. "You best get that team ready. They'll be showing up any minute."

Will pulled his pocket watch from his vest, checked the time, and jumped to his feet, following Clay to the door.

Clay took Griffin's gunbelt and shoved him outside. Will passed them going to the barn.

"Hands against the wall," Clay said.

"I got leg irons in the barn if you need 'em," Will said, as he passed. "Presidio sheriff left a set here. Told Bessie she never knew when she might need to put 'em on me, but I think he just wanted a spare here."

"No thanks," Clay said. "I've got a set of cuffs in my bags. I'll use them if they're needed." He turned back to Griffin. Finished checking for weapons, Clay spun Griffin around. "You hungry?"

Griffin, surprised, took a moment, then said, "Yep, I sure am, but more'n that, I'm thirsty. You reckon you could work that pump while I get a drink?"

"Sure," Clay said.

He pumped a couple of times, and the water ran clear and cold. He figured Griffin was liable to founder before he stopped drinking. After pumping twice more, Griffin finally raised up.

"I got one question. Was that thong really over my hammer?"

Clay grinned back at the gunman. "I guess your head's about as weak as your legs, after that long walk you had." He lifted the gunbelt so that Griffin could see the holster. The revolver sat free and easy, the leather thong out of the way.

For a moment Griffin's face hardened. Hate filled his eyes. Then he diverted his head and mumbled. "You shouldn't have tricked me."

"You're still alive. Be thankful for that. Now go on inside."

They walked in, and Clay indicated where Griffin was to sit. Once the gunman was seated, Clay moved to the other side of the table, facing the door. "Aunt Bessie, if you wouldn't mind feeding this fella, I'll take care of it."

She nodded, fixed up a plate, and set it on the bar. "Ranger Barlow, do you like buttermilk?"

Clay turned toward her. "Yes, ma'am, that's almost as good as ice cream."

She laughed, pulled a pitcher and a glass from beneath the bar, and filled the glass. She came around the bar and dropped the plate in front of Griffin after giving him a dirty look. Then she set the buttermilk and a fresh bowl of steaming peach cobbler in front of Clay. "I got you a fresh bowl. Yours had cooled off. Ordered me some dried peaches and had 'em sent out by stage, a couple of months back. Makes fine cobbler. You enjoy it." She turned to Griffin. "You want cobbler?"

He looked up expectantly. "Yes, ma'am."

She dropped the bowl of cobbler she had originally dipped for Clay, just before Griffin showed up.

Clay watched the man race through the steak, potatoes, and beans, then pull the bowl of cobbler in front of him and devour it, too.

"A mite hungry?"

Griffin let out a long belch, then said, "I was, and thirsty. That dirty breed left me with nothing last night. I woke up and he was gone—took the food, water, everything."

Clay nodded. "Must be nice to have friends you can trust."

Griffin gave him a sour look. "I ain't had any of those since I was a kid."

Griffin studied him. Clay knew he was dying to ask.

"The rain."

"What?"

"The rain softened the ground enough so I could pull out the stakes."

"You beat the flash flood?"

"I'm here, aren't I?"

"Yeah, you're here. I want you to know that wasn't my idea."

"Griffin, you didn't stop Beck, and you seemed to be enjoying it."

"You don't know him. Anybody goes against him and he'll kill 'em. That's the honest truth. I swear, that man has no heart. You should've seen what he done to Cobb."

"The third man that escaped from Presidio?"

"Yeah, he was Arlo Cobb. Not the sharpest ax in the barn, but not a bad feller."

Clay nodded. "I did see. I trailed you from Presidio. If Cobb wasn't pretty after what Beck did to him, you should have seen him when I got there. The buzzards had several hours to work on him."

Clay noticed it didn't faze Griffin to hear it. Obviously, there was no love lost between Cobb and Griffin. "Where's Beck?"

"I don't know."

The wide-set, hard gray eyes drilled into the outlaw. "I'm not playing a game, Griffin. Just because I fed you, doesn't mean I wont beat you so bad you'll toss all that food and water you just ate. You got me?"

Griffin nodded.

One more time. "Where's Beck?"

"We were supposed to go to Fort Stockton, and from there, strike out up north. We'd decided it's gettin' too hot for us down here—why, we heard that Billy the Kid was killed by Pat Garrett in July. Our plan was to take the money from the Presidio bank and head up to Montana."

"Two bad decisions, Griffin."

"Whatcha mean?"

"Presidio was stupid, as you found out. But you were planning to go north with winter only a few months away. You'd get there just in time for the coldest part of the year."

"Cain't be no colder than Texas."

Clay shook his head. "How do you know that he followed your plan?"

"I got out to the edge of the mountains in time to see his dust. He was heading straight for Fort Stockton."

"He has my horse?"

"That blue roan?"

"Yes, the one I was riding when you grabbed me. The blue roan."

"Beck's hard on animals. He don't treat horses no better than the people he deals with."

Griffin tried to look sincere as he said, "I tried to treat your horse real good, Ranger Barlow. He's a fine horse."

"I know he's a fine horse, and the marshal saw you cutting him with a quirt when you were racing out of town."

"I was just scared."

"Does he have my shotgun?"

"Yeah, I had it, but he took it away from me. That's a fine gun. It shoots four times. Can you believe it?"

"How long do you think he'll be in Fort Stockton?"

"Till his money runs out. That breed loves to gamble. We didn't get much from the robbery, but he has all of it, plus what you had."

Griffin looked up at Clay with the mention of the ranger's money, but Clay's expression didn't change.

"Is there a place he likes to stay?"

"Anywhere liquor's served and gambling's available. He'll sleep a couple hours and go right back to gambling."

Skunk started barking, and Will stuck his head in the door. "Stage'll be here mighty soon."

"Everything's ready in here," Bessie said.

Clay stood and slipped the shoulder holster on. Normally, he wore it under a coat, but he had no coat, and it was too hot for the poncho. He removed his gunbelt with the single Colt in the holster —Miguel's Colt. He needed to get it back to Miguel. Maybe Will knew the old sheepherder. Picking up the gunbelt with the two Smith and Wesson forty-fours, he noticed the increased weight. It felt good. Now all he needed was his horse and his shotgun. If he could get any more of his things, they would just be gravy.

The stage rolled into the yard, creaking and harness rattling. "All right, folks," the driver called, "we'll be here for thirty minutes. This is your best chance for grub until we hit Del Rio, and that's a mighty fer piece. Eat up, stretch yore legs, and be ready to roll when I call."

Aunt Bessie had already set out six plates of food, steaming and waiting for the hungry travelers, along with big glasses filled with water and cups of hot coffee. There was also a bucket full of water with a dipper on the table, and, next to it, a full coffeepot.

Six people came through the door, walking strangely and stretching their backs. Clay recognized one of them. "Ransom," he called, "grab a plate, and come on back here."

Ransom Priest, Texas Ranger tried to make out who had called to him as his eyes struggled to adjust in the dark room. "Well, I'll be dipped, if it ain't Clay Barlow."

Holding his plate, Ransom strode back to Clay. They shook hands, and the wide-shouldered ranger sat down across from

Clay. "Who's this?" he asked as he pushed by Griffin, knocking the outlaw forward and into the table.

"His name's Earl Griffin."

"Griffin, huh? There's enough paper on this ole boy to stretch his neck two or three times."

"Where you headed, Ransom?"

Ransom shot a sidelong look at Clay. "Why?"

"I'm after a real hard case. He's supposed to be in Fort Stockton, and I need to get moving. If you're heading as far as Austin, or even San Antonio, I'd be obliged if you could take this one off my hands." He nodded toward Griffin.

"What'd he do recently?"

"He and his friends caught me napping and staked me out over an ant bed. I'm not real appreciative of that. They also tried, unsuccessfully, to rob the Presidio bank. There was eight of them. Now there's only one remaining."

"Who you going after?"

The driver and shotgun came in and sat down to their plates. "Fifteen minutes, folks," the driver said.

"Shifty Joe Beck."

"Beck? Half-Apache?" Ransom asked around a mouthful of steak.

Clay nodded.

Ransom returned to his meal and worked on it for a few minutes, disappearing the steak, potatoes, and red-beans, plus his coffee. Clay let him eat in silence.

Finally he looked up. "I understand that feller was born with the bark on. Wish I could go with you, but I'm due back in Austin."

"Ransom, you're doing me a big favor by taking Griffin off my hands. I'm obliged."

"Glad to do it, just be careful."

"Time to roll, folks."

The two rangers shook hands and followed the driver out the door. The shotgun rider turned to Clay. "You riding with us?"

"Clay shook his head. "No, only this one." He held Griffin's arm, while Ransom climbed up on the coach. He reached up to the roof, slid his saddle where he could get to his saddlebags, opened them, and pulled out handcuffs.

"I ain't gonna have to wear those, am I?" Griffin asked.

"Only until we get to Austin," Ransom said, as he closed up the bags, jumped back to the ground, and fastened the iron cuffs around the outlaw's wrists.

"Safe trip," Clay said to Ransom as he followed the outlaw into the coach.

"Good huntin'," Ransom said, and waved from the window as the coach jerked away from the yard, turned out onto the road, and headed east in a cloud of stifling dust.

Clay walked to the barn where Will was unhooking the old team and stripping the harness. He pitched in. With his help, they were done with the six animals and had them fed and watered in thirty minutes.

"Thanks," Will said.

"Glad to do it." Hombre was standing in the adjacent corral. Clay opened the gate from the barn, and stepped in with his rope. He made a short toss over the dun's neck and led him inside.

"You leavin?"

"Yeah, I've got to get moving. I'm after a killer who's in Fort Stockton. I want to get there before he leaves."

"It's getting late."

"Still have a few hours of daylight."

Hombre was saddled and ready. Clay led him to the front of the barn where Skunk sat watching a patch of greasewood.

Will looked at the greasewood about fifty yards away. "I sure hope there's no skunk out there. It's been nice around here for the past week. The smell has finally worn off. You'd think he'd kill 'em out."

Clay walked over to the pump and filled both water bags and the canteen. Will stood watching.

"You'll need all of that for you and your horse before you get there. With the rains we've had, you might find a waterhole but not likely. Best chance of water is Comanche Springs, and that's where you're headed, Fort Stockton. That's at least a day and a half away, north of us."

Clay walked inside with Will following. "What do I owe you folks?"

"Ranger Barlow," Aunt Bessie said, "we have never charged a lawman, and we ain't startin' now."

"Aunt Bessie, this comes out of the coffers of the state of Texas. It isn't out of my pocket."

"Makes no never mind. You don't owe us a thing. Thanks for keeping this country safer."

"Well, I'm much obliged. I'll be on my way now. Everything was very good, and the cobbler was delicious. You folks take good care of yourselves. Maybe I'll be back through here sometime."

"Goodbye, Ranger Barlow," Bess said, smiling over the compliment.

Will followed Clay outside. The ranger swung into the saddle and pulled Hombre around to trot by the west side of the house. He reached down to Will. The two men's hands clasped, and Clay said, "Thanks for your hospitality, Mr. Chambers. I'll not forget it."

Will nodded. "You just take care of yourself. I've heard of this Beck, and he's an evil man."

Clay touched his finger to his hat, bumped Hombre in the flanks, and turned for Fort Stockton. "Adios," he called.

IT HAD BEEN a tough push from the stage station to Fort Stockton, but Hombre had shown his mettle. They arrived late in the afternoon of the second day, having used all of the two bags of water and half of the canteen. Clay had pushed hard. Hombre had lost some weight, but the horse never stopped. He gave Clay everything asked of him.

Clay came upon the livery and let Hombre drink for a bit before he pulled him off the trough. The horse would have to wait a bit before he drank more water. Clay turned the canteen up and emptied it down his throat. That might be a good idea for him, too. He patted the big dun's neck and said, "That's a good fella."

At his first word, he heard a soft whinny from inside the barn. Clay felt his heart tug. Could it be Blue? After all this time. He led Hombre into the barn. He was met by a small worried-looking man with a big mustache.

"Can I help you?"

"Two things," Clay said. "The first, I need this horse well taken care of. He has worked hard for the past few days. I'll put him up here, but he'll need good feed and more water. We just came in from the south."

"I've got corn and oats," the little man said, his worried countenance remaining steady. He had seen the badge, and Clay suspected that might be what was worrying him.

"The second thing, where's the horse that whinnied?"

About that time the whinny came again, weaker.

"The funniest thing," the man said. "That horse is sick. It hasn't eaten or demonstrated any kind of spirit since he's been here. I've been trying to doctor him as best I can."

"Where is he?"

"Back in the fourth stall."

Clay pushed Hombre's reins into the livery owner's hand. "Take care of this horse." He dashed toward the fourth stall.

He rounded the corner. Blue. The big horse lay on the straw, his sides heaving.

"Hi, Blue," Clay said. "What's wrong, boy?"

The horse strained and tried to raise his head. He got it high enough to see Clay. He kicked out his feet several times, trying to get up, but couldn't make it.

Clay rushed around in front of the blue roan so the horse could see him, and Blue settled down, still breathing hard, sides rising and falling. Clay sat on the straw and held the horse's head in his lap, scratching between the alert ears that turned toward him and rubbing the muscled cheeks.

Clay was a teenager again. This was his horse. He looked up as the liveryman came into the stall.

"Is this your horse, Ranger?"

Clay nodded, not trusting his voice.

"The feller that rode him in must have ridden the life right out of him. The horse was stumbling when he made it to the livery door. The man was going to shoot him until I threatened him with the fort provost. He said he didn't want him, stripped his saddle and gear, and put it on the other horse, which wasn't in much better shape."

Clay pulled himself together while the man was talking. "Did the man look like he's part Indian?"

"That's him. Scary character. I thought he was gonna shoot me when I threatened to report him."

"This is Blue," Clay said. "I've had this horse since I was a boy." He looked over the big animal that meant so much to him. There were cuts from a quirt along his neck and flanks. His forehead had lumps and bruises from being struck with some type of hard object.

"I'm right sorry, Mister. I've seen animals mistreated, but this poor boy rates right up there. Man do something like this ought to hang."

Clay said nothing. His mind didn't have room for Beck right now—later. He sat with Blue for several hours, his mind replaying the good times the two of them had over the years. When his pa first brought Blue home, he fell in love with the big, gentle horse right away, and Blue reciprocated. Blue was with him when his folks were murdered. The horse helped him make it through those first hard days and then carried him through the chase.

Blue never faltered. He was a special horse. He waited two years while Clay was in New York learning more about the law. Then, when he returned, he made that miserably cold trip in the snow from Austin to Uvalde.

Clay had been deep in thought, tenderly rubbing the roan's cheek. Now he noticed Blue's labored breathing had gotten louder. The liveryman had never left their sides. He rubbed a cooling liniment over the horse's back and shoulders. Clay looked at the man through the dim lantern light. He shook his head.

The horse's big eyes never left Clay's face. Tears hadn't passed his cheeks since Ma died, now they were slowly making their way down his sharp features and disappearing into his mustache, to later drip out the ends. The liveryman looked away, giving Clay a semblance of privacy in his grief, and continued to rub the horse's back.

The other horses in the stalls were unusually quiet, as if they knew what was taking place. A great horned owl hooted once, "Whoo?" and was silent. The tinny pianos in the saloons competed with each other for the loudest award, and Blue's breathing slowed.

The great horse who had carried Clay from boyhood to manhood released one last, long breath, his eyes still gazing at Clay, and died.

Clay continued to stroke his horse after he was gone.

The liveryman finally stood, and said, "He's gone, Ranger."

Clay nodded. He sat with his horse for a while longer, then gently laid the big head on the straw, stood, and checked the loads in all three of his Smith and Wessons. Satisfied, he made sure that each of the revolvers on his hips was loose in their respective holsters. He removed his bandanna and wiped his eyes.

All the liveryman could see was the stark outline of the man's face. In the dim light, he couldn't see the hard, unforgiving gray eyes.

Clay spoke to the liveryman, his voice as cold as a Texas blue norther. "Which saloon is best known for its gambling?"

Without having to think, the liveryman replied, "The Pecos."

"Up the street?"

"Yeah, it's the second one. All three are right there together."

"Where do you bury horses?"

"Uh, Ranger, we don't bury 'em, We just drag 'em out onto the plains."

"Get a wagon, and hoist Blue into the wagon. Then hook up a team and figure a good place to bury him. Then toss in a shovel."

"One shovel?"

"Make it two, in case one breaks.

"Get Blue loaded as quickly as you can. Hire some men to help you. I'll provide generous pay for each man." Clay pulled a couple of gold double eagles from his vest and dropped them into the man's hand.

The man stood staring at the gold. "Yes, sir!"

Clay nodded and walked into the dark street. He felt cool, even cold. A chilling calmness had come over him. He had no thought of his ranch, his grandpa, or even Dee. He had only one mission—Shifty Joe Beck.

22

W hen he reached the Pecos Saloon, Clay stepped up to the batwing doors and peered over the top, examining the men in the room. The place vibrated with noise, noise from the men shouting to be heard, noise from the women's shrill laughter, and noise from the piano. He continued to look, finally spotting Beck at the roulette wheel, shouting at the girl operating the game.

Clay pushed the doors open, stepped through to the interior of the smoke-filled room, and listened to them squeaking as they swung back and forth until they stopped, finally quiet. He stood there—motionless.

It started slowly. Each of the men was concentrating on his cards, or wheel, or the painted woman in the low-cut dress next to him, but it started. One man looked up and saw the big man, the Texas Ranger star on his left breast, the two revolvers hanging at his waist, and the one, which they seldom saw, in a shoulder holster. The man stopped his gambling and stared, first at Clay, then in the direction of the ranger's gaze. Then another man looked up, and another.

Gradually, the whole room quieted, until Shifty Joe Beck was the only one yelling, and then the girl looked up at Clay and froze, for the ranger's cold stare looked like it might be on her. Beck, through his drunken fog and gambling euphoria, looked up at the girl to see her staring at the door. He slowly swung his head. And saw the ranger.

Clay could see reality gradually make it through to the man-killer.

Beck grinned and growled in his gravelly voice, "Hey, kid, how are those ant bites?"

"You are under arrest for the murder of Arlo Cobb, and for the theft and subsequent murder of a blue roan named Blue." Clay started walking toward Beck.

"You want a little bit of Joe Beck, Ranger? I think you do. Come on over here, so I can be sure I don't miss."

With his last word, Beck went for his gun. He was fast, he knew he was fast, but two guns appeared in the ranger's hands before his Colt had cleared the holster. He turned loose of his gun like it was the wrong end of a branding iron.

"Don't shoot, Ranger. I ain't got a gun. You wouldn't shoot an unarmed man now would ya?"

Clay continued walking toward Beck, never changing his stride. Patrons of the Pecos Saloon jumped, knocking over chairs and tables, to get out of the way of those two big Smith and Wessons. Several of the soldiers from the fort gathered at the bar and started taking bets, and Clay kept walking.

When he was within reach of Beck, the breed went for his big knife, the knife that had cut Cobb's throat and sliced the dying man's stomach open.

Clay moved like a striking snake. The barrel of his right-hand revolver slammed into the killer's skull. He collapsed on the saloon floor.

Clay holstered his weapons, carefully checked Beck for more weapons, throwing three other knives and a derringer to the floor, and tossed the unconscious man over his shoulder like a rag doll.

He turned and started out of the saloon. The patrons followed, at a respectable distance. Several ran to the other saloons to spread the word what was happening. Before Clay had reached the livery, his entourage had grown to over half the town.

When he walked into the livery, the liveryman and three other men had just lowered Blue into a wagon. The horse's head hung over the seat. Clay tossed Beck in a space just behind the seat and climbed up on the wagon, taking Blue's head in his lap. He motioned for the liveryman to drive. The man climbed up and looked at Clay. He nodded, and the liveryman popped the reins.

The horses pulled them a short distance, to a sandy knoll on the west side of town. The liveryman stopped the horses just as Beck was starting to wake up. Groggy, he looked around.

"What the . . . what's going on?"

Clay grabbed the man by the scruff of his neck and, with one hand, threw the killer off the wagon and watched him slam into the ground. When Beck staggered to his feet, Clay tossed down a shovel.

Beck looked at the horse and then at the shovel. "You're crazy, I ain't burying no horse."

Clay climbed down and, with his big open hand, slapped him, knocking the outlaw to the ground again. No man had ever treated Beck like this, not since he was a little boy, and it made him furious. He jumped up and reached for a knife that wasn't there. Then he jumped at Clay and was slapped down again.

"I can do this all night long, and you're still going to dig. Now or later, your choice."

Beck, his voice a guttural growl, said, "You can't do this."

Clay pulled a water bottle from behind the seat, that the liveryman was nice enough to include, and took a long drink. "Dig."

Beck looked at the horse and then at Clay. He picked up the shovel and started digging.

By daylight, almost all of the residents of Fort Stockton were gathered around the deepening grave. Even the camp commander of the fort had ridden out. He watched for a few minutes, then spoke with Clay who explained who he was and what was going on, watched for a little longer, and rode back to the fort.

It was another hot day on the plains of Texas. The late summer sun drilled down without mercy, and Joe Beck continued to dig. He would be allowed a break and a little water, then would start again.

Just before the sun set, he had dug a six-foot deep hole wide and long enough to allow the blue roan to be lowered into it so that he lay on his side, legs and neck extended. Several of the men observing what was going on had volunteered to help move Blue to his final resting place.

Once the fine horse—who had loved Clay as much as he had loved the blue roan—was laid respectfully into the hole, Clay walked to the edge. He stood, taking a final look at his friend and companion. The crowd grew silent in respect. Clay removed his hat, and the men around him followed suit. Some of the people swore they could see his lips moving and could hear words of a prayer, but others said that he just stood there with his eyes closed.

Then he raised his head, put his hat back on, and looked over at the limp and shaking Beck. "Fill it."

The man looked around wildly. Clay could see hope for rescue in the man's eyes. The ranger walked over to the killer, the man's eyes pleading. Clay bent down, picked up the shovel, and handed it to him. In concert, a low moan issued from the crowd. When Beck threw his first shovelful of dirt on Blue, another man moved up, picked up the extra shovel, and started throwing dirt into the grave. Then another man stepped up with his shovel. Within minutes the edges of the hole were crowded with men filling it in.

It filled quickly, and Beck collapsed. The liveryman was one of the men filling the hole, another was the mayor.

The two men walked up to Clay, and the mayor spoke. "We didn't do it for Beck, Ranger Barlow. We did it for you. There's a room waiting for you at the hotel. Jim, here, will take you back in his wagon, and we'll take Beck to jail. Don't worry, he isn't going to escape. I don't think he could crawl five feet. Stop by the marshal's office when you wake up."

Clay was in a daze as he rode back to town. Jim stopped at the hotel. Clay, feeling as alone as he had when he lost his folks, turned to Jim and said, "Thanks."

His legs were heavy as he climbed the steps to the hotel entrance. He vaguely saw the people, gathered solemnly around the entrance, both inside and out. He went inside.

The clerk handed him a key and said, "Number seven, Ranger Barlow, and don't fret about signing in now. You can do that when you're ready."

Clay slowly made his way up the stairs, managed to focus on the room number printed on the key and made his way down the hall to door number seven. He unlocked the door, closed it, and removed his guns, placing them on the chair. Sitting on the edge of the bed, he thought of Blue and the punishment his horse had gone through. He started to reach down to take his boots off and collapsed on the bed. He fell on his left side, with his feet dangling over the edge.

Sometime in the night, he thought he remembered an angel coming into his room, removing his boots, and lifting his legs onto the bed. He dreamed of leaning forward over the neck of a blue roan, his hat gone, and the wind whipping through his hair, as they raced across rolling hills of hip-high green grass.

IN THE AFTERNOON of the next day, a beam of light lanced through a crack between the warped interior window shutters of the west-facing room. It drove, as if aimed, into the closed eyes of Ranger Clay Barlow. Keeping his eyes shut, he moved his head and was out of the light. Immediately, his breathing leveled, again becoming deep and steady.

The beam, persistent in its mission, gradually moved across the pillow, climbed across his black, stubble-covered chin, across his mouth and nose, and found its goal, settling on both eyes.

Clay yawned, raised up on the bed, and stretched his long arms. He looked at his legs, stretched out on the bed, his feet sticking out from under the comforter that had been pulled up to his chest. He raised an arm and took a whiff, pulling his head back and grimacing. Then he swung his feet over the side of the bed, reached for his hat that was on top of his guns, and put it on his head. Next, he beat out his boots. A nasty-looking scorpion fell out and raced across the floor. He watched it for a moment before he stomped on his boots.

After arming himself, he walked over to the wash basin. The face that gazed back at him from the mirror didn't look twenty-five years old. "I'd guess fifty," he said to the mirror. The thick stubble aged him. He looked at his eyes, more red than gray. He needed a shave, a bath, and some new clothes. These needed to be burned, or at least washed real good.

Clay turned to get his razor from his saddlebags. Then he remembered his good razor was gone, with Griffin and Beck. His momentum carried him around, and he spotted a pair of saddle-bags sitting next to the chair. He knew he hadn't brought up saddlebags. He walked over and picked them up and immediately saw the engraved initials CJB. These were his. Reaching in he felt a moment of relief—his binoculars. Laying his binoculars aside, he dumped the remaining contents out on the bed. His pocket watch rolled across the bed. Several boxes of Smith and

Wesson forty-four cartridges, and his razor. His cup, brush, and shaving soap were gone.

I hope they didn't use it to whittle, he thought, slipping the precision instrument that he had purchased in New York out of its wooden container. There it lay, clean and pristine. He picked it up and looked at the blade. No nicks. Then he checked the sharpness by cutting a few hairs on his arm. A little dull. He sat and crossed his legs so that he could strop it on his boot. When satisfied, he moved to the mirror and the water basin. The water was cool.

What am I doing? After putting the razor back, he headed downstairs for a barber.

"Good afternoon, Ranger Barlow," the clerk behind the desk greeted him.

Clay turned and walked to the desk. "Afternoon. I think I need to sign in."

"Yes, sir." The clerk swung the register around to face Clay. "It's all around town. This morning, when the marshal went in to check on Shifty Joe Beck, he found him hanging from the window bars. I guess he was wanted all across Texas."

Clay finished filling out the register, slid it back to the clerk, and said, "Good riddance—saves the state some money. I need to buy some clothes and get a bath and a shave. Where's the general store and the barber?" He wanted to get cleaned up, and not think about Beck.

"Store's just across the street, and the barber shop is right next door to your left when you leave the hotel. That was quite a sight, you making Beck bury your horse. I think the mayor is having a monument erected."

"Much obliged." Clay turned and headed for the door.

∼

CLAY STEPPED out of the barber shop feeling like a new man and turned toward the marshal's office. He'd left at least ten pounds of Texas in that bathtub. It was a wonder what clean clothes and a clean body did for a person. He had found himself a new hat while he was getting clothes and supplies. The short-crown, black Stetson felt different after wearing the big, heavy sombrero —not necessarily better, just different.

While he was in the store, he had realized that he was way past hungry, and the storekeeper had recommended The Stock-man's Cafe. For all of its name, it was just a hole in the wall, but the food was good. He put away enough for three men and felt much better.

His mind drifted back to Miguel and the sheep. He owed that Mexican a lot. It'd be good to see him if he ever got back to this country, but for now, he needed to get the man's Colt back to him.

The thought of Dee pushed Miguel, unbidden, to the back of his mind, sending a smile to his face for the first time in days. He could see her, vibrant and alive, leaning across the table with her lovely hand on his arm. He hadn't thought it much before, but he just might give up rangering. He'd have to see.

Clay opened the door and stepped into the sparse office. The marshal was leaned back in his chair reading an old El Paso newspaper.

"Well, if it ain't the man of the day. Everybody's talking about you and Beck. Come on in, and have a seat."

"Thanks, Marshal. I'll stand. I need to be getting back to Austin. Can you tell me what happened to Beck, for my report?"

"I'd be glad to, but you sure you want to rush off? That's a long way to Austin."

"You're right, Marshal, but it doesn't get any shorter with me standing here."

The lawman nodded. "You're right about that. Well, tough Mister Beck decided he couldn't live with being humiliated like you did to him, and he hung himself to the bars of his window last night." The marshal stopped to take a sip of his coffee. He held it up to Clay. "Want a cup? It's terrible but better than no coffee at all."

Clay shook his head. "How'd he do it?"

"Now, that's a funny thing. He used his britches, twisted 'em up and looped 'em around his neck. But what was really funny, he was tall enough to look out that window, so he must've been mighty serious about hangin' hisself. When we found him, he was hangin', his back against the wall with his feet stretched out touching the floor." The marshal shook his head. "All he had to do, at any time, was to stand up. He must've been mighty serious. Sometimes you just can't figger them Injuns.

"Oh, I got something for you." The marshal opened a drawer, pulled out a drawstring bag, and set it on the table."

Clay recognized it immediately but waited.

Then the man got up and walked over to the gun cabinet, opened the door, and pulled out Clay's Roper shotgun.

"This was with Beck's gear, what little he had. The rest of it is at the livery. He was braggin' about the stuff he took off a big ranger, especially this shotgun. I'm thinkin' that big ranger must've been you." He handed the Roper to Clay.

It felt good to have it back in his hands. The Roper had been with him throughout his rangering days. It had gotten him out of a couple of tight scrapes, and besides Blue, this was what he'd wanted back the most. He eared the hammer back slightly to make sure a shell was in the chamber, then let it back down. "Yeah, Marshal. It was me he was talking about. They got the drop on me. I was thinkin' about something when I should've been keeping an eye out."

The marshal nodded. "Yeah, it's hard to be alert all the time, but in this business, relaxing can sure be hard on your health.

"The rest of Beck's gear is at the stables. You can look through it and take whatever you want."

"Thanks, Marshal, thanks for everything. You'd been within

your rights to stop me with Beck. I'm obliged you didn't." Clay reached into his vest and pulled out ten dollars. He laid the coins on the desk. "The state of Texas is always glad to pay for the burying of Beck's kind."

"Obliged." The marshal picked up the money. "As far as the other thing, it seemed like just punishment for the man. That must've been a fine horse."

"None finer. I need to ask you a couple of favors, Marshal. First, a Mexican sheepherder found me and saved my life. He loaned me his Colt." Clay pulled the weapon from behind his gunbelt. He laid it and two boxes of forty-four ammunition on the desk. "His name is Miguel Lopez."

"I know Miguel. He's had like three or four wives and a passel of kids?"

"He's the one. Now, for the second request. Do you know Cesar Garcia in Presidio?"

"Danged right. Marshal Butch Ironside happens to be a good friend of mine. Why, before he became marshal, I was down that way chasing a horse thief, and Butch—"

"Sorry to interrupt Marshal, but I've got to be on my way. I need to get back to Austin."

The marshal waved his hand. "Sure, sure. Sometimes I get long winded. You were saying."

"Cesar loaned me a set of binoculars and a shotgun. I don't have them with me, but you can pick them up from the hotel desk clerk. I need to get all these things back to both of them. It's no rush, but the next time you're down that way, I'd be obliged if you could return them."

"It'd be a pleasure. I don't get down there often, but the army does. Is it all right if I ask the major? He won't mind at all."

"That'll be fine. You've been a great help Marshal. Now, I best be getting on my way. Thanks again." Clay reached across the desk and shook the marshal's hand, left the office, and headed for the livery.

As he walked, his thoughts drifted back to the short message from Jake that had started all of this. Hard things had happened, but he'd met some fine people. Strong people who had made a way for themselves in this unforgiving land. He thought of Rory. Jake's son was a tough little boy, who would have the opportunity to grow to manhood with his folks. That was worth all of the difficulties he had faced, even the loss of Blue.

Clay stopped by the hotel to pick up his gear, settle his debt, and leave the binoculars and shotgun with the desk clerk, before continuing to the stable. Everyone he had met today greeted him by name. He didn't care for this much attention, but unfortunately he'd earned it. *Not necessarily in a good way,* he thought. But he found he felt no remorse for what he'd done to Beck.

The liveryman was outside the stable, sitting in a chair, leaning against the barn, whittling. He looked up when he heard Clay.

"Headin' out of town?"

"Yep. I understand you've got Beck's gear."

The man's face fell. He obviously had planned on selling it. He got up and walked into the stable. "Follow me."

In the tack room, Clay saw it piled in the corner. His saddle and bridle looked to be in good shape. "I'll ride this one out of here. When the stage comes through, if you'd send the saddle I rode in on to Austin, in care of the Texas Rangers, I'd be obliged." He couldn't bring himself to sell the saddle Señor Garcia had given him.

"Sure. By the way, I didn't tell you when you was with your horse, but that blue roan had heart. When they came in, a man could see the horse was completely done in. He was shaking all over, wouldn't eat or drink, but he stayed on his feet until he was in the stall. Never seen such heart."

"One of a kind," Clay said. He walked to Hombre's stall and dropped his saddlebags. Laying the Roper across them, he turned to go back for the saddle.

The liveryman was behind him with his saddle and equipment. Clay patted Hombre on the flank and laid the blanket across the dun's back. Then, while he finished getting the horse ready, he asked the man, "How many men did you have helping you?"

"Three others."

Clay finished with Hombre, sliding his Roper into the boot last. He turned to the man. "I'm much obliged for all you did. Give those men my thanks for their help, along with this." He reached into his vest pocket, pulled out a small bag, and opened it. From the bag, he counted out three twenty-dollar gold pieces, dropping them into the man's hand. "That's for the three men." Then he pulled out two more. "That's for taking such good care of Blue and everything else you did."

The liveryman looked at the money in his hand. With the two the ranger had given him earlier, that totaled eighty dollars and was almost two months' income. "I'm beholden."

"Are we square?"

The man was still staring at the gold. He looked up at Clay and nodded his head. "More than square, Ranger."

Clay looked around the stable. It was time to put Fort Stockton behind him. "Adios." he said to the liveryman, then trotted out of the stable and turned toward Blue's grave. One last thing to do.

He rode up to the fresh dirt on the little knoll and looked around. A lot of country could be seen from here. *Blue would've liked that,* he thought. In the late afternoon on the Texas plains, shadows were starting to lengthen. *I didn't realize the hole was so big,* he thought now as he surveyed the work Shorty Joe Beck had done. He sat for a moment more, then swung the big dun around and pointed him east, out of town. "Adios, Blue."

23

C lay pulled Hombre up at the Comfort turnoff. It would take him no more than two hours to be at the Davis ranch. "What am I gonna do, Hombre? Do I head on to Austin? Grandpa was in a bad way when I left for Presidio. That seems the right thing to do. Or do I ride down to see Dee?"

The big horse's left ear shifted back toward Clay as if he was listening.

Clay's heart prompted him to make the turn, but what if his grandpa died before he got back? He'd never be able to forgive himself. He sat at the turnoff, pondering. Normally, he made decisions quickly, but today he was torn. The young blonde beauty tugged at him. During the short time they had spent together, Dee had captured his heart. Every thought of her pulled at him to go to her.

He had stepped down, poured water into his hat, and was giving Hombre a drink when he heard the stage approaching from behind him. He moved the horse off the road and continued to let him drink.

The stage rattled and rocked to a stop.

"Well I'll be double-danged and took for a Yankee, if it ain't the scourge-of-the-west, Texas Ranger Clay Barlow."

Clay shook his head. "That can't be Whip Bingham. I heard he was turned out to pasture 'cause he was too old to handle those big, mean horses."

"You best stop that blather, young feller. Keep that kind of talk up and I'll climb down from here and give you the lickin' you deserve."

Clay left Hombre ground hitched where he could crop a little bunchgrass while he walked over to the stage and thrust his hand up to Whip. "Good to see you, amigo. How you been doin'?"

"Why, Clay, I'm as fine as a daisy. Reckon I'll be driving this here stage when you got grandbabies crawling all over you."

Clay laughed. "I'm thinkin' you just might, Whip. You headed into Austin?"

"Yessiree. We'll be pulling in there late tonight. Wanna ride?"

"No, thanks." Clay nodded to Hombre ."He wouldn't much like trailing along behind the stage."

Whip's face turned grim. "I hate to tell you this, but I got some bad news. A few days back, we got news a ranger was killed."

Clay's face stiffened. "Do you know who it was?"

"Reckon I do. It was that young feller. Came on with the rangers just before you did. I think his name was Priest. You know him?"

"I know him. It was Ransom Priest. Any idea what happened?"

"Just what I heard. It was at a stop over near Del Rio. Seems the ranger was transportin' a prisoner, and whilst they was eatin', this feller got ahold of a drummer's gun. The coyote still had his cuffs on—don't know how he managed that. Anyway, he shot Ranger Priest, what was sittin' next to him eating, in the side. Bullet went right through him and hit the wall. He then shot and killed the feller that was riding shotgun. He got him a horse and lit out. I imagine he's deep in Mexico by now."

"You hear the shooter's name?"

"Reckon it was a lowlife by the name of Griffin."

Clay nodded. "I was afraid of that. Earl Griffin."

"That's the one. How'd you know?"

"I turned that prisoner over to Ransom at the station east of Fort Davis. I was chasing Shifty Joe Beck."

"I mighta knowed it. I wondered why you weren't ridin' ole Blue. You're the ranger that made Beck bury your horse in Fort Stockton."

"You heard about that?"

"Son, I reckon that story's done covered the state of Texas. I'm right sorry about Blue. That was one fine—"

A man with a bowler hat shoved his head out the stagecoach window and, in an exasperated voice, said, "Driver, are you going to sit here and talk to this man for the rest of the day, or can we expect to be on our way soon?"

Whip turned around and shot a long stream of brown spit at the ground next to the passenger door. "Keep yore shirt on, feller. That ticket you got provides you ridin' space, not jawin' room. Sit back inside there before you get a busted head on that door.

"You take care, boy, I've got to be moving on. Looks like folks —" He indicated the people riding in the coach. "—is gettin' antsy."

"Hold up a second, Whip. Have you heard anything about how Senator Barlow is doing?"

Whip shook his head. "Sorry to bring you more bad news, boy, but when I left, 'bout a week past, he was doing might poorly. I reckon he just never got over those bullets in the back. I did hear that the feller that shot him died in the Huntsville prison."

"Thanks, Whip. I'll be coming in behind you. Maybe I'll see you in town."

The older man nodded, unfurled his whip, and cracked it above the horses' heads. "Hiyah, you hay burners," he yelled at the horses. The stage jerked away, kicking up dust from the dry road. Clay stepped back and watched them roll out of sight.

"Well, boy," Clay said to Hombre, "I guess my mind's made up. We better get on into Austin. I sure hate it about Ransom. It's too bad I didn't kill Griffin at the stage station."

Clay cast a wistful look down the road to the Davis ranch. He clucked at Hombre, and as the horse stepped out toward Austin, said, "One more night under the stars, boy, and then you'll be resting and getting fat on corn and oats."

THE WIND HAD CHANGED last night. Now blowing from the west, it picked up dust and deposited it on everything and everyone. The change brought only wind, no rain or cooler temperatures. Hombre stepped off the east side of the bridge over the Colorado River and into Austin.

His hat pulled low to protect his eyes, Clay turned Hombre left on San Antonio Street, and, at the next block, right onto Cedar. Near the end of the block, Clay guided Hombre to the hitching rail in front of the Texas Rangers' office in the courthouse.

When he stepped down from Hombre's back, the horse turned and looked at him. Clay patted his neck. "I know. I'll be through here pretty quick, and you'll be in the barn soon."

The big man pulled two envelopes from his saddlebags and walked up the steps, entering the office. It was empty, except for the sergeant at the desk. The man wore his hat on, shoved to the back of his head. "Howdy, Clay. Welcome back. Have you heard the news?" The ranger stood and walked around the desk. He had a slight limp from an old leg wound.

Clay extended his hand. "Sergeant Bellows, I talked to Whip on the trail. He told me about Ransom, said he was shot by Griffin."

"Yeah, that's the information we have. As soon as we got word, the captain took a detail out to Del Rio. Not much hope of finding any sign of Griffin. He's probably in Monterey by now."

Clay nodded. "Yeah, I sure hated to hear it. I turned Griffin over to Ransom. I was chasing Shifty Joe Beck and needed to keep moving. Ransom just happened along at the right time, or wrong time from his viewpoint."

"We heard of the Beck incident." The sergeant looked up at Clay, and his hard eyes softened for a moment. "Sorry to hear about your horse. It takes a pretty lowdown skunk to treat a good horse like that. How'd he get Blue?"

"Long story, Sergeant. It's in here." Clay handed the man the envelope containing his report.

The sergeant looked at it for a moment. "That's fine. I'm bettin' this is pretty interestin' reading. What's happening with Jake? I don't suppose he came in with you?"

Clay had dreaded this moment. "No, he sent a letter." He handed the letter to Sergeant Bellows.

The sergeant moved back behind his desk and sat. Clay knew what the letter said. It was short, but Bellows took some time reading it. Finally, he looked up.

"You know what this says?"

Clay nodded. "Yep."

"It doesn't tell me much, just that he's resigning. Do you know why?"

Clay thought about that for a moment. He knew why Jake wanted to leave the rangers, but he also knew his friend wanted to keep his family out of it.

"I reckon he just got tired."

The sergeant continued to look at him for a long moment, then nodded. "I can see why. He's been in the rangers for a long time. I'll let the captain know when he gets back."

"Have you heard anything about Senator Barlow?" Clay asked.

"I have. He ain't doin' so fine. Ran into Raymond yesterday. You might want to get up there pretty quick."

"Thanks," Clay said. He spun around and headed out the door. *I shouldn't have stopped,* he thought. *I could've taken care of this anytime.*

He rode straight to the livery. The doors were closed to keep the wind and dust out. He looped Hombre's reins over the hitching rail that stood by the watering trough. The horse immediately shoved his head in and started drinking. Clay went to the small door that was cut into one side of the two large sliding doors. He opened it and stepped inside. It was almost dark, but there was no dust blowing.

"Welcome back, Clay," Platt, the stable owner said, stepping out of his office. "Reckon you want to put Blue up."

"No, sir. Blue's dead."

A shocked look on his face, Platt said, "I'm right sorry. That was a fine horse. You got another one out there?"

"I do. A dun, lineback. His name's Hombre."

"Go ahead and get him, and I'll open the door."

"I can give you a hand with that," Clay said, as Platt walked toward the big doors.

"No, I can get it. That way, it won't be open any longer than it has to be. Keeps the dust out, at least most of it."

Clay went through the smaller door to get Hombre. By the time he had unhitched and swung up on the dun, Platt had the door open just wide enough for him to ride through. As soon as they were inside and clear, it started rumbling again as Platt pushed it closed.

"Second stall, and just leave your stuff. I'll take good care of Hombre and your things. You need to get up to the senator's apartment right now. Raymond said that if you came in to tell you to git there quick."

"Thanks," Clay said.

As soon as he was outside, he turned right and started

running. It was several blocks to his grandpa's apartment. *I just hope I'm in time.*

Clay took the steps three at a time. The door jerked open as he reached the second-floor landing.

"You made it. Thank God," Raymond said. "He's been holding on to see you. We thought he died a week ago, but he's the stubbornest man I've ever known. The doc had pronounced him, but a few seconds later, he takes a deep breath, opens his eyes, and looks around. First words out of his mouth: 'I need to talk to Clay.'"

Clay stepped around his grandpa's good friend and, spurs jangling dashed to his grandfather's bedside. He stopped as he stepped into the room. His grandpa was propped up on a bank of pillows. He hardly recognized him. The thick neck now looked pencil-thin, and his wide shoulders looked like sticks propping his pajama top open. It was his face that looked the worst. Always strong and powerful with wide-set gray eyes that could be either soft and kind, or hard like granite. He and Pa had looked a lot alike, except that grandpa was bigger.

All of the physical strength appeared to be gone. Although his body almost disappeared under the covers, the eyes hadn't changed. Though they now were hollow and deep-set with the loose skin hooding a good part of them, they were still bright and intelligent.

"Come on over here where I can see you better, boy." The voice was weaker, hoarse and raspy. "Don't look so danged surprised. Haven't you ever seen a dying man?"

Clay continued into the room, taking a seat in the chair next to the bed. His grandfather reached for him, and Clay took his hand. His grandpa had never lied to him, nor he to his grandpa. "You've looked better, Grandpa."

The old man gave a gravelly chuckle. "I guess that New York school taught you to be diplomatic without lying."

Clay grinned at the man who had done so much for him. "It's better than lying, isn't it?"

"It sure is, son. How was your trip?"

"Long and dusty. It's good to be home."

The front door closed quietly and Clay heard steps coming into the room.

"Son, this here is the sawbones who's been taking care of me. Dr. Mason Eggleton, and this other fellow is Senator Luke Weber. I asked them here as witnesses. Gentlemen, this is my grandson, Clay Barlow, rancher, attorney, and Texas Ranger." The pride in the old man's voice couldn't be missed.

Clay found himself embarrassed at the introduction but rose to greet the men.

The doctor said, "Yes, I'm familiar with your grandson, Senator. I fixed up a couple of ruffians who had the misfortune to resort to the manly art of fisticuffs with Mr. Barlow. One fairly recently."

"Doctor Eggleton, as far as the last one is concerned, I think the young lady did more damage to that buffalo hunter than I did."

Both Senator Weber and Doctor Eggleton laughed at Clay's comment.

"You may be right, Clay," the doctor said. "I don't think that man will ever breathe properly through his broken nose. That young lady smashed quite a bit of cartilage with her little fist."

Senator Weber took Clay's hand. "Your grandfather speaks very highly of you. May I call you Clay?"

"Yes, sir."

"I admire any man that has accomplished as much as you have by your age." Senator Weber cleared his throat. "You should consider getting into politics. I think you could do great things for Texas."

Before Clay could reply, his grandpa said, "Luke, stop trying to recruit him. He's got enough on his mind. I'm the one that's dying, and I need to talk while I can."

Raymond had been standing behind the men.

"Raymond, you pull up a chair next to Clay. This is about the both of you. Son, go ahead and sit back down." He turned to Senator Weber. "Luke, did you bring the document?"

"I did, Joseph." He produced an envelope from his pocket and, leaning over Clay, handed it to the dying man.

"Where the Sam Hill's my glasses?"

Clay reached to the side table and handed the specs to his grandpa.

The old man slipped them over his large nose. He blinked a couple of times, opened the envelope, and took out the document comprised of several sheets of paper. He fixed Clay and then Raymond with his gaze.

"What I'm holding in my hands is the last will and testament of Joseph Stedham Barlow."

"Grandpa," Clay said, "I don't need anything. Why—"

"Son, don't interrupt me again. I don't have a lot of wind or time. Understand?"

Clay sat back in his chair and nodded.

"Where was I? Oh, hell, I don't need to go through all of this. Clay's an attorney and can read it later, and Raymond doesn't care any more than Clay does. I'll just tell you what it entails." He stopped and looked around at the four men. Clay and Raymond looked extremely uncomfortable.

"All right, let's get this over with. Pearl goes to Clay. You took to him on that winter trip to Uvalde. You ought to have him. Raymond gets all the rest of the horses and mules. Raymond, you also get that fine shooting Winchester '73. It's mighty pretty, with all of that silver and gold engraving, and I know you like it. You also get whatever handguns you want. What you don't want goes to Clay. I'm leaving you this apartment."

When he saw that Raymond was going to object, the old

senator held up his hand. "Raymond, I know you like it. I'm leaving it to you for as long as you're alive. When you die, it reverts back to Clay, unless you get married, then it goes to your wife, but the office below remains Clay's."

Raymond lowered his head to prevent anyone from seeing his eyes tearing up.

"That ain't all, Raymond, I'm leaving you a hundred thousand dollars and that little spread just east of here that you love so much."

"You ain't oughta do that. All that rightly belongs to Clay."

Clay watched his grandpa's gaze soften. "Raymond," his grandpa said, "you've been my best friend almost longer than I can remember. You and Maude made me a part of your family, and you two took care of me almost as good as my sweet wife had." Now a devilish twinkle returned to his eyes for a moment.

"In fact, if Maude was here, I might just give everything you're getting to her."

Raymond grinned. "She'd deserve it more than me."

"Yes, well, let's get on with this. Clay, are you all right with this so far?"

Clay nodded to his grandpa. "I don't want anything. Give it all to Raymond, he deserves it."

"No, I'll not do that. Besides, I don't have the strength to make another will. Clay, I want you to have the Barlow Law and Land. You can do whatever you want with it. We've got Harry Baldwin working in the office. He's a good attorney, and I believe he's honest. You can let him run it, and just check on him occasionally."

Clay realized he couldn't argue with his grandpa, so he nodded.

"Good. Like I said, you get Pearl. He's a fine horse with plenty of years left. As far as the remaining property, I want you to have all the rest of my land."

Clay had no idea what that entailed, so he just nodded.

His grandpa stared at him for a moment. "I know you're doing well, son. You've improved your ranch with the Herefords, and I know you like rangering, but I have substantial properties across the state."

Clay watched his grandpa pause to cough, the pain obvious on the older man's face.

The doctor pushed his way past the two chairs. He lifted the old man's wrist, once thick and strong, now frail, almost floating from the bed in the doctor's grip. He checked the pulse. "Joseph, you *must* rest."

"Doc, before long I'll be getting all the rest I need." He turned back to Clay. "I'd hoped to leave some of this property to my great-grandkids, but I didn't hang around long enough." At that, he smiled.

"Hear your rescued girl found you?"

Clay was puzzled. "Sir?"

"The girl you saved on the stage five or six years ago. What's her name?"

Self-conscious, for he was a private person, Clay chuckled. "Oh, you mean Dee Davis."

"That's the one. She stopped by the office with your message from Jake. She seems very nice and is a lovely girl. She's grown substantially since our prior meeting. I think it was in the restaurant that she said she was going to marry you. So is she?"

Clay looked into his grandpa's eyes. "If I have anything to say about it, she will."

"Good. Any girl that can take care of herself like she can will make you a fine wife." Another fit of coughing overtook the old senator.

The doctor started forward again and was waved back.

"Leave me be, Mason. You've done all the doctoring you're gonna do on me."

Veins stood out like dry creeks on the old hands. He patted

Clay's arm. "You've grown into a fine man. I have only one more request."

Wearing a questioning look, Clay waited.

"I'm dying, son. I know it's a lot for an old man to ask, but if you're going to marry that girl, I'd be almighty happy to see it happen before I leave this world. I'd love to know that the Barlow name was continuing."

Clay shook his head. "Grandpa, she could say no."

"You're right, but she could also say yes. If you're going to do it, I'd be pleased to see it happen. But if I am going to see it happen you best get moving."

Clay mulled the idea over, looking at it from every direction, then a big grin spread across his face. "You're right, Grandpa."

"Of course your old grandpa's right, boy. Now, git." Color had returned to the old man's face. "I'm not going anywhere. I'll be waiting for you. You'll need a fresh horse, so why don't you take Pearl? He's yours anyway, or soon will be. Now be on your way, and bring your future wife back. I'll send Raymond to put Supreme Court Justice Gould on notice. He owes me. Go!"

24

The doctor stepped forward when Clay walked into the room. His face was sad at the approaching loss of a friend. "I'm sorry, Clay, but he doesn't have much longer. I'd say one, maybe two days. That'll give you time to tie up whatever business you need to at Joseph's law firm before the funeral."

Raymond had just walked in and stood watching.

Clay's face was set. "Doctor Eggleton, I've got to go to Comfort, but I'll be back. I think you give my grandfather too little credit. He's come back once. I don't think he'll be leaving until he's ready, and that won't be for a while."

Senator Weber stepped forward. "Clay, you can't mean that. That's your grandfather in there. He could go at any time."

Clay's presence, much like his grandfather's had, filled the room as he addressed both men. "Didn't you hear what he said? He wants me to leave, now. I'll not choose to disobey my grandfather at this late date. Trust me, he'll still be alive when I get back."

The senator was used to winning arguments. In a persuasive tone, he said, "Clay, I understand how you must feel, but you have to understand, your grandfather is a dying man. Quite often, the dying want to save the feelings of those remaining behind. I'm sure he didn't mean you should leave."

Clay shook his head. "Senator, I know my grandpa respects you, as do I, but I can't believe what you're saying after hearing how emphatic he was."

Raymond stepped forward. "Doc, Senator, you're both good men, but you're dead wrong about this. Senator Barlow is sane and is danged sure about what he's saying. If it comes out of his mouth, he means it, and he wants to see his grandson married."

Raymond turned to Clay. "You talk to the senator, and I'll go fix you some grub to take with you. Won't be but a few minutes." He turned to the doctor. "Doc, I reckon there ain't much more you can do. I'll get you if we need you."

The doctor looked at Senator Weber, then at Clay. "I disagree with your decision, but I can see your mind's made up. Good luck to you. I'll let myself out."

"Thank you, for all you've done. Please continue to check in on my grandpa," Clay said to the doctor. The two men shook hands, and Clay turned back to the senator as the doctor pulled the door closed.

"Clay, I, too, disagree with what you are doing. This will not look good with you leaving town just before your grandfather dies. People will say you had no respect for a great man. That could hurt you in the future, in business, and possibly politics. I do believe you could be quite successful if you decided to follow your grandfather's example."

"Senator, first, thank you for being here. I know my grandpa thinks very highly of you, but I need you to know, I care not a whit about what other people think of me. Politics is not a path I care to follow. I have my ranch, and I have the rangers. They both keep me very busy."

"But, Clay, you are an attorney, not a lawman. Use your education, be successful, build a future for yourself."

"The way I see it, I'm building a future for myself and a lot of other people by being a ranger." Clay felt himself getting exasperated with the argument. "Senator, I don't have time to argue. I need to get on the road. My grandpa trusts you and I trust you. I'll check in with you when I return."

Raymond came back into the room with a full grub bag.

After shaking hands with the senator, Clay turned to Raymond and took the sack. He had seen the color return to his grandpa's face. In his heart, he knew the old man would still be here when he returned. At that thought, he could feel his heart start to pound. He was going to ask Dee to marry him!

"You're doing the right thing, son. He wants you to go. Trust him. He'll be here when you return."

"I know, but I sure hate to leave."

"He wants it this way. Now, you hit the road. This'll give you something to eat when you camp tonight. You oughta be in Comfort in the morning. I'll take care of everything here. Now, like your grandpa said, go."

Clay grasped Raymond's hand. The old man pulled him close and gave him a quick hug, then pushed him toward the door.

The wind and dust cut into Clay when he stepped outside the apartment. He walked down the stairs and turned toward the livery.

The barn door caught in the force of the wind and banged closed behind him. Frank Platt was sitting on the steps of his office, scraping manure from his boots. "Hazard of the business. If I had a dollar for every horse apple I've stepped in I'd be a rich man." He continued to scrape, then stood and kicked each boot against the bottom step, dislodging most of the remaining deposits. "What can I do you for?"

Clay looked over at Pearl in the stall next to Hombre. "If you'll tell me where my gear is, I'll saddle up Pearl. I'd be obliged if you'd bag me up a few oats to take with me."

"Glad you made it in time, Clay. Yore granddaddy puts great store by you. Yessir, he shore does." The liveryman turned aside and loosed a long stream of tobacco juice. After wiping his mouth with a dirty rag taken from his canvas vest pocket, he continued, "You ain't leaving before the funeral, are you?"

"Just get my gear or tell me where it is, Mr. Platt, and I'll be on my way."

Platt pointed toward the tack room. "You know where the tack is. I'll get yore other things from the office." He started up the steps, and as his hand hit the door, he turned. "That wind's cuttin' up right smart outside. Might be a good idea staying till it dies down." He was talking to Clay's back, for as soon as he pointed to the tack room, Clay headed for it. Platt shook his head and mumbled something about all of the Barlows being hardheaded, then pushed on through the door, returning quickly with Clay's saddlebags, Winchester, and Roper. Clay already had Pearl saddled and was slipping on the bridle while he talked to the horse.

Hombre watched Clay as if he couldn't figure out if he had gone crazy. Clay patted the big dun on his neck. "Rest up, boy. I'll be back in a few days." Then he moved to Pearl and swung up into the saddle. He pulled his hat down tight, making sure the loop of leather was under his chin, and yanked the brim down lower over his eyes before he nodded to Platt.

"Thanks, Mr. Platt. I'll be back in a few days."

Platt raised a hand in salute and shoved the barn door open. The wind slammed into them. Clay could feel Pearl shudder, wanting no part of the biting sand. He bumped the reluctant horse in the flanks, and they started forward. Once he was in the street, he turned left and headed for Cedar Street. *I hate to stop back at the ranger's office,* he thought. *I'd like to just keep on riding.*

Then, a brief picture of a vivacious young blonde with bright blue eyes flashed through his mind. A smile broke across his melancholy face. *It'll be good to see her.*

He almost missed his turn on Cedar. Crossing Congress, normally the busiest street in town, was no problem. There was almost no other horses or wagons in the streets. A lone tumble-weed bounced and raced past Clay, continuing down the vacant street. He pulled up at the office where he had been no more than an hour ago, tied the horse, and tramped up the steps.

He stepped inside to see all of the papers fly off the desk. Closing the door, he said, "Sorry."

With Clay helping, the sergeant went about picking up the papers. He put them on his desk, strode into the captain's office, and came back with a large book, which he dropped, unceremoniously, on top of the papers. He looked at his paperweight with satisfaction, then looked up at Clay. "Twice in an hour. In this weather, it must be important."

Clay got right to the point. "Jim, my grandpa is mighty sick. I'm headed West for a while. I'll be back pretty soon, but then I may go back East. I could be there for quite a while. I need to take a furlough until I make up my mind as to what I'm going to do."

"Clay, I'm right sorry about your grandpappy. We all like and respect him. As far as a furlough, I ain't got the authority for that."

Clay reached into his vest pocket, pulled out his badge, and tossed it on the table. "I understand, Jim. Tell the captain I quit."

The sergeant looked at the badge and rubbed the growing bald spot. "Dang, Clay. I hate to see you do that. The captain's gonna be almighty upset, losing Ransom and Jake *and* you." He sat there staring at the badge. Then he picked it up and handed it back to Clay. "Well, I might be in a passel of cow patties over it, but take this. Consider yourself on indefinite furlough. Let us know when you're ready to git back to it."

Without hesitation, Clay took his badge back from the ranger. "Thanks, Jim. All I can tell you is that it'll be a while. I'll stop by when I get back in town."

The sergeant stood, and the two men shook hands, each respecting the other. Clay turned, grasped the latch, and looked back. Jim was grinning back at him, the book, and his hand, over the papers.

"Adios," Clay said. He went out the door and down the steps. After untying Pearl, he swung into the saddle and turned the Tennessee Walker into the wind.

CLAY PULLED PEARL UP, reached forward, and scratched the horse between his ears. He searched the open grassland, broken by patches of oak and ashe juniper. Other than a small band of whitetail standing in one of the near oak patches, their white tails facing the blowing wind, and a big, lean jackrabbit sitting several yards away using a scrawny mesquite for cover, nothing moved. The wind still blew, but the dust had moved on toward Bastrop and Columbus.

In the failing light, he could see the tall pecan trees that marked Browns Creek as it flowed through the prairie. Farther to the west, Twin Peaks stood out in silhouette against the dust-reddened sunset. He'd thought to push on to see Dee tonight, but there just wasn't enough time, and he didn't want to take the chance of an injured horse from traveling at night.

He entered the thick forested zone along the creek and picked his way to the bank which rose at least ten feet above the rocky creek bed. Easing along the edge of the bank, he found a trail that had been cut by cattle and wild game and eased Pearl down into the creek. This was summer, and the creek was dry in this area, except for a few deep holes holding water. Adjacent to the crossing was one of those holes.

Stepping down from the saddle, he allowed the horse to drink. After Pearl had his fill, Clay walked, leading his horse to the west bank. He found a game trail out of the creek bed and moved up into the thicket on the west side. He wished he had arrived a little earlier. This had been a long day. He'd had no lunch, only a couple of pieces of jerky and a hard biscuit. Earlier, he could have caught a few fish from the hole, but daylight was gone, and he still needed to take care of Pearl.

There would be no fire tonight, not with the wind. He knew what one burning cinder could do to this dry countryside. After staking Pearl out on a grassy area, Clay moved back to where he had dropped his tack and gear. He hauled the Roper from its scabbard. Next, he pulled out the sack Raymond had given him and laid them next to his gear.

The small bag of shotgun shells he laid alongside the shotgun, his gunbelt, and shoulder holster. A moment of humor struck him in the twilight. *Jake may be right,* he thought. *I do look like I robbed an armory.* The lightness of spirit was only momentary. The bleak and gloomy mood returned to grip his soul.

He spread his groundcloth next to his saddle and dropped to the ground, using his saddle for a backrest. The traveling wind through the treetops left an uneasy moan in the deepening darkness for anyone who might be around to hear it.

I sure would've liked a fire tonight, Clay thought. *It always helps lift the spirits.* He glanced over at Pearl. The white horse had stopped pulling at the bunch grass and was watching him. *You're a fine-looking horse. Can't say I've ridden one with a smoother gait. Grandpa was really proud when he got you. Claimed you could cover twenty miles an hour in a smooth walk.*

Pearl tossed his head a couple of times, as if he heard and understood what Clay was thinking. The horse brought a smile to the ranger's lips—over the past few weeks smiles had been at a premium.

Then Blue pushed back into his memory, and Clay could almost feel the big roan nosing at his coat pocket to find an apple.

The big man sat in the darkness and hardly noticed the taste of the fresh food Raymond had prepared. He chased it with water from his canteen. It was dark now, as dark as his thoughts.

He sat, thinking of his grandpa and Blue. Suddenly, a bright picture pushed the darkness from his mind. Dee. He couldn't wait to see her. Thinking of her brought happier thoughts. *Was it possible for a person to fall in love, if that was what he was feeling, so quickly?* He shook his head and sighed. *I figured you had to know a person for a while, learn about them, grow close. But this just leaped up like an ornery bronc. I have to admit that I've never had these kind of feelings, not with Sarah nor Lynn. Dee and Lynn are so different. Lynn put me aside because I used a gun, and Dee accepts me for what I am.*

Clay had been sitting, leaning against his saddle. Now he slid down to make it his pillow. Though this was late summer, it was Texas. The west wind brought cooler air, and it was almost downright cold. He rolled to his left side, pulled the Smith and Wesson from his shoulder holster, and reached down spreading his blanket over his long legs and slipping it up over his shoulders.

Thinking of Dee made him restless. Clay usually fell asleep on his way down to the saddle or pillow, but tonight, sleep was hard to capture. His mind ran constantly. He pictured the lovely blonde woman and her flashing blue eyes. He could imagine pulling her close and feeling her warmth. *I think she really loves me. Maybe it's time I put away my badge for good. We could raise a family.* Then a thought struck him so hard, he raised up on his forearm.

I've got the finances. I could take her to New York and introduce her to the people I know there, take her to Columbia, where I received my law degree. Maybe stay a few weeks, take her to a play. We can even stay a couple of months. I think she'd love it. Then we can come back to the ranch or law practice, whichever she wants, and have that family —no more shooting, no more chasing, and, most of all, no more killing.

Clay woke to the sound of turkeys yelping and crashing through the trees as they left the roost only a short distance down the creek. He thought about slipping along the creek and shooting a couple to take to the Davis home but ruled it out. He didn't need to waste his time with the birds when he should be on his way. It had been difficult for him to get to sleep, but he had slept soundly. Daylight was already here.

He took a long drink from his canteen, slipped on his shoulder holster and his gunbelt, and took Pearl to water. When they were back at camp, the creek sounds intruded on his thoughts. He could hear a couple of squirrels barking, then the sound of claws scratching on bark as they raced through the trees. A cardinal tuned up nearby. He looked up at the treetops. They were still. The wind had moved on, leaving a haze in the sky that would be there until the next rain, but it was quiet and still. The thrashing of limbs and constant moaning of the wind were gone for now.

He saddled Pearl. Once mounted he allowed the horse to work his way through the thicket and onto the grassy prairie. He should be at the Davis family home by lunchtime. He grinned to himself with the thought of seeing Dee.

On the trail, a morning without wind and dust, and with the crashing of the turkeys, his gloom flew away, and he had started thinking. *Pa always said, 'Death is a part of life.' And I know it is. No telling how long Grandpa will be around. He's always proven to be a powerful adversary. If anyone could, he'll give death a mighty tussle. He wants to see me married, and I believe he'll do it, and Blue would have wanted me to help save Rory.*

He passed a small herd of longhorns grazing on the dry, yellow grass. One old, rangy cow looked up. Her horns spanned at least six feet. She watched, with a threatening glare, as he rode past. He waved to her, feeling much better today. Taking a deep breath of the cleaner air, he looked across the prairie at the clusters of dark green oaks and ashe junipers interspersed with the pale green of the mesquites, set in the yellows and browns of the late season grasses. A smile played across his face as he thought, *This is a good day.*

25

I t had been a good ride—a smooth ride, thanks to Pearl. The countryside seemed to celebrate the passing of the wind-storm. He had seen several coveys of quail. Even a pair of gray wolves had loped up a hillside, stopping near the top to turn and stare at him. He felt sure they wanted to know why he was intruding on their land.

It was nearing noon, and Clay expected the ranch to come into view any time. He had never been there, but from Dee's description, he knew he was close. Rounding a small knoll, he pulled up. In front of him, about a half mile away, sat the Davis ranch house. It looked like there was some kind of get-together going on. There were saddle horses and several buggies parked in front of the house. He could see people standing in the yard and on the front porch. He could faintly hear a fiddle playing. *Must be some kind of party,* he thought.

Clay was dusty from his travel. He climbed down from Pearl and took off his chaps, rolled them up, and tied them with his bedroll. Using his hat, he started dusting off his pants and shirt. It wouldn't help much, but maybe he wouldn't look too bad. Then he poured water into his hands and rinsed his face, combing his black hair back with his hand and thinking he should have taken a razor to his face this morning on the creek. After drying with his bandana, he retied it around his neck and swung back up on Pearl.

He was surprised he didn't see Dee's blonde hair bouncing around outside with so many people but figured she must be inside helping her ma. He clucked a couple of times to Pearl and started the horses walking down to the house. Several younger folks came dashing outside and ran toward the ranch headquarters entrance, then, when they saw the stranger riding toward them, they raced back to the house and leaped onto the porch.

Nearer now, he could hear the laughing going on inside. The men stood outside, talking. When the young people had dashed back to the house, all the men had turned and now watched Clay approach.

He rode into the yard, dismounted, and led Pearl to the water trough.

"Clay!" he heard the familiar voice shout from behind.

He turned to see Dee dashing toward him, dressed in a short-sleeve, green satin dress that seemed to float across the hard-packed Texas dirt. When she reached him, she flung her arms around his neck and gave him a long kiss, right on the lips.

That stopped all the action and conversation. He could faintly hear some of the gasps from the women who had come out on the porch to see who this Clay was.

He couldn't help himself. He wrapped her in his arms and returned the kiss. Then good sense returned, and he lowered his arms and stepped back. "That was quite a welcome," he said into those blue eyes.

She tilted her head to one side, her breathing rapid. "I thought so too."

A gruff cough brought his attention back to his surroundings. He took his eyes from Dee's face to see Niles and Nancy standing on each side of their daughter. He could feel his face getting hot. "How are you? Sorry about the display."

Nancy tried unsuccessfully to keep a smile from replacing the stern look on her face. "Sometimes it's difficult to rein in our daughter."

Niles had no difficulty retaining the frown on his face. "It's good to see you, Clay. Although I woulda been happier with a less dramatic entrance."

"Yes, sir," Clay said, totally at a loss for words. He could hear chuckling coming from the group of men near the doorway.

"Dee," Nancy said sharply, "don't embarrass Clay or your father."

Through all of the stern greeting, Dee continued to beam up at Clay. "Yes, Mama. I'm just so happy he's back safe. Come on, I want you to meet everyone." She grabbed his arm and started off.

"What's the big occasion?" Clay asked, while they were still with Nancy and Niles.

Beating her daughter by only a fraction, Nancy said, "It's Dee's nineteenth birthday. We invited a few friends and family over to celebrate."

"Well, happy birthday," Clay said.

She gave a half-curtsy and said, "Thank you. I'm not so big on parties, Clay, but you're here, and that makes this one wonderful." She tugged on his arm. "Now, come on."

As they were walking away, Clay heard Niles say, "Did you see your daughter kiss that ranger?"

Nancy responded, "Yes, dear, I did. That's the same ranger that saved her twice, and the one she has professed to love for the past seven years. Now, relax."

And so it started. Dee, laughing, took Clay around to all of the adults, introducing him to each individual or couple. For his part, Clay put on his attorney meet-and-greet hat. It wasn't difficult for he liked people, and his ma had, on occasion, thrown parties that he had enjoyed. Plus, in New York, he had attended and found enjoyable, many of the parties, except for the stuffy airs put on by a few. No airs here. These were hard-working folks who had to fight for an existence in this land and were taking time off to have a bit of fun. Most had been around since either before or shortly after the Civil War and had fought their share of Comanche warriors. They worked hard, fought hard, and played hard.

The first person Clay met was the top hand for the Davis ranch, Wendell Nelson, who had been outside with the group of men when Clay rode up. Everyone called him Windy, for obvious reasons, especially on cattle drives, a short while after eating a big plate of beans.

"You'd better be Clay Barlow, or you two are in trouble."

Dee had her left arm linked through Clay's right. She made a fist and hit Windy on his bicep, which elicited a fake groan and a wide grin.

"He *is* Clay Barlow, Windy. Now you be nice." With no pity, while Clay shook hands with Windy, Dee wrinkled her nose and sniffed. "Windy, have you been eating beans again?"

The other men roared while Windy shook his head. "No, I ain't, Miss Dorenda. Why cain't you be nice to an old cow nurse?"

She turned, dragging Clay with her, and said over her shoulder, "Don't dish it out, *Windy,* if you can't take it."

The rest of the time was spent meeting all of the guests. Many of the folks Clay knew, some personally and others by reputation, and many of them knew about his exploits before and after he joined the rangers.

Clay ran into only one problem—a fella younger than him and about his size, by the name of Avery Stanton. Clay had spotted him right off. The young guy was with some other cowboys near his age and had a loud mouth. He wore a Colt low on his right leg, and tied down. Niles had gone over to the group and assured them they were welcome, but if they became rowdy they'd have to leave. After Niles had walked off, the big kid had let out a raucous laugh. Niles started to go back, but Nancy grabbed him and talked him into waiting a little longer.

Now Dee was taking Clay to that group. The rest were fine, even though he could tell they had been drinking. But Big Boy couldn't hold his liquor. When Clay and Dee walked up, the guy tried to reach his arm around her and pull her to him. Clay stepped between them and knocked the young man's arm away.

"Whatcha doin', *Ranger?*" The kid said belligerently, taking an exaggerated gunman's stance.

Clay said nothing. He stepped closer and quick as a snake, flipped the leather thong off the man's gun and yanked it from the holster. The crowd had again grown silent.

Clay leaned in even closer, where only the kid could hear. "I've killed men faster than you. Don't even think about trying anything like that. Even if you were successful and beat me, every Texas Ranger in the state would be looking for you. Now, apologize to the lady." He turned the Colt up and emptied the cartridges from the cylinder, then looked back at the young man.

"Sorry, Dee."

"Thank you, Avery. Now stop embarrassing yourself."

Clay nodded and handed the empty Colt back to the man. "Don't load until you leave." Then he dropped the cartridges into the man's other hand, put his arm around Dee, and guided her into the house where introductions continued.

Having met almost everyone, Dee guided him to a young woman of familiar features. She was older than Dee, and her black hair had been pulled back in a severe bun that couldn't begin to hide her beauty. Dressed in a plain black dress, she turned her violet eyes to Dee, and then to Clay. "Why, hello, Clay," she said. The words felt like they traveled over ice before they struck his ears.

Clay grinned. "Hi, Lynn, how's the banking business?" She was just as pretty as he remembered, but the happy, laughing girl was gone. Those eyes were just as violet, but harder, less kindness resided there.

"It's fine, Clay."

"Dee," Clay said, "Lynn and I knew each other when we were much younger." He turned back to Lynn. "How's your ma and your grandpa?"

"You're not concerned about my father?" The barb was fired with practiced ease.

"No, Lynn, I'm not concerned about your pa. My question was—"

"I know what your question was. Both my mother and grandfather died, within months of each other. My father took care of me."

Now I know where the coldness comes from, Clay thought.

"I'm sorry to hear that. They were both very good to me. Nice seeing you," Clay said, attempting to withdraw tactfully.

"Oh, you're not curious as to why I'm here?"

"No, Lynn. I'm only curious about things that interest me." *That didn't come out right,* he thought.

Lynn continued as if he had said nothing, while Dee looked bewildered. "I'm here from San Antonio to look at the possibility of opening a bank in Comfort, and I received an invitation to attend Dee's birthday party."

"That's nice. You have a good day." He once again attempted to walk away.

"I hear about you often. It seems you're killing someone new every time I turn around, now with the blessings of the law. It certainly appears you are doing quite well." She looked pointedly at Dee.

Clay could see that Dee was getting mad. He didn't want her to break a banker's nose, so he tried once again. "Busy keeping you and your banks safe. Now, good day."

"I see you're still seeing little girls."

Clay thought Lynn's barb was funny, since Dee was at least

four inches taller than her. He started to respond, but Dee stepped forward, pushing him back. "You listen to me, you sharp-tongued hussy. You will not come into my home and insult one of my guests. I am thankful that I'm younger than you, and I hope that by the time I reach *your* age, I will have learned to be more respectful of a man that risks his life every day to protect ours. Now, I'd suggest you pay your respects to my mother, and then get the hell out of here. Now!" Dee's hands were squeezed into fists so tight that her knuckles were white.

Lynn, her face pinched tight and pale, lost the beauty she had shown moments before. She stared at Dee for a moment, then, without a word, whirled and walked stiffly to Nancy. Dee, her cheeks flushed, watched as the woman spoke briefly to her ma and then went out the door.

"Whew," Clay said, "I guess I better stay on your good side."

She glared up at him, then her look softened. She giggled. "I guess you better, Mister."

Nancy walked over and asked. "What was that all about?"

"Oh," Clay said, "I met her in Brackettville when I was chasing the killers that murdered my folks. We saw each other for a while, but when I caught up to and ended several of the killers, she threw me over. Said she couldn't be seen with a murderer."

Dee smiled up at him and took his arm again, squeezing it. "Her loss is my gain."

Clay looked at Nancy, a grin relieving the tension on his face. "Your daughter flat told her off. I don't think anyone has taken up for me like Dee just did, at least not over the last few years."

Nancy gave her daughter a mock glare. "I heard every word."

"Mama, I'm sorry. I didn't mean to use that kind of language in your house."

"Don't apologize to me, sweetie. You made me proud. Now, go finish saying goodbye to your guests while I talk to Clay."

Dee gave her ma a kiss on her cheek, flashed Clay a smile,

and walked over to the people who were speaking to her pa as they filed out.

"Finally some time to talk. I've heard what you went through out in Fort Stockton. I'm so sorry about Blue. How are you doing?"

"Nancy, I hate whiners, but I've got to say, I'm a little worn down. You know about my grandpa?"

"Yes, Clay, I do. How is he doing?"

"Not well, but he is looking forward to something, and Jake's son is safe. Those are both positive things, but I'm here to see your daughter."

"I'm glad you mentioned her. What are your plans where she's concerned?

"Nancy, it's all honorable. I need to talk to Niles. I know it's quick, but I feel like I've known her for a long time. I can't imagine my life without her."

Nancy smiled up at the big ranger, who, as confident and tough-looking as he was, still showed signs of the uncertain boy he had once been. "Clay, she's done nothing but talk about you since the stage holdup. I thought it would change as she got older, but I think she saw something in you that she recognized. She is a woman now and fully capable of making her own decisions, but her pa would appreciate you asking."

Clay watched the last of the guests ride out of the yard. "I intend to right now."

He walked outside, looking for Niles.

"Over here, Clay," Niles called from the barn, where he and Windy were feeding the horses.

Clay walked into the large barn. "What can I do?"

Niles pointed to a sack of cracked corn standing with some other bags. "Look inside the bag. There's a scoop. Fill it and bring it over here."

Clay walked to the bag and found a large can. He pushed the can down into the corn and pulled it out full. Turning, he walked over to Niles, who took it and split it into two feeders. "Windy, take care of the rest, will you?"

"Sure thing, Boss."

Niles tossed him the can. "Let's walk outside," he said to Clay.

They walked toward a large mesquite tree with a swing hanging from one of its big limbs. When they reached it, Niles put one boot on the board that was polished smooth and grasped one of the ropes. Looking up at Clay, he said, "You wanted to talk to me?"

Clay felt his chest tighten. He took his hat off and glanced toward the house. He could see the two Davis women standing side by side, their arms around each other, watching him and Niles. He turned back to the ranch owner. "Niles, I'd like permission to ask your daughter for her hand in marriage."

Nile's foot slipped off the swing, but he maintained his balance by hanging onto the rope. Once both feet were on the ground and he was again stable, he looked up at Clay. "Are you serious? You haven't even called on her. I thought you'd be asking me if it was all right to take her for a ride, not marry her."

"Mr. Davis, I'm hoping Dee loves me, and I know I love her. I've had all these weeks to think about it. You don't have to worry about her financially. I have my ranch and significant investments."

Niles waved his hand. "That don't matter, Clay. I mean, of course we want her to be taken care of, but what we want most is for the man that marries her to love her. Are you sure about your feelings?"

"Mr. Davis, I'm as sure as any man can be at a time like this, and I promise you, I'll do everything in my power to provide her with a happy home."

Niles looked up at the big ranger. Clay's reputation of being fair and honest in his dealings was well known, especially to the folks who lived in the hill country and had known Clay's parents. "Of course, it'll be up to her, but if she say's yes, I'd be pleased to have you for a son." He shoved his hand toward Clay.

"Thank you, sir," Clay said, grasping the rancher's hand in his and giving it an enthusiastic shake. "You won't regret this decision."

"I'm sure I won't. Now, can you go back to calling me Niles?"

Clay grinned. "I sure can, Niles. If you'll excuse me." He turned back toward the house to see the mother and daughter in each other's arms. His walk to the house felt like it took forever, but he could see a glowing Dee watching him approach. Nancy still had no idea of his plan to ask for Dee's hand.

Nancy smiled at Clay and said, "Are you two going for a ride?"

Clay felt around in his vest pocket for the object that he had been carrying around in a secret compartment in his saddlebags for years. "Not right now, Nancy. First, I need to ask Dee a question."

26

Both Nancy and Dee looked puzzled. He had walked up on the porch facing the two of them. Now he dropped to one knee. Nancy's eyes got so big it looked like they would fall from her head. Dee first looked astonished, then tears sprang to her blue eyes.

Clay pulled the package from his vest pocket and opened the little box. Nestled inside was a ring with a small single diamond set in it. He took Dee's left hand, and said, "Dee, this was my ma's. My pa and ma dearly loved each other. I love you and hope we can have a life as good as theirs. Dorenda Lynn Davis, will you marry me?"

Tears of happiness streamed down her cheeks. She started to say something and had to first clear her throat. "Oh, Clay, yes. Yes, I'll marry you, and I know we'll be the happiest two people on this earth."

Nancy was still in shock, her hand over her mouth, eyes filled with tears.

Clay slipped the small ring on Dee's finger, or at least he tried to, but unfortunately, it wouldn't fit. It was much too small. With a look of consternation, he looked up at Dee. "I never thought about size. Ma was a tiny woman."

Dee grabbed Clay by the shoulders and pulled him up. When he stood, she gazed up into his eyes. "We can get it fixed. Now, kiss me." With her arms around his neck, she pressed her lips to those of the man she loved and the two of them stood on the porch alone, except for Niles and Nancy.

Finally, Niles cleared his throat.

Clay broke the kiss but kept one arm around his future bride. His face was red. "Sorry, I guess we got carried away."

"Marriage?" Nancy said. "I certainly didn't expect you to ask Dee this soon."

"Do you think it's wrong, Mama?"

Nancy looked at her happy daughter, at the young man she thought so highly of, and then at her husband, who smiled back at her. The confusion and surprise turned into a big smile. "No, sweetie, I think it's perfect. I don't know why I'm surprised. You told us, all these years, that you were going to marry this man. I've known it would be perfect. I was just surprised at the sudden question."

Clay spoke up. "There's something else I need to talk to all three of you about."

Nancy said, "Come in the house. We can sit in the kitchen. I need to sit down, anyway."

The four walked inside and turned toward the kitchen. Clay held the chair for Dee, while Niles did the same for his wife. Then the two men sat.

Nancy jumped up. "I'll make some fresh coffee."

"I'll do it, Mama," Dee said, also rising. "Clay, would you like some water? I know you don't drink coffee."

"How'd you know that?" Clay asked.

"The first time in the hotel, after the stagecoach. You told the waiter you didn't drink coffee."

"You remember that, from all those years ago?"

"Yes, Mister Barlow. I have a good memory—now, water?"

Clay shook his head. "I can't believe it. You were only twelve."

"Just because you're young, doesn't mean you can't be observant. Papa always taught me it was important to see my surroundings, not just look at them." She smiled at her papa.

Clay nodded to Niles. "Looks like you did a good job."

"Clay Barlow, do you want any water?"

Clay laughed. "That would be great, thank you."

Dee gave an exasperated sigh, pulled a glass out of the cabinet, and, using a dipper that was floating in a bucket of fresh water, filled a glass for Clay. Nancy had the water on to boil for the coffee.

They both returned to the table. Nancy said, "What else is on your mind, Clay?"

He made eye contact with each person at the table, finishing with Dee. "I don't know what kind of plans you have for Dee's wedding, but I may be throwing a wrench into the plans. One of my grandpa's wishes is that he be able to attend our wedding." He could see the concerned look on Nancy's face.

"Clay," Nancy said, "isn't your grandfather quite ill?"

"Yes, ma'am, he sure is. In fact, the doctor said he's already died once. So no one knows how long he'll be with us." Clay turned back to Dee and took her hand in his. "But if you could see your way clear to get married fast, in front of a judge, and forgo a big church wedding, Grandpa will have it set up in his apartment with Justice Gould conducting the ceremony."

Dee clapped her hands. "Yes! That's such a wonderful idea and being married by a supreme court justice. I can't wait." Then she saw the disappointment on Nancy's face. "Oh, Mama, I know you so counted on me getting married in the church with all of our friends there, but you know I never liked that idea. I've never wanted a big wedding." She looked back at Clay, her face alight with happiness. "I just want to marry Clay."

Nancy gave a small smile to her daughter. "I know, Dee, and if that will make you happy, it is fine with us." She turned to her husband. "Isn't it, honey?"

Niles nodded. "As long as everyone's happy, it's fine with me. Clay, what do we need to do?"

"That's the other thing. We need to leave right away." Clay looked out the window, to the sun lowering in the west. "As late as it is, I'd say if we leave early in the morning it'll be fine. That should put us in Austin late tomorrow. We can make the wedding on the following day, if that works?" Clay looked at everyone. All three nodded, with Dee nodding enthusiastically.

Niles laughed at his little girl. "Dee, baby, you really want to marry this big galoot, don't you?"

Dee stood up, moved around the table, and wrapped her arms around her papa's neck and gave him a big kiss on his cheek. "Oh, Papa, you know he's all I've talked about since the stagecoach robbery."

"Well, Clay," Niles said, "looks like you're gonna be stuck with her. I promise she'll keep you guessing. She doesn't stop." He shook his head, a mock frown on his face. "Always into something." Then he sobered and held his daughter's face between both of his rough hands. "But we are going to miss her." He leaned forward and kissed Dee on her forehead.

Clay could see the tears welling in Dee's eyes. "Oh, Papa. I love you and Mama so much."

Nancy laid her hand on her husband's arm and squeezed, her eyes also full. "We know, baby, we know."

Niles cleared his throat. "All right. We've all got a lot to do. Clay, come with me, and you can give me a hand."

"Yes, sir, I'd be glad to, but there is one more thing."

Everybody stopped and looked at Clay. "After the wedding, if it's all right with Dee, I'd like for us to honeymoon in New York."

Niles leaned back like he had been punched. His eyes were wide, and his mouth was open. Finally, he said, "New York City?"

"Yes, sir. You might remember L.M. O'Shea. He was the one

who first gave us the information about the coming market crash. He handles all of Grandpa's investments and several of mine. I need to take him a copy of Grandpa's will and set up some new guidelines for him. I thought that might be a perfect time and place for us to honeymoon."

Niles thought about it for a moment, then nodded. "That makes sense. How long do you think you would be gone?"

Clay studied over the question. "I can't say for sure, but I'd think at least a month and possibly as many as four months."

Dee pulled her chair around next to Clay and slipped her left arm around his. "That's where you went to school, isn't it?"

"Yes, at Columbia. I'd like for you to meet a few of my instructors." He turned his head and looked into her blue eyes. "Is there anything you don't know about me?"

She gave him a sweet smile. "No, there isn't, and don't forget it, Mister."

"Well, that's a lot to digest," Niles said. "Married and gone to New York City within the week. My goodness."

"This is something we could postpone for a while, Niles, if that would make it easier."

Niles looked at Nancy who gave a slight nod and tilt of her head.

"No, Clay. This is the life you and Dee are building. We won't interfere." He grinned and winked at his wife. "'Course we might toss out some opinions ever once in a while."

Niles slid his chair back and stood. Clay followed.

Dee jumped up. "I've got to start packing." She almost made it out of the room before she spun around. "Mama, we forgot to tell Clay about his friend."

"You're right," Nancy said. "Yesterday morning, right in the middle of that terrible sandstorm, a horseman rode into our yard and watered his horse. We have no problem with strangers helping themselves to water. After he was finished, he walked his horse over here and knocked at the door."

Dee piped up. "I let him in. Mama was upstairs and Papa . . . I don't know where Papa was. This man said he was your friend and was looking for you. I saw Mama looking around the door facing from their bedroom. She had her shotgun. I told him you weren't here and offered him a meal. He ate and left."

Clay had headed to the door behind Niles. He turned back, listening. "Did he say who he was?"

Dee shook her head. "All he said was that he was a friend of yours and was looking for you. I didn't especially like him. He was really dirty, but the sandstorm was blowing like crazy, so that could explain it."

"What'd he look like?"

"Big man, maybe five ten or five eleven. Unshaven, and he smelled really bad."

"Any identifying marks?"

"Nothing."

Clay shook his head. "Can't imagine who he might be." He stood thinking for a bit longer. "Thanks, Dee."

Nancy spoke up. "I didn't like him either. There was just something about him. I can't put my finger on it, but he gave me the shivers." With her last comment she shook for a second, like she was having chills.

Clay puzzled over the description. "I can't think of any friends that are like that."

"Oh well," Dee said. "I've got to pack."

"I'll help," Nancy called as Dee disappeared into the hallway. She flashed a smile to Clay and Niles, then followed her daughter.

"Let's tell Windy and the boys," Niles said, and headed out the door, Clay following close behind.

~

CLAY'S FACE showed a calm countenance, much like the duck smoothly gliding across the water while, beneath the surface, his feet paddled like crazy. Like the duck's feet, Clay's heart pounded so loud he was sure everyone could hear it. He looked over to his grandpa, the old man smiling as he sat in his favorite chair. The chair had been moved around so that he had a full view of the bride and groom.

I sure enjoyed the ride back to town, Clay thought. *It was so much different from the one going out to the ranch. I don't think I've ever been so happy. I just wish Ma and Pa could be here.* He stood next to the minister, looking anxiously at the front door of his grandpa's apartment. The street in front of the *Barlow Law and Land* office was packed with people. In fact, he didn't think another person could be squeezed into the apartment's living room.

Word had gotten out that Clay Barlow, the attorney and Texas Ranger, was getting married and it looked like everyone had turned out. When the local Presbyterian minister heard of the proposed wedding and that the bride was, in fact, Presbyterian, he approached Nancy at the city hotel and offered his services. She was thrilled. Justice Gould, always the gentleman, graciously stepped aside, although he was in attendance.

Raymond stood behind and slightly to the right of Clay's grandfather, the dutiful friend, willing to provide whatever service the old man needed. *Old man,* Clay thought. *He looks better than I've seen him look in months. In fact, he walked into the living room under his own power. He sure doesn't look as sick as he did when I left.*

Clay ran an index finger around the inside of his collar. He had worn suits everyday when he was back East, but after returning, he very seldom wore one, unless helping in his Grandpa's law office. Now the collar irritated his neck. He was used to the feel of a soft bandanna against his neck instead of a stiff, starched white collar. He unconsciously straightened the hunter green puff tie he wore with his white shirt. Over the shirt was a four-pocket, gray, pinstriped vest, covered by his charcoal gray frock coat. The frock coat was custom made, so that the bulge under his left arm, where his shoulder holster rode, was hardly visible. He felt naked without his gunbelt and his hat, but Raymond had convinced him, that neither gunbelt nor hat would be appropriate for a wedding—no Indian or bandit attack was imminent. Against his better judgment, he relinquished both. Now his thick, wavy, black hair hung just over his ears framing the strong jawline, and piercing gray eyes that hid the anxiety he felt.

The Davis family had stayed at the City Hotel. Niles and Nancy would be bringing Dee to the apartment by buckboard when she was ready. Clay unbuttoned his frock coat and pulled the pocket watch from his vest pocket. A gold chain, attached to the watch, hung across the vest, terminating in the second buttonhole of the four-button vest. He popped the watch open— two minutes past the last time he'd checked it. After closing the watch, he slipped it back into his pocket, buttoned his coat, and looked up. Several of the seated ladies were smiling at him. *I must be making a complete idiot of myself,* he thought. *Dee, could you please get here, and put me out of my misery?*

No sooner had the thought crossed his mind than he heard cheers and clapping from the crowd below. *She's here.* He straightened his tie for the umpteenth time, unbuttoned his coat and pulled his vest down, tight, and, once again, buttoned his coat. Clay turned so he could face the door. He heard footsteps coming up the stairs, and the door opened. In walked Nancy, looking the proud and beautiful mother, and stood to left of the door, followed by Niles, who stepped to the right. He looked stressed but impressive. A moment passed.

And she stepped into the room. Clay's eyes couldn't believe the vision floating through the door was about to become his wife. Her golden blonde hair fell about her shoulders with a royal blue ribbon tied at the crown of her head, the brilliant blue ends floating down the contour of her hair. Her eyes matched the color of the ribbon, and he could see they were focused on him. She took her father's arm and glided toward Clay.

He had time to fully take her in. A lace ruffle caressed her skin as it traveled in a line over her shoulders and across her upper body, exposing a small portion of the soft, white skin and accentuating her long, graceful neck. The light blue sleeves were puffed with a white under sleeve that stopped just above her elbows, and it, too, was trimmed in white lace. Beneath the light blue blouse was a skirt of the same color that hugged her body, emphasizing her small waist and slim hips as it flowed to the floor, a ten-inch ruffle at the bottom completing the dress.

As she neared him, he was further unnerved to see she was outwardly calm and relaxed. Then her full lips spread in a wonderful smile, just for him. Her father placed her hand in his, and he felt the warmth. He could feel her heartbeat in her fingertips. Now facing him, in front of the minister, she reached out with her other hand. He took it and lost himself in her touch and her beautiful eyes. And the minister began.

He remembered them saying "I do," and slipping the ring on Dee's finger. He was thankful that he had remembered to have the rings resized this morning, but no matter how hard he tried, he would never remember the ceremony, for he was feasting on the vision of his wife through the entire service.

"You may kiss the bride," the minister said.

It was done. He reached out and scooped her up in his strong arms and pulled her to him. The meeting of their lips was like the balls of fire that danced across a room during a lightning storm. They separated and, arm in arm, turned toward the guests.

27

Grandpa was on his feet, and he proudly said, "Ladies and gentlemen, I present to you, Mr. and Mrs. Barlow." The room erupted in applause. When the crowd below heard the commotion, they joined in, and the celebration was on. Nancy and Niles stepped forward, and Nancy hugged her daughter and then her new son-in-law.

"We are so happy for you both," Nancy said.

Dee grinned at her mother. "I told you I'd marry him."

Nancy shook her head. "Yes, you did. I shall never doubt you."

Niles gave his daughter a hug and said, "I never doubted a moment."

All four of them had a good laugh at that. Clay turned and was surprised to see his grandpa standing there, waiting his turn. The old man stepped forward, leaned down, and gave his new granddaughter a kiss on the cheek. "Welcome to the family. You have no idea how happy I am to see this wedding. I was afraid the Barlow name would die with my grandson, and now there's hope."

Dee looked up at her new grandfather, stood on her tiptoes, and returned his kiss. She whispered in his ear: "I promise you, there is more than hope. We will fill our home with the sound of many Barlows."

He looked down at her, a tear in his eye. "Thank you, my dear. Now, go have fun."

Clay looked at his grandpa, and then at his new bride. "What'd you say?"

She tossed a conspiratorial grin to her new grandpa and then turned back to Clay. "That, Mister Barlow, is for me to know, and for you to make happen."

He looked at her, his brow wrinkled, and then at his grandpa. The older man laughed and shook hands with his grandson. "Congratulations, son. I think you've got your hands full."

Dee winked at him and said, "You are so right, Senator."

Clay, still puzzled, said, "Don't forget, we've got to catch the train in two hours. It leaves at three o'clock."

"I'll be ready, husband, dear. Now let me meet some of these fine folks."

Clay nodded. "I'll introduce you."

"No, you talk to Grandpa. I'm capable of introducing myself." She turned and immediately started talking to a senator and his wife.

Clay turned back to his grandpa. "Do you need to sit down?"

"Surprisingly, no. I'm feeling better."

"Grandpa, I hate to leave again with you feeling bad."

"Son, this is perfect. If I die, I at least die happy, but your trip to New York is a great boon. You can see L.M. and give him a copy of the will. You can also check on our investments. There is a power of attorney enclosed with the will, and don't you worry about me. I aim to be around to see my first great-grandson."

Clay grinned at his grandpa. "Good, it might be awhile."

His grandpa slapped him on the back and grinned back at him. "I'm betting it won't be much longer than nine months."

Clay's cheeks turned a little pink. "We'll see."

"Yes, we will. Now, you go meet your guests. Too bad more of the rangers couldn't have been here."

"Yes, sir. Most of the Austin bunch are out West looking for Griffin. When he killed a ranger, he signed his own death warrant. If they don't kill him themselves, he'll hang."

"Good riddance. Now, go. You got a lot of folks downstairs waiting to see the bride and groom."

Clay looked around and found Dee and her folks talking to Justice Gould.

When he came up to them, he heard the conversation. The justice was asking Niles what he thought of the new Hereford breed.

"Excuse me," Clay said. "Sorry to interrupt. But we need to go out on the porch. There's a lot of folks waiting to see us."

"Oh, you're right," Dee said. "Sorry, Judge, but those folks have been waiting."

"You go right ahead. Clay, when you get back from New York, come see me."

"Yes, sir." Clay slid his arm around his bride's slim waist and walked with her out the door. When they stepped on the landing, the crowd erupted and almost immediately started shouting, "Speech, speech, speech."

Clay held up his hands until the crowd quieted. "We want to thank all of you for being here. You know we'll be heading back East for a while. Thank you for a great Texas sendoff. There's refreshments in the *Barlow Law and Land* office. Thanks again."

The crowd erupted once more, but quickly died down in its push to get to the refreshments. Clay turned to his wife. "I didn't get to tell you, but you are mighty pretty in that outfit."

She smiled up at him. "Oh, yes, you did. It looked like you were devouring me when I came through the door, and I enjoyed every minute of it. Oh, Clay, I don't think I've ever been this happy. Thank you for making a long dream come true."

He pulled her to him. "The dream is just starting, honey.

We're going to have a great life ahead of us." He bent and kissed her, forgetting they were still in sight of everyone. A loud cheer went up. He pulled back, sheepishly. "I guess I forgot where we are."

"I didn't," she said, and pulled his head back down, giving him a long kiss, to a rousing cheer. "There, they need something to talk about. Now I've got to go get changed. I'll get Mama and Papa. Why don't you pick me up at the hotel?" Then she said, a teasing glint in her eye, "By the way, where are we spending the night?"

"Dallas. We'll change trains there. Our train isn't scheduled to leave until noon tomorrow."

"Oh, goody." She turned, swinging her hips suggestively, and went after her folks.

Clay shook his head and grinned to himself. Life was going to be very interesting.

GOODBYES HAD BEEN SAID. Clay and Dee stood on the train platform, watching the men load the baggage and mail. Niles and Nancy had to leave to get back to the ranch. Besides the other passengers who were almost all boarded, they were the only two.

Dee turned to Clay. "Have I told you how happy I am?"

"I think I lost count."

"Maybe this'll jog your memory." She pulled his head down to hers, and he felt her soft, warm lips on his.

"Now ain't that about the cutest thing I ever did see."

Clay knew the voice immediately. He broke the kiss, put his bag in her hands, and shoved Dee toward the train steps. "Get onboard. Now!"

Without hesitation, she ran up the steps and found a seat where she could see the man through the open window. It was the same man who had been at their ranch. His gun hung low and was tied down. She snapped her head back toward Clay. The only gun he had was the Smith and Wesson in his shoulder holster—under his coat.

As soon as Clay knew that Dee was clear, he turned back to face the killer. "Hello, Griffin. This is pretty bold, coming into Austin."

"I figure I can kill you and be out of town before the sheriff or any of your rangers come after me. Works in my favor, all those rangers out West lookin' for me. Guess I'll just fool 'em and kill me another ranger."

"You're making a big mistake."

"I don't rightly see it that way. Anyhow, I owe you. You tricked me at that stage station. You had me thinking I had my gun dogged down when I ain't. That ranger what was escortin' me made jokes about it all the time—until I killed him."

Several people had walked out on the platform and were watching. "Folks, get out of here," Clay said. "Bullets are about to be flying, and you don't want to be anywhere around."

The people ran from the platform, making sure they were well clear.

"Well, ain't you nice, Mr. Ranger. Only you was nice for the last time. Where's yore fine guns? I sure liked 'em. You got that shoulder rig on under that coat? Well, it don't make no never mind, cause I'm gonna have you filled full of holes before you can even git that coat open."

"Griffin, you kill another ranger and the manhunt will never stop."

"It ain't gonna stop now, Barlow. I know that. But afore I'm gone, I'll have the pleasure of sending you along ahead of me."

Griffin pulled his revolver from its holster. He took his time. There was no way Clay could get the Smith and Wesson out of the shoulder holster. It wasn't meant for a fast draw. The man stood with an awful grin on his face, exposing brown and broken teeth. Two dogs sat at the end of the platform, barking at the train engine.

Clay looked around and took a deep breath. The sky was a crystal blue, almost the color of the ribbon in Dee's hair. Spotted around were white, fluffy clouds drifting aimlessly across the heavens. *If it's my time, Lord, I couldn't think of a better day. Thank you for this day.*

"When that train whistle blows, Barlow, you're a dead man." Griffin brought his revolver up to shoulder height and aimed down the barrel. "I want to be dead sure of this shot." Then he laughed. "Dead sure, get it Ranger?"

The train whistle blew, Clay leaped to his right, going for his Smith, knowing that he didn't have a chance. The gun blasted. Clay expected to feel the punch of lead but felt nothing. On his right knee, he brought up the Smith, after finally getting it out, but Griffin was doubled over, his gun lying on the platform. The killer dropped to his knees. He was there only a moment before he rolled over on his back, his blank eyes staring up at the same clouds Clay had been admiring, moments before. The train started moving.

The station agent ran out and helped Clay up. "Get on the train, Ranger Barlow. I saw it all. He was trying to kill you. Get on the train, it's leaving!"

Dazed, and wondering what had happened, Clay watched the train, as it gradually picked up speed.

Dee stuck her head out of the window and yelled, "Come on, Clay!"

Her voice snapped him out of the haze. He dashed down the platform, and just before reaching the end, leaped for the train steps. His foot landed on the bottom step where he teetered for a moment, then grabbed the rail of the caboose to steady himself. He looked back and saw Austin gradually disappearing in the distance.

His mind was in a quandary. What had happened? How was

it that he wasn't lying dead on the train platform? The conductor walked back to the end of the caboose. "Come on, Ranger. Your wife is waiting for you."

Clay followed the conductor through the caboose, across the next platform, and into the pullman car. There was Dee, looking back at him. She had a little smudge on her right cheek. As he got closer, he could see his valise sitting open on the seat next to her and one of his Smith and Wesson forty-fours lying in her lap, a thin rope of smoke lifting from its barrel. He moved the valise and sat down beside her. "You shot him?"

She looked into his eyes, her deep blue eyes clear as a spring morning. "Yes."

Clay shook his head. "I can't hardly believe it."

A drummer, sitting across the aisle from them, spoke up. "Believe it, Mister. Why, she came running in here, threw that bag down on the seat, and started ripping at the strap, trying to get it open. I think she even cussed at it."

Clay looked at Dee, eyebrows raised. She shrugged, and the drummer went on.

"Finally, she got that bag open, pulled one of those big Smiths out of its holster, and sat down in that seat where she's sitting. It wasn't hardly any time at all before she ups with that Smith, ears the hammer back, and shoots that fellow right in the chest. Yessiree, that lady knows how to shoot."

Clay turned back to his wife. "Are you all right?"

"I am. That's not something I want to do every day, but when someone threatens my husband, he's also got me to contend with."

Clay took the revolver from Dee, reached into his valise, took out one cartridge from the gunbelt, broke the Smith open, and reloaded it. He then slid it back into the holster and closed the valise. He stood and placed the bag in the overhead storage and took a deep breath.

He sat back down next to Dee. "I really thought I was dead. You know what went through my mind?"

She looked at him, taking his hand in both of hers.

"I thought that if I had to die, this was the perfect day. Now you've made it even better. Are you sure you're all right?"

She released his hands and grasped his head, a hand on each cheek, and pointed his eyes directly to hers. "Listen to me, Clay. I am fine. You didn't marry a helpless wallflower. I've grown up on the frontier, and though I don't like taking a life, I'll do it everyday to defend my family if I have to, and you are now my family. Besides, you've saved me twice. I thought I'd return the favor. Also, I need you to help me keep a promise I made to your grandpa."

Clay put his arm around Dee, and she leaned her head on his chest. "What kind of promise did you make Grandpa?" he asked.

His hand hung over her right shoulder. With a knowing smile, she reached up and held the big, sun-browned hand with her right hand, patting it with her left. "Don't worry, I'll tell you when we get to Dallas."

AUTHOR'S NOTE

I hope you enjoyed *Lonesome Justice*. This is the third book in the Justice Series, following Clay Barlow, Texas Ranger.

I have to admit, I like Clay. If you've read the preceding two books in the series, *Forty-Four Caliber Justice*, and *Law and Justice*, you are well aware of the hard times he has gone through.

If you have written a review or written to me, you have helped me to make the decision to continue the Justice Series novels. It may be a while, since I am working on a three book project in the Logan Family Series. But when that is completed, Clay will get the attention he deserves.

Thank you. Should you care to share something you liked, or didn't, please feel free to let me know. My email is: Don@Donald-LRobertson.com, or you can fill in the contact form at:

www.DonaldLRobertson.com

I'll be looking forward to hearing from you.